REIGNING FIRE

JASMINE KAH YAN LOO

First published in Australia in 2025

House of Ember Publishing, Melbourne, Australia

This revised paperback edition first published in 2026

This book contains themes of abuse, trauma recovery, power imbalance, and institutional harm. Reader discretion is advised. For a full list of trigger alerts, please visit www.jasmine-loo.com

Jasmine Kah Yan Loo has asserted her moral rights.

 NATIONAL LIBRARY OF AUSTRALIA

A catalogue record for this book is available from the National Library of Australia

ISBN 978-0-6458960-0-8

To all of you who are forged in fire,
this tale carries your embers and flame.
May we rise from the ashes.

Jasmine K. Y. Loo

ALSO BY JASMINE K. Y. LOO:

Reigning Abyss

2026

Book Two of Reckoning in Smoke

Nurturing Neurodivergence:

The Late-Identified Adults' Guide to Building

Healthy Relationships with Self and Others

2023

(Non-fiction)

For all media enquiries, please visit:

Author Website

https://jasmine-loo.com/

Instagram

@jasmineloo.author

Facebook

/NurturingNeurodivergenceBook

Chapter One

所賜之名

THE NAME I WAS BESTOWED

The strip of silk lay cold against my throat. It always was—as they said—tradition, not cruelty. But our tradition came in a myriad of flavors, and many burned.

I knelt at the center of the Ancestral Hall, my hands resting folded across my thighs, fingers loose, head bowed. The jade-inlaid floor gleamed like a mirror made of knives. Not smooth—never smooth.

Above me, the carved wooden beams loomed like watching ancestors, each one etched with a different face. Some solemn, some serene, but all looking away. Smoke rose curling from the offering braziers, slow and silver, like the breath of a spirit, filling the air with incense and remembrance.

When the chanting began, signaling the commencement of my Binding Rites, Father entered, moving like a verdict already passed—Prince Yan

Yun, third son of House Yan, clad in solemn black silk robes. The rising smoke motifs stitched with pale silver threads wrapped around his arms like whispered law. His long silver hair, threaded with a single carved jade hairpin, swayed behind him as he walked.

Only when Father was on the move, his robes billowing out around him, would his Emberkin show. Even then, it was only possible to catch quick glimpses of some sinuous portion from the majestic serpent's smoky body coiled around his leg. Unlike Weavers of Yan flourishing their Emberkin as a power display, Father's perpetually half-concealed Emberkin added to his cold, intimidating presence. The glimmer of deep green at his ankle, so intense it was almost black, looked like a bolt of dark lightning riding his heel into the room.

The clerics began to chant my name, the one I was bestowed. Yan Xun—the miracle child and sole heir of the Prince Regent. The heavens' doting response to my parents' thousand prayers for my arrival. Just like my granted name, I was the precious gem they'd *found*, as if to seal my fate to be a passive thing. Something to be chiseled and faceted into any shape and form the Empire found palatable.

The ritual moved forward, oblivious to my inner turmoil. Yet, beyond the ceremony and the ancestral drums, I heard something else. A beat that wasn't supposed to be there. One that didn't belong to the ceremony, to the Empire, to the Mortal Realm.

Boom. Pah. Boom. Pah. Boom-boom-boom. Pah.

The qilin drummers from the Dream Realm reached across boundaries to kindle my fortitude, their beats thundering as I entered a battlefield disguised as celebration.

The head cleric approached with the binding ink, holding it like something holy. It smelled of smoke and blood and something older—the ghosts of those before me, made to revel in the crushing of their own will. He dipped the brush, and I breathed in, shallow. It was then that a wisp of ember-red smoke grazed the edge of my vision.

My eyes flicked inconspicuously toward Mo, my bonded Emberkin—visible only to me. Because to reveal her to the world would be to sign her death sentence. And possibly mine. Emberkin were only meant to come to us *after* our Binding Rites, once our powers had been tamed, our legacies sealed. So, perhaps only heavens knew how I'd bonded Mo eighteen moons before this day.

But beyond the bewildering timing of my bonding, the crux of the issue was that Mo didn't take on the form of an extant creature in the Mortal Realm, as expected of Emberkin. Looking indubitably mythic, Mo was shaped like a phoenix but … wrong. Her wings tattered, her form dim, she'd looked broken from the

outset. To this day, I still couldn't tell if that broken-
ness was hers or mine.

As soon as the brush touched my skin, the ink
hissed. My name was drawn in strokes of flame and
ash. The silk around my neck tightened briefly as the
Smokecraft was sealed, marking the end of the em-
blematic ceremony. My birth mother, Lady Linhua,
wept with pride. Father only nodded grimly from his
throne on the upper dais. I played my part, smiling
demurely as they extolled the divinity of the Rites.
Everyone thought the Empire had gained another
amenable pet to maintain its dominance over the
Smokeveil. But I'd never had more clarity.

After the conclusion of the ceremony, the palace was
awash in congratulations. Scrolls delivered from distant provinces, courtiers smiling too widely, servants
folding into bows like they could smell power clinging onto me. I supposed simply surviving to the age
of sixteen could be considered an achievement when
royals often died young. Through lamentable accidents and by the will of the heavens, of course.

At the high table, Lady Linhua patted my hand
with false delicacy, then held her a corner of her silk

handkerchief to her cheek, dabbing at the tears she always kept just under the surface.

"You shone, my treasure," she whispered. "Your mother looked pleased with you. Did you see?"

I murmured something obedient and sweet, an acceptable response from a Princess. Even though the Princess Consort did not birth me, I had to call her Mother. Because I was to do as I was told—the way it had always been.

I was five when I'd first experimented with overt defiance. Right in the Grand Pavilion, in front of Father, the Consort, and a full circle of court officials. It was Father's birthday, a day of ceremony and filial display. I was supposed to bow, present the jade scroll, and offer my reverent wishes: *"Father and Mother, long may your wisdom guide the Empire's flame."*

Instead, when my cue had come, I said, "Father and the *Princess Consort*, may your day be bright."

Lady Linhua had gasped. The silence had cracked like a dropped teacup, my words construed as an insulting reference to the absence of a blood heir in the Consort's household. The Consort, having gone as still as a statue, didn't speak. But Father did. Later. Privately. Severely.

I was made to kneel in the Ancestral Shrine for six hours—no food, no water, no shift in posture. The inked names of my ancestors had stared down at me from the walls, weighing my worth. Father had stood behind me as I bled the words from my mouth:

"I will honor what has been given to me.

"She is my mother in all the ways that matter.

"There is no room in legacy for disobedience.

"Respect is not earned; it is owed."

I'd repeated those words mechanically. Because if I wasn't devoid of thought and emotion, I would have screamed. I was five—but childish tantrums, like genuine affection, had no place in the royal court. So, I'd stared at the floor to keep my focus.

The mosaic was pieced together from razor-thin jade slivers, forming a spiral of sacred geometry that extended from door to altar. It was beautiful and brutal in equal measure. A stellar design engineered to keep those kneeling from moving a single muscle. Skin would break if you wobbled. Flesh would tear if you lacked experience in the art of kneeling. Reverence was measured in stillness.

Later that night, Lady Linhua had visited me. Crouching beside me, she'd smoothed my hair back, her expression wet and tragic.

"You mustn't cross them," she whispered. "You know I love you. But I'm not the one the world will listen to."

Holding her gaze, I said, voice hoarse from hours of silence and dehydration, "But I already have a mother. You're right here."

Reigning Fire

She'd looked away. "You will say no such thing ever again if you value my life."

And so, since then, I'd been croaking the word "Mother" whenever I addressed the Consort.

Lady Linhua dropped some food presented by the Imperial Food Tester into my bowl with a pair of silver chopsticks, snapping me out of my memories. Across from us, Father was eating silently while reading his news scrolls.

If he was paying attention to our exchange, he gave no indication of it. This wasn't unusual, since my idea of a father was a magnificent stone statue. One that gave no warmth but still required tiptoeing around. For that slab of stone might just smite you, if you weren't cautious.

That said, over the years, I'd made it a private game to see if I could make that slab of stone twitch without getting smote. Not with tantrums or dramatic antics—just petty things using surreptitiously drawn glyphs. I tapped my fingers against the underside of the table, restless. The ashwillow brush I carried in my sleeve all morning itched against my wrist. Though it was only out of habit, not necessity, since I'd been practicing finger-glyphing in secret for weeks now.

Most students only started learning finger-glyphs in their final year at the Academy, but I'd picked it up faster than expected. Perhaps an unintended advantage from all my efforts copying Xiao's movements in the Dream Realm.

Might as well give it a test now, I thought. Holding out my index and middle fingers, I flicked a few quick strokes under the table for a Scramble glyph. One that would make the words on Father's scroll reorder themselves into gibberish for a few breaths. Something harmless and reversible that Weavers used in mischief spells or puzzle trials.

My strokes shimmered before vanishing, too quick for ordinary eyes to catch. But apparently, not quick enough. Without even glancing up from his scroll, Father's Emberkin, Zhu Feng, uncoiled beneath the table and flicked his tail across the glyph before it had a chance to activate. A perfect counter-swipe—exact, effortless, and thoroughly humiliating.

I blinked. Zhu Feng didn't hiss, but if snakes could form facial expressions, his would be a perfect imitation of Father rebuking, "Childish nonsense."

Except Father hadn't said a word to me. Just pulled out a second scroll and resumed reading.

I kept chewing, my expression blank. But I swore the next time I glanced down, the serpent's focus hadn't shifted. Not sight, exactly, but something that felt just as piercing. I hadn't succeeded in getting Father to react, but at least I'd confirmed one thing: he was paying more attention than he was letting on.

Well, I'd done my part today, and he'd approved. I was now *officially* his miracle. No one asked how I felt. That was never part of the ceremony.

That night, I sat alone by the window, watching the wispy leaves of the willow tree sweep across the surface of the pond. Though I was never truly alone—not since Mo. She curled at my bed's edge, like an ember that refused to go out. I used to flinch whenever she'd manifested before me, but I'd grown accustomed to her presence.

"I still don't know what you are," I whispered. "But I'm grateful I didn't have to go through the Binding Rites alone today. Thank you for being there."

Her ember-eyes glowed just a little brighter at my words, her posture mellowing deeper into repose.

We were told we wouldn't remember much about our Binding, but I remembered *everything*. I remembered glyphs drawn in the air with smokeink, and the way the flat stone tablet was passed from hand to hand, until it was finally placed into mine. It was smooth as river glass and cool to the touch, like it hadn't been held in centuries. Its surface was etched with concentric glyphs, said to represent the circle of will, vessel, and veil.

I remembered the discomfort when the glyph ink seared across my palm—meant to leave no physical mark, but nonetheless symbolic of the Binding. Despite all the ceremony, it didn't feel mystical. It felt clinical, like a medical procedure dressed in poetry.

And I remembered looking up at the rows of bonded Weavers—our Empire's finest—who'd lined the edges of the chamber, each accompanied by their own Emberkin, visible and proud. Towering over me from the stands, they were all robed in the same silver-gray silk robes for court assemblies, watching with measured interest, as if calculating what kind of Emberkin I would be suited for. No one asked me who I was, or who I wanted to be. They just wanted to see who would answer the call from the Smokeveil.

They always spoke of the Binding Rites as if they were a sacred milestone—a young aristocrat's first step into adulthood. But it was never about readiness or maturity. Not even worthiness.

Rather, it was about *control.*

The Binding Rites took place the day we turned sixteen, which happened to align with the final phase of our studies. By then, we were expected to have developed not only discipline and loyalty, but most importantly, openness and pliability. We were no longer children, yet we weren't powerful enough to challenge the order of things.

The grueling training we'd been put through over the last six years made time for rest scarce. A tremendous amount of pressure and a lack of repose made perfect ingredients for long-term suggestibility. Hence, the Empire considered this the ideal window to mold us into the way we *should* be, at least from the way they saw it. And so, the ceremony was framed as a gift—a rite of passage—when in truth, it was a leash.

Emberkin weren't random familiars arriving in our lives like lightning strikes. They were always around us, watching and waiting. Most would never manifest to bond with any Weavers. Only those who'd sensed a compatible tether, a kind of resonance with a human who'd been "shaped"—made predictable and palatable—might dare cross the Veil.

Of course, not all Emberkin were the same, any more than all humans were the same. But the ones that bonded easily? They were the ones who knew how to follow the Empire's expectations. Just like us.

For Weavers who bonded, their Emberkin usually arrived within a moon of their Binding Rites. Sometimes six. And if still no Emberkin manifested? The Empire would wait twelve moons. That was the grace period. The "reasonable" time it supposedly took for the Smokeveil to respond, if it ever would.

After that, the child would be quietly labeled as *unbonded* at the lack of progress. Not *broken*—the court avoided that word—but *incomplete*. Destined for support roles. Steered away from inheritance. And never again considered for anything that required a voice of power.

In the case of noble houses, it would be considered deeply unfortunate. For a royal? Unthinkable. Historically, unbonded royals had been married off in political deals, their names slowly erased from succession records. Few ever returned to the inner circle. It was a mercy, the court said. A dignified fade, not an exile.

So, the Binding Rites weren't just a ceremony; they were a silent contract. The Empire trained us, molded us, filled our heads with the illusion of choice. And once they were confident that we were ready, they offered us a single opening into the life they wanted for us. That was the "gift."

Truth was, most of us weren't bonding to Emberkin, but being chained to the Empire itself.

There were myths about the early Binding Rites. Before they were sanitized and turned into orchestrated performances. Back when Emberkin had come in all shapes, sizes, and shadows. When the powers of Smokeveil weren't bound by class, and Weavers without noble blood once roamed the lands, forging their own meaning, determining their own cultivation.

They claimed the result from that system was pure chaos. That when the Smokeveil was being interpreted in that way, it couldn't be trusted. But I wondered now, who was it chaotic *for*? The ones with something to lose, or the ones who had everything to gain from the narrative? The Binding Rites hadn't always existed. They'd only been introduced when the Empire began to fear what happened when the people bonded freely on their own. When the people chose.

And if I could return to the moment that stone tablet was placed in my hand, accompanied by prayers laced with containment, I would have smiled. From the bottom of my heart. Because they were never taming me. They were handing me the torch I would one day use to set it all alight.

With all the fuss throughout the day, it didn't take long before sleep claimed me. Falling into the Dream Realm felt like being dunked into an icy pond, the scent of temple ash invading my senses. Then came the pounding from the drums—deep, wild, and invigorating. Twenty-four qilin drums were arranged in a great crescent, flanked by veiled drummers half-shrouded in mist.

Standing before the drum formation was a masked figure in white, their sword in hand. They'd never spoken, so I didn't know their name. But I'd been calling them *Xiao* in my head—breathy, soft, like the sound of snow landing on stone. Xiao's movements carved through the air like the muscle memory of a warrior—graceful, devastating, precise, and in complete synchrony with the drumbeats.

For over a year now, whenever we met in the Dream Realm, Xiao skipped all exchanges of civilities and sprang right into action, like there was no time to waste. And I would simply start copying their moves, circling through the five foundational stances and a range of sweeps, kicks, and strikes. Then they would have me pick up a stick and mimic their movements with their sword.

Night after night, that was what we'd been doing. While I never had a chance to practice Swordcraft outside of the Dream Realm, what with all the palace surveillance, the nightly repetition seemed to activate an indescribable strength in my body and mind. Even when I was battling a bone-deep fatigue throughout the day in the Mortal Realm, I felt *alive*.

But tonight was different. Without forewarning, Xiao tossed a sheathed sword toward me in full swing, to my utter bewilderment. My hand shot through the air without thinking, catching it by the hilt. I blinked, stunned in total disbelief. Next thing I knew, Xiao was already charging toward me, led by their sword.

Sucking a sharp breath through my teeth, I drew my sword and spun to a defensive stance, just in time

Reigning Fire

to deflect the tip of their sword from my chest. Our swords met with a hiss of metal. Pivoting without missing a beat, they sent another strike low. I dropped, barely catching it with the flat of my blade. Sparks flew, and pain flared in my wrist.

Before I could regain composure, the hilt of their sword cracked against my ribs. I staggered, air knocked from my lungs. Then another blow to my thigh, not enough to wound but enough to teach. Xiao didn't pause. Their strikes curved like water, effortlessly flowing past my defense as their sword danced—no, *sang*—around me. I scrambled to catch up with them, blood roaring in my ears, every muscle screaming for balance.

Then it all stopped. Their blade rested lightly against my shoulder, a whisper of cold metal against fevered skin. Panting like I was just moments away from being sick, I was a sweating, shaking mess. I would have doubled over if it wasn't for the sword still on my shoulder. Out of nowhere, a laugh escaped me. And once I started, I had trouble stopping.

For the first time ever, I was neither Princess nor prey. *So, this is how it feels*, I thought.

If Xiao thought I'd lost my mind, I couldn't see it through their veil. They simply stepped back, sheathed their sword, and disappeared into the mist without a word. By now, words were no longer needed between us. The message was loud and clear:

To be continued.

When I woke, the soles of my feet felt raw, as if I'd danced barefooted all night on stone. My thighs ached and my hands trembled, but my heart was light. I chuckled. Progress didn't have to look pretty.

My nightly trips to the Dream Realm remained a secret of one. It wasn't something that any other Weaver could do. And a realm-crossing Princess wasn't a rumor one would wish to go around, not if they didn't find the idea of torture and violent interrogations appealing.

In class, I sat with the stillness expected of a royal heir. No one ever noticed I was often hovering barely an inch above my seat, my knees wobbling with effort, core locked tight. I'd been doing this every day since starting training with Xiao. At first, I'd only managed to hold a few breaths at a time. Now, I could manage at least half a stick of incense-burning time.

Playing the role of a dutiful student, I always offered to carry scrolls and sacred bowls. No one knew it was to teach myself to lift with breath control, keeping the tremor in my arms invisible. Others only saw me wearing all the finest hairpins. No one knew I picked the precious stones on them for their weight, not adornment. These shoulders were now strong enough to carry fifteen pounds on them all day.

No one could feel the weighted silk wraps beneath my sleeves and skirts—hand-stitched from discarded fabric, threaded with iron wire. Their sand panels weighed just enough to strain my muscles throughout the day without changing how my silk robes draped on me. It was something I'd created when the palace was still asleep and the ache in my chest wouldn't let me be.

Once, I'd read that centuries ago, noble girls wore weighted sleeves to train for elegance. To perfect the lines of their shoulders and the tilt of their wrists. Their weights were for beauty; *mine were for survival.* Every step, every word, every motion was training. To what ends, exactly, I didn't yet know.

It wasn't as if I could ever leave these palace walls. And within them, learning self-defense was never deemed a relevant skill for royals. Not with all the best trained palace guards, assassins, and Warriors. No one would ever acknowledge that the deadliest threats were rarely external, appearing in forms neither tangible nor overt.

I could just feel it in my bones—a war I hadn't yet fully understood, looming on the horizon. And I would not enter it soft.

Chapter Two

烟中有序

ORDER IN SMOKES

The Weavers' Academy at the outer palace was quieter than the rest of the palace—not out of reverence, but fear. The paintings of the great scholars and Weavers of Yan adorning the walls served as a solemn reminder of what we should aspire to be. The students were one another's allies and rivals in equal measure, influenced not only by personal rapport, but also by clan dynamics.

In class, it mattered not if we'd had a full night's sleep, or if we were perpetually tired. Looking alert and ready to learn was the only acceptable way to present ourselves. We filed in just before sunrise, our Emberkin trailing behind us like silk shadows. Or, in my case, hidden and invisible to all others.

The classroom was built for nobles, and it showed in every detail. Rosewood desks lined the room in perfect symmetry, each paired with a matching chair whose legs curved like calligraphy strokes. Mother-of-pearl inlays shimmered along the borders, catching the light from the open-panel doors that let in the sun once it'd risen. In one corner, a coil of sandalwood incense curled smoke through the air, softening the sharpness of ink and effort. Above each desk, a golden Lighting glyph hovered—a flicker of Smokecraft left behind by Master Dan.

Those of us born royal had our places etched long before we'd learned to write our own names. I took my seat at the center row, third from the front—the position reserved for the Prince Regent's sole heir. While my desk didn't look any different from the others', I could feel the pressure pressing inward from every direction. But Mo remained a comforting wisp of warmth curled near my elbow.

As usual, the class started with a silent bow to the "First Flame," an ancestral concept of weaving powers as duty, led by School Master Dan. At his side, a pale blue heron Emberkin stood motionless, his long neck curved like the tail of a comet. He blinked slowly—once—then resumed watching the class as if memorizing each movement. Only nobles with bonded Emberkin were permitted to teach royal heirs.

"Today," announced Master Dan, brushing ink across the board with practiced elegance, "we'll revise on Emberkin classification and lineage theory.

After six years of intense training on all the essential Smokecraft, many of you have now either bonded an Emberkin or are within your window to do so."

A few students sat a little taller. Minister Lee's eldest let her Emberkin—a slender white crane—perch on her forearm with poise. When her wings flicked open, a whisper of admiration swept the room.

"Lee's crane Emberkin is perfect for amplifying her strengths in Sealbinding and Illusory Grace, amongst other Smokecraft disciplines," someone eagerly offered.

Indeed, since bonding her crane, Lee's usual sturdy presence had now become almost impossible to overlook.

Councilor Wu's young rising star from across the aisle leaned back in his seat and let his fox Emberkin stretch across his shoulders. The tail of the fox twitched with lazy confidence. *Subtle.*

"Enterprise, influence, and tactical shrewdness," Master Dan said without looking up. "Classic House Wu traits, as expected."

All highly regarded qualities in the political sphere. Looked like Father would have to endure at least another generation of Wus at court.

I focused on the board, carefully maintaining a neutral expression. Mo flickered, then stilled. Her shape was far too large, far too broken to mimic elegance—and far too *mythic*. More times than I could count, I'd seriously considered my odds of convincing others she was a regular bird-type Emberkin, instead of a phoenix. But each time, I would quickly dismiss the idea. I wished I could keep Mo hidden forever and pretend to be unbonded, but that was never going to be an option for me.

Since the Emperor's illness over five years ago, Father had been ruling in his stead as the Regent. Though he hadn't officially ascended the throne, no one mistook where the true power lay. Being the least favored son, Father wasn't the first choice; not even the second. Like me, he wasn't a natural at Connate Charisma. He'd had to work extremely hard at this particular Smokecraft discipline.

However, he was a prodigy in Tradeweaving, which was a driving force in the Empire's economic stability all these years. Tradeweavers could bind glyphs to goods and contracts alike: preserving produce through weeks of travel, keeping silks flawless despite bad weather, sealing Smokecrafted trade deals that enforced fair terms—or unfair ones, if the Weaver knew how to veil it. The most skilled could nudge regional demand or tilt negotiations without ever saying a word, weaving influence as subtly as shifting of the tide.

But if I'd learned anything about court politics, it was that barely anything could beat Connate Charisma.

Unless they were Prince Yan Yun, of course. He'd made it to the very top, even when he wasn't dealt with the best starting hand. That had to count for something.

Unfortunately for the Emperor's favorite children, my two uncles were too impatient and power hungry, which could be a dangerous combination. Like two vultures smelling opportunity, they could hardly wait to be the first to dive in once they'd learned about the Emperor's illness. I wondered what had hurt Grandfather more—his most treasured sons' complete lack of care for his welfare, or the risks they had put the Empire under.

Father had eventually stepped in to settle the political unrest. Overnight, the political scene was completely overturned. Two noble Princes—one permanently banished from the royal family, the other in indefinite solitary house arrest far from the palace. Their Emberkin were sentenced to lifetime incarceration in an enchanted glass prison at the top floor of the Lifeng Pagoda.

Like his serpent Emberkin, Father made no false strikes. But when he did strike, one could be certain it would be deadly. So, naturally, nothing short of absolute excellence was to be expected from me. And to remain unbonded by the end of the year would be to bring unspeakable shame to the royal family.

The only problem was, there was no way I could allow Mo to be visible to others without sending an open invitation to unknown perils. At least not before I could find more information. After all, I'd never known of any Emberkin taking the form of a beaten-up phoenix. All known Emberkin took the form of real-world creatures.

While our legends and mythical creatures were core to the Empire's culture and tradition, they were considered sacred and celestial. Entities from a different realm, inaccessible to us. So, any such manifestations in, or associations with mere mortals—even Smokeveil Weavers—were considered unholy and a taboo. Which meant I couldn't exactly walk up to Master Dan, or anyone else for that matter, and simply ask about it.

Over the last year, I'd been thoroughly searching through both the Academy and royal archives. But I had come no closer to finding any clues than when I'd started.

Master Dan turned, cuing an end to my daydreaming. "Can anyone remind us of the social functions of Emberkin visibility?"

Three hands rose.

"Status," offered one. "If you've bonded, you display. If you haven't, you try harder."

"To bond within a year of the Binding is considered a baseline for all noble bloodlines," said another.

A third voice—sharper—added, "There could always be … exceptions."

The Wu boy.

Several pairs of eyes inconspicuously glanced toward me. The smile that accompanied the voice was pleasant but also instructed and scheming.

"After all, some bond on the day of their Binding Rites. Others, not at all. We can't all be like our ancestors. Not even if our mothers tried their hardest to whip us into shape."

The jab landed gently, precisely. I returned the smile, small and regal.

"Or perhaps we would exceed them," I retorted, my voice soft as ash. "Eventually."

Master Dan said nothing, but I saw the smallest twitch of his ink brush before he turned back to the board. *If this exchange was a test, I should have absolutely aced Illusory Grace*, I thought.

My clever riposte aside, all I could hear now was the drip of an invisible water clock. My twelve-moon countdown had officially begun, and I was still pretending Mo didn't exist. But if I'd thought that was going to be the worst of my woes, I was very quickly proven wrong.

"Now that we've had a refresher," Master Dan continued, setting his brush on the inkstone, "it's time to start discussing the mid-year Concordance Trial."

A rustle of excitement swept the room. Chairs were straightened. Even the Emberkin perked up—feathers twitching, tails curling.

"This is no mere assessment," he explained, "but a simulation of court. Of power. Of real-life consequences. You will be divided—not by me, but by *yourselves*. Alliances will be forged, betrayals will occur. That is the point."

A hush settled over the class. I resisted the urge to collapse into a ball. I'd barely survived the tea-circle politics of breakfast. A public alliance? That was asking for war.

"You're to form your own alliances," Master Dan elucidated the rules. "Three to five student Weavers per faction. You must recruit a candidate from the adjoining Martial Academy to act as your General. Your task will be to secure influence, extract intelligence, and position yourselves favorably ahead of the final day of ritual combats, which marks the end of the Trial."

He paused, letting that sink in before emphasizing, "Yes, close combat between Generals from different factions is involved. No, it will not be optional. Its outcome will be the final measure."

He turned to face the class once more. "Once your factions are formed and Generals selected, each faction leader will draw a plaque by lot. Each plaque will indicate the arms your General will be granted during the duel. One plaque, however, will be blank. Leaders will have full liberty to decide whom to disclose the outcome of their draws to."

A few murmurs sparked among the students.

"If your faction draws the blank plaque," Master Dan explained, "your General will enter the fight with no assigned arms. You may try to bargain for one or steal from other factions at any point up to the deciding day of the Trial, but that is your burden to manage. The arms draw is part of the Trial; so is how you respond to imbalance."

He shot a warning glance at Wu, who was sounding all too excited, then added, "You're to attempt to extract intelligence on the other factions' arms. Any manner of sabotage and misinformation to steal or trade plaques, as well as to win the Trial, will be permitted—*if* you believe you can get away with it. But if *caught* breaking a Sealbinding agreement or engaging in any undisputably unlawful acts, your entire faction could be disqualified. Or worse."

Master Dan's gaze swept across the room, solemn. "What matters more is how you *navigate*. Who you protect. Who you deceive. And what you're willing to sacrifice."

The room crackled with tension. A flicker of nervous energy buzzed down my spine. Mo pulsed under my skin—hot, then cold, then gone, almost completely in sync with my internal clash of dismay and resignation.

"Put your years of Smokecraft training to good use," he advised. "But remember, those without an Emberkin won't be able to tap into the powers of Smokeveil, so choose your allies wisely."

He tapped on the character for *breath* written on the board, hard. "All Weavers' true powers begin with the Smokeveil. It is a conglomerate of spirit and skill—a current that can only be tapped into through our bonded Emberkin. Without them, we are capturing smoke with our bare hands. We may mimic, but we will never truly grasp."

His voice lowered as he gave a final cryptic reminder, "To bond is to breathe. To breathe is to act. Let this be the year you learn the difference."

Master Dan's voice was still echoing in my mind even as I crossed over to the Dream Realm. Night after night, I'd been getting my phoenix tail handed to me sparring with Xiao, both in hand-to-hand combat and in Swordcraft.

The twenty-four qilin drums pulsed in the distance, low and steady, and Xiao was ready and waiting, as always. It occurred to me that my unusual training with my enigmatic mentor might have been the first constant in my life I could count on.

Mentor?

"Master" would've been more respectful. There it was again—we'd never even decided on titles.

Xiao nodded once, the same way they always did before drawing their sword in a fluid arc, barely disturbing the air. I mirrored them, adjusting my grip, and we began. The fog was lighter than usual tonight, like breath on glass.

I moved first, which was a mistake. I was always faster when I reacted—not out of skill but survival instincts. Most nights, I was too busy absorbing everything I could to mind how unglamorously I'd failed time and again. But ever since the Concordance Trial announcement, the vines of desperation had coiled itself around me, tight as a python's grip.

Too stiff.

Too slow.

Again.

My own inner voice was as curt as Father's.

Xiao shifted their weight, parried without effort, then swept forward in a blur. I braced for the sting— the same sharp tap of steel on skin I'd come to anticipate. But this time, I moved. Not perfectly, not even well, but I *moved*. My shoulder twisted just far enough, and Xiao's strike missed by a hair's breadth. My blade was already rising when I saw an opening, albeit a momentary one. I took it.

The tip of my sword touched the hem of Xiao's sleeve before they recentered and deflected my strike with a smooth, circular motion, like a master calligrapher spinning a brush. Then Xiao turned away wordlessly, which I'd learned meant the night's lesson was over. Any moment now, they would be vanishing into the mist.

Whenever they turned their back on me while I was still armed, I wondered: was it out of confidence in my character, or just assurance of my incompetence? The latter made more sense, but it still stung.

I stood there, panting, sweating, heart thundering in my ears. It wasn't a victory. Not even close, but they hadn't landed their final blow, either. Then across the clearing, Xiao turned back. For the first time, they inclined their head by just a fraction and tapped the fist holding their sword's hilt to their open palm.

An acknowledgment.

Then they were gone. I sank to my knees, taking it all in. It wasn't much—a little step's worth of progress, but it was real.

The memory of the first time I'd met Xiao drifted to mind like the fog around me. I hadn't meant to cross over to the Dream Realm. I didn't even know

I could. It'd been another sleepless night, and I'd abandoned my bed in spite. I remembered curling up on the cold floor in my quarters, Mo pressed tight against my chest. My mind wouldn't quieten. My body felt heavy and wrong, like it didn't know how to rest.

Next thing I knew, I was stepping on obsidian ground veiled thinly by snow in a vast, open plain. My breath was fogging up before me in the bitingly cold air.

I turned, and the drummers were already there—twenty-four of them standing in a perfect formation, arms raised. Without looking at me, they began striking on the drums, one by one. I wasn't sure if I was visible to anyone at all. That was when I saw Xiao walking forward from behind the drum formation.

Their eyes found mine—black as ink and unreadable—before they lifted a hand in a slow, beckoning gesture. I knew then that I wasn't invisible. I took a step. Then another. The sound of the drums thrummed into my bones, a rhythm that seemed to rearrange something in me, as if I was longing to answer to battle.

Xiao stood in the center of the clearing, still as a mountain. A sheathed blade was hanging loosely on the cord around their waist, but they didn't reach for it. Instead, they stepped forward and lifted a staff—just wood, nothing ornate—and began to move, slow and deliberate. No words were exchanged between us, just instruction through motion.

I stood frozen at first, until Xiao paused and pointed their staff toward the edge of the clearing, signaling me to a stick lying on the ground. I hadn't noticed it before. Picking it up, I tried my best to copy them. I was clumsy and always a few beats behind, but the rhythm of the drums helped pull me into movement. I didn't know what I was doing but knew I wanted to keep going. To learn.

That was all we'd done for hours, maybe more. Time was a fluid construct in the Dream Realm. We'd trained until I'd collapsed on the ground, my arms trembling from effort. Xiao didn't help me up, only signaled for the drummers to stop.

When my consciousness had slipped through the borders of realms again, I'd awoken on the floor in my chambers as if I'd never left, Mo still curled against me. But my muscles were sore in ways no dream had ever left me before.

That was the first time I'd realized I might be dangerous. And the first time that didn't scare me.

Chapter Three

深藏不露

THE RETICENT STRATEGIST

Prince Yan Yun

The Lifeng Pagoda stood at the southmost edge of the palace grounds, rising like a shadow just before the cliffs dropped into the Gorge of Echoes. In the daylight, its structure looked deceptively elegant—its smoked black flying eaves carved with the ancient sigils of Smokeveil law, obsidian roof tiles glinting in the sun. But no one ever mistook it for a sanctuary. Lifeng was where the Empire buried its sins under the guise of salvation.

Yan Yun didn't take the usual path through the pagoda's main hall. Not when he could access the secret corridor exclusively reserved for the possessor of the Empire's jade seal of governance. His personal guards never followed along when he came here. It was understood that he demanded privacy.

The air grew colder the deeper he went, and the scent of redroot smoke thickened, laced with something metallic and dry. The lifewardens stationed at each descending level nodded stiffly as he passed, eyes fixed ahead, hands unmoving at their sides. Silent and loyal, they were bound to never speak of what they saw while on duty.

He descended the spiral staircase until he reached the deepest level, far beneath the main Lifeng prison on the top floor—the one that all others assumed held every incarcerated Emberkin. But of course, he would never leave his brothers' fates in a place so obvious, so vulnerable.

Two doors made of smoke-glass awaited him. One bore the etching of a five-clawed dragon lazily coiled over a cauldron. The other shimmered, carved with the outlines of a smoke serpent—its iridescent coils draping over a cypress branch. Yan Yun always entered the left chamber first.

The moment the door sealed behind him, the scent of spiced incense thickened. Hammocks made of woven Smokecrafted threads hung from the ceiling, mostly unused. At the back, sprawled atop a mountain of embroidered silk cushions, lounged his second brother's Emberkin—Hu Wei. He was a stately white peacock Emberkin. Or had once been.

Wei's once glorious plumage now hung limp, the tail feathers dulled to a ghostly sheen. The crown of feathers atop his head drooped slightly, and his eyes—once sharp with amused indifference—now blinked slow and disinterested. One talon lazily flicked a gemstone across the floor, nudging it toward a shallow lacquer bowl brimming with similar trinkets—all polished, gleaming, and utterly useless.

The peacock did not look at him. Could not. But his brothers' Emberkin would recognize his aura from anywhere in this realm, even from the depths of hell. A slow blink told him he was right. Then a puff of plume in the direction of Yan Yun's Emberkin. As if acknowledging the presence of Zhu Feng, his serpent Emberkin, but not him. Hu Wei had always been theatrical like that. Everything was a performance, even now, with no one left to perform for.

Yan Yun didn't react to his irreverence. Folding his arms behind his back, he stared down at the creature he'd once admired, sometimes feared. Now, he felt only the weariness of recognition. Hu Wei had been shrewd in his day. Not necessarily cruel, just endlessly entitled. The brother he'd bonded with had always sought brilliance without burden—clever schemes with no cost. And when the cost eventually came, as it always did, he'd wept and blamed fate.

Yan Yun moved to the next chamber. The other Emberkin acknowledged them with a low growl and a glint of silver eyes. His fur was the color of cold smoke, tipped in soot, and his large paws stepped lightly across crystal floor tiles as if it weighed nothing at all. This was the lynx Emberkin of the eldest Prince—the favored heir before his self-invited downfall. He'd called the lynx Li Shuang.

Shuang padded through hanging veils of chain-linked crystals, creating soft, melodic chimes as he passed by. He liked beautiful things. Gold, mirror-glass, smoke-infused jewels. His chamber looked more like a ruined treasure hall than a prison cell.

"I swear I still marvel at your collection, no matter how many times I've dropped by," Yan Yun muttered, though he knew Shuang wouldn't hear him. Yan Yun wondered how many of those trinkets were offerings, and how many were embezzled.

The lynx Emberkin blinked slowly, then glided lightly across the crystal floor, pawing at a shattered piece of mirror-glass. His reflection fractured, then re-formed in a dozen angles. The creature paused to gaze into one—not seeing, but lingering, as if sensing the warmth of presence in the smoke creature coiled around Yan Yun's feet. Shuang had always believed in the permanence of beauty. Even now, surrounded by ruin, he curated his surroundings like a shrine.

Yan Yun stood there a moment longer, then turned, letting the door seal itself behind him. There was a narrow hallway that overlooked both chambers through thin slits of smoke-glass. A one-way viewing corridor. He stood stolidly between them, watching the silhouettes of the white peacock lounging and the lynx pacing.

The past came back unbidden—memories of two older brothers fighting over relic swords, racing Emberkin through the training forests, calling him a "little flower" when he'd trailed behind. Back then, he hadn't bonded an Emberkin of his own. He'd only watched, in silence, until the day he'd bonded

Zhu Feng—the serpent of green fire that submitted to him alone. The same serpent that now rested in his shadow, silent and coiled.

He breathed in deeply, his attention still fixed on the blurred smoke figures. "You were the Emperor's favorites. Chosen. Indulged. Ruined." The words weren't spoken in cruelty, only in fact. "I was the afterthought. And yet, here I stand."

Behind the glass, the two Emberkin stirred. Not in overt protest, nor in assent. Zhu Feng hissed at his feet, sensing the tension threading through his bonded human's spine.

Glancing down, Yan Yun murmured, "Stay at ease."

This wasn't a visit of finality. He didn't come here for revenge or forgiveness. Only remembrance. It was ritual, a reminder. That strength without control led to ruin. That favor without scrutiny led to downfall. And that even monsters still echoed when broken.

He stepped back, shadows clinging to the folds of his robes like old regrets.

"Seal the corridor," he told the lifewarden at the entrance. "Report any anomalies with those two to my personal attendant. Directly."

"Yes, Your Highness."

As he ascended the spiral stairs once more, the air warmed, but the cold in his bones did not lift. Behind him, the Lifeng Pagoda stood lofty and solid, holding its ghosts, as always.

The palace was the quietest in the mornings, before the scholars began their recitations and the heralds started announcing the arrival of those requesting an audience in their booming voices. It was in that hush that Yan Yun read the day's news scrolls—left thumb smoothing the edge of the brocade backing, index finger curled in thought, attention fixed not on the words but on the *silence* they granted him.

The silence he so appreciated was not a lack of sound, per se—there were always echoes, footfalls, and soft greetings from attendants who were constantly on the move. No, this was a different kind of quietude, where no one asked what he wanted, nor apprised him of what was needed from him.

There was a time in his distant memory that he'd felt peace without needing the news scrolls as an excuse. A life of careful diplomacy and cultivated gardens, of days spent wandering book alleys in the Capital and evenings reading by glyphlight, untouched by the hunger that ruled court politics.

But the court had its own appetite, and so did the family he was born into. His rise to power was hardly a surprise to most in court, even when it was still such a hard pill to swallow for the Emperor. For … complex reasons.

Yan Yun's eldest brother, spoiled to ruin. The second, consumed by vice. And then there was their father, withering in his chambers, refusing physicians one day and summoning them in fury the next.

Yan Yun had simply waited patiently. For it was foolish to try to destroy what was already headed for destruction. An ineffective use of his time and energy. Vultures would always be vultures. He'd always known he was playing the long game.

When their father had finally collapsed, it was Yan Yun who'd stayed. Who'd wiped his mouth and watched him still mourn the sons he once loved most. Yet, Yan Yun insisted on personally powdering the ginseng roots for his daily concoction. He knew the exact temperature that his father's medicinal tea had to be steeped in.

He'd never resented the work. It was, in fact, the first time he could be so close to his father without any interference, any competition. It was tough to care for an ailing father, yet so easy at the same time.

Yan Yun had never quite known how to be around the Emperor before his father *needed* him. Being a carer came with a clear list of tasks, albeit a long one. But being a worthy son? That was like being on an ever-shifting domain, with a vague target you could somewhat make out but never quite reach.

He was never the favorite, but he would be the last one remaining by his side. Others said he was cunning, that he found the law's seams and stretched them without ever tearing the fabric. They weren't wrong. He did not believe in chaos, only in leverage and artful maneuvers. In loopholes, yes, but never in lawlessness. Let others call it deviousness. For him, it'd always been about living up to his full potential.

He thought of Linhua sometimes, of the way she'd looked when she'd first entered his study. She was still a palace attendant then. Quiet and keen-eyed. Not in a coy or docile manner. Just … measured. A woman who'd learned the shape of power from the outside looking in.

He'd offered her safety; she'd offered him silence. They didn't speak much of affection. That wasn't the kind of bond they had. But when she'd asked for her adoptive brother, Wan, to be found, he did it without hesitation. The man who arrived was sharp-eyed and coiled like a knife. Loyal, but only to Linhua. That suited Yan Yun just fine, for loyalty often made the best leverage.

The court had jeered at first. At Linhua, at Yan Yun. Taking a concubine with no clan, no heritage— a foxglove in silk. But she'd never broken under the weight of both the court and the inner palace, even as the years had passed with no heir. There were whispers, of course. Always whispers. That she'd cursed him. That she was the reason no children had come. That he could have chosen almost anyone else.

He heard them. Ignored them. But deep within, he had felt the pressure mounting then—social, political, ancestral.

Then came Yan Xun, a child born as a long-awaited miracle. She was quiet, even as a baby. He'd always been a man of few words himself, but there was always something brewing beneath his quietude. Like the surface of a tranquil pond—no one could know its true depth, or what might be lurking underneath.

Yan Xun's quietness felt different. She was like Linhua, yet not like her at all. With all of his astuteness in judging characters, he could never be certain if there was much going on in that child's head. For all he knew, it could simply be meekness or resignation. Observance, he would hope, at the very least.

He should have immediately named her heir at birth, but he hadn't. Not until he became the Regent, and the matter couldn't be delayed any further. Because she wasn't exceptional, not in the way he needed. She had his face but not his clarity. And that, more than anything, had unsettled him. He never told her that, just read his scrolls without looking up while she spoke to him. Let her sit near him in silence. Let her think proximity was presence.

He'd taught her how to write her own name as soon as she was old enough to grasp a brush. Got her to practice it again and again, from sunup to sundown. For days on end. She needed to learn the weight that her name carried. It was never too early to let that sink in for her.

He'd imagined that when he could finally experience fatherhood, it would be different from what he actually felt. But it ended up panning out just like how he felt about his own father. Now that the child was here in flesh and blood, he didn't know what to *do* with her. What to *say*. How to *be*.

Déjà fucking vu.

The mission to teach, to instill excellence, however—that came with a much more straightforward framework. A clear start and end, a way to track progress. That was easier, or so he'd thought.

To his utter bewilderment, the child had found *everything* so difficult—anything from basic numeracy to Smokecraft. It blew his mind to see someone so … slow. And he'd tried teaching her—heavens knew he'd tried—but most of these things had come easily for him. He was at a loss at how he could teach something that was instinctive for him.

A familiar voice from outside his study caught his attention, nudging his thoughts back to the present. He looked out and recognized the figure passing through the eastern colonnade below as Fu Kai, Wan's son. Yan Yun abruptly recalled reading a report that he was now back from the borders and freshly reassigned to the palace as an Imperial Guard. His uniform was crisp, sword at his side, gait as arrogant as ever.

Kai had never been to his liking. Loud, haughty, and just sharp enough to irritate, but never to impress. Still, there was a time when even someone like him served a purpose. Linhua had insisted that Yan Xun needed someone who could be close enough to feel like kin, but distant enough to pose no threat to her position at court. Someone who could speak and act freely around her, without invoking political calculation. A "brother," she'd called it. Someone Yan Xun wouldn't have to impress. And in turn, someone who wouldn't be compelled to treat her with reverence or fear.

Yan Yun had granted it. He always granted the small requests, especially when it cost him nothing. Besides, with how much Yan Xun tried engaging him in trivial conversation, he thought perhaps she did need more human connection than he ever did or could ever offer. A brother might be exactly what she needed, as Linhua had said.

While Yan Yun had never cared for the self-professed royal, Fu Kai had been lingering in Yan Xun's orbit long enough that even the palace stewards began referring to him as part of her circle. He made a racket but not waves, drew attention but not influence. And, more importantly, he'd never truly *belonged*. In other words, all noise and no bite.

Yan Yun had observed them once in passing. Yan Xun was seated beneath the cherry pines, Fu Kai throwing pebbles into the koi pond and narrating each ripple as though it held some grand significance. She'd said nothing, just stared ahead. A sight, Yan Yun thought, of imbalance, but also of strange companionship.

So, he let it be. If Linhua wanted her daughter to have a stand-in for Wan, so be it. Wan had been loyal to Linhua beyond reason, beyond blood. Perhaps she hoped that Fu Kai might someday be the same for Yan Xun. Though that was sentiment, which had no real bearing on power distribution at court.

He'd never once considered Fu Kai to be family or a member of the nobility. As far as he was concerned, Fu Kai was nothing. But Linhua didn't need to know that. Yan Yun would do well to keep the mother of his child happy, especially when he was at a loss as to what to do with that child.

As a father, he'd found nothing about raising Yan Xun easy, even when it came to getting her fed. It was as if she wasn't even equipped with the most basic of survival instincts—to acquire sustenance.

For over twelve seasonal changes as a young child, there'd been only *one* dish she would eat. Prepared in the *exact* same way. Even when he'd conjured his most terrifying demeanor, Yan Xun would rather cry herself to sleep than to take a bite of anything else.

The royals were forbidden to eat more than three spoonfuls of the same dish, or to repeat a dish. A system designed to complicate the poison work of any possible assassins. If no one could guess what their favorite dish was, it would be onerous to determine what to poison.

But no, this child would rather die of self-imposed starvation than to yield. No need for poisons and assassins. He wasn't the Regent then—not yet—so it was still easier to bend the rules. Every meal, he'd personally tested her food after the Imperial Food Tester had approved it, before letting it be served. Even with just three bites a day, it didn't take long before he'd had to suppress a dry gag whenever he as much as smelled that damned dish from afar.

He could shape policy but clearly not determine the destiny of his child. He could subjugate courtiers but not influence his daughter's obstinate refusal to learn the ways of court life.

He was more relieved than he'd cared to admit when Yan Xun was finally old enough to enter the Weavers' Academy. Because then, there would be someone he could rage at if she'd continued to fail to rise to the occasion.

So, he'd summoned the School Master to his private study the night before Yan Xun was due to move into the Academy. Made sure he was crystal clear that there was to be no special treatment for her over the next seven years of her studies. And that he had his full permission—no, in fact, his *orders*—to work her harder than anyone else.

Based on the reports Yan Yun had been receiving, she'd been making considerable progress. So, it wasn't entirely hopeless. But he knew she was still nowhere near where she needed to be.

He'd once taught her how to write her own name; now, he would read that same name in reports that praised her efforts but never her brilliance. It was one thing to be named the heir, but everyone knew keeping the title was the true test.

As of now, he wasn't certain she could subdue the influence of her closest rival in the succession game that was already forming. Perhaps if he was extremely strategic about the perfect alliance for her through a heavenly union sometime in the future …

Well, that would be a future problem. The burning issue before the year ended was the bonding of an Emberkin.

Yan Yun cast his gaze on Zhu Feng, coiled up near him under the desk and hidden from passersby, as he should be. There was something incredibly powerful in staying evasive, so that no one could know when he might strike, or where from. Sensing the attention on him, Zhu Feng lifted his head in Yan Yun's direction with a lazy flick of his tongue. Satisfied Yan Yun wasn't in any trouble that required his assistance, he returned to his nap.

Yan Yun had bonded Zhu Feng on the very day of his Binding at sixteen. It was interesting how no one—be it parents, siblings, women, courtiers, or child—knew him like Zhu Feng did.

He clearly remembered his own lesson as a child, on a day of storming heat and roiling clouds. His father, the great Emperor Yan, had summoned him to the inner courtyard, where the old School Master had waited with a brocade-bound tome in one hand.

"Emberkin," the School Master explained, "are fragments of the Weavers' soul, melded with the very powers pulled from the Smokeveil itself—their ultimate forms are shaped, not born. They reflect not your bloodline, but your innermost truths."

His father had said nothing, simply watched him appraisingly from beneath the shade of a parasol.

"They determine if they will tether themselves to you, embrace a part of you as their own the moment your will meets the world. Not a breath earlier. What results is a familiar that carries the essence of both Emberkin and Weaver," the Master continued.

"Do they think?" a young Yan Yun, barely a scrawny little thing with curious eyes then, asked.

The School Master blinked. "They *feel*. Deeply, and with devotion. While they cannot see, hear, smell, and taste like humans do, their sentience is interwoven with your own."

"Can others see them?"

"Only when you choose to, provided you've bonded one. Mortals aren't blessed with the sight to detect all the unbonded Emberkin around us. However"—the School Master paused—"not all Emberkin are interested in manifesting and bonding with a Weaver. Some may choose *never* to."

At the time, Yan Yun had wondered why that was so. But before opening his mouth again, he'd habitually glanced up at his father, studying any smallest changes in his composure. While the Emperor had remained impassive, his grip around the handle of his cane had tightened infinitesimally.

Yan Yun had decided against asking any more questions.

"Emberkin are their bonded Weavers' unique conduit for the Smokeveil's mighty powers," the School Master continued, "keepers of our secrets. And sometimes, a trial that the heavens have written into our destinies."

That was the first time Yan Yun understood that power didn't always come with the blare of a horn. Sometimes, the heavens laid it to slither beneath your feet when you had proven yourself deserving.

Denied the privileges of his brothers born into power, Yan Yun had been forced to learn how to seize it for himself. And, most importantly, how to *conserve* it.

He turned toward the window, scrolls tucked under one arm. Outside, the day was already beginning in full. Somewhere, students were preparing for the Concordance Trial, alliances being formed, and arms drawn. He wouldn't interfere; that was never a question. He wouldn't try to reach for the threads of Yan Xun's fate. Not anymore.

She would either learn, or she would fall.

And if she fell, he would not catch her. Not because he didn't care, but because to rule this Empire one day, she needed to become someone who didn't need catching.

燕

yān

云

yún

Reigning Fire

Chapter Four

致命联盟

DEADLY ALLIANCES

They called it the *Resilience Residency*. A seven-year boarding scheme for all students of the Weavers' and Martial Academies—high-born children and sponsored commoners alike, enforced without exception.

"To build bonds of merit," the scrolls proclaimed. "To shield future pillars of the Imperial Court from the boundless indulgence of their clans."

Such virtuous aspirations for cultivating young minds—the beautiful work of many crane Emberkin through time, no doubt. The art of politics, distilled: if "conditioning," "surveillance," and "control" unsettled the people, veil them beneath nobler names, like "camaraderie" and "resilience by shared ordeal."

No one should mention the way Detection glyphs lined the Academies' perimeters, or how the School Master's heron Emberkin was said to perch in shadowed corners. Still, the student Weavers adapted. The nobles treated their private annexes like family estates in miniature, complete with embroidered banners and ceremonial meal deliveries. The sponsored lowborns shared narrow dormitory halls, all harsh wood and flimsy window panels.

We were allowed leave on the weekends. Most of the nobles seized the opportunity to return to their manors, relishing luxurious baths, home-cooked delicacies, and embroidered slippers delivered by trembling servants. But most low-born students stayed behind, unwilling or unable to afford the travel—and the reminder of how far they'd strayed from home.

As for me, I kept my sizable wing stripped down to the bare essentials by choice. No attendants, no personal guards, no warmth. Just a string connected to a bell in the servants' quarters near my bed—the only allowance I'd negotiated after Shan had gone.

Since then, I'd mostly chosen to stay back over the weekends, on the pretext of catching up on my studies. The one reason that would never be questioned by my parents.

The empty familiarity of my old annex in the inner palace began to feel colder than the court. At least here, I could enjoy the tranquility of empty courtyards and dormitories.

The formal announcement came with ceremony—just a piercing bell chime echoing through the courtyards, followed by scrolls nailed to the entryways of every hall. It read:

The Concordance Trial begins in thirty days.
Afternoon lessons suspended for strategic preparations.
Reward: An artifact chosen by the victor
from the Vault of Smokeveil Relics.

That changed everything. The students buzzed like struck chimes. Everyone knew the artifacts existed—scrolls of foresight, whispering blades, old soul-ink that bound secrets into silence. But most wouldn't remotely dream of laying their hands on one. And now ... one of us would. Student access to the Vault was unheard of. In fact, I wouldn't have thought more than a small fraction of those at court had ever been granted access.

The halls had never felt so dangerous.

The Concordance Trial itself had evolved over centuries—from a ceremonial sparring match to a full-scale strategic simulation, designed to test more than just brute strength or weaving adeptness.

To the public, it was a rite of passage. A dazzling tradition designed to prepare the Empire's future leaders. Royals, nobles, and officials would flock to witness the final matches, casting judgments behind their fans and clan banners. Some came with match-makers in tow. A faction's performance at the Trial could shape reputations, launch careers, or even secure political marriages.

Internally, we all knew what it really was: an orchestrated battleground. A test of who could plan three steps ahead, form fragile alliances, and betray them before being betrayed. It was a public interview masked as a game.

And there were always popular stories about past Trials—the infamous duels and miraculous underdog victories. Like the year a noble heir turned the tide by swapping arms mere moments before their General had entered the duel. Or whispers of how certain clans had risen or fallen at court depending on how their heirs had performed in the Trial.

For most of us, however, the message was simpler: Your success and defeat were never just yours alone—they were bound to your family's legacy.

No pressure at all.

I did not rush. Slipping from the briefing chamber before the murmurs reached full pitch, I cut through the crowd like smoke through lattice. Behind me, students began to form clusters, false camaraderie blooming like poisonous flowers.

The Trial played right to my fatal weakness— a deadly lack of skill in Connate Charisma. But being who I was, life was already perilous either way. Sooner or later—what difference did it make? I allowed myself all but a moment to wallow in self-pity and had already decided on my strategy before class was dismissed: *strike early*.

While the rest of them squabbled over alliances, I would visit the Martial Academy. The real path to victory wasn't through whispering campaigns but Generals. But first, I turned down the southern corridor, away from my annex, past the gilded classrooms, down the eastern walkway where stones cracked beneath the roots of ancient trees.

The shared dormitories were quiet this time of day. Most had gone to gossip and speculate over lunch. All but one remained, sitting cross-legged in a sliver of courtyard sun. Her hands formed a blur of well-practiced movements, driving a heavy pestle into her mortar to crush dried roots into a salve. Nearby, a row of clay bottles stood ready, the scent of pine, clove, and bitter orange thick in the air.

I lingered in the doorway a few moments longer than I'd meant to. Though I'd rehearsed no fewer than four different openings, I found myself doubting every one of them now that I was here, unsure where to start.

Without glancing up, Yue said, "You're thinking too loudly."

I stiffened. For a moment, I wondered if she could actually read thoughts, or if I was just becoming that easy to decipher. Chuckling awkwardly, I slowly stepped forward.

"Hi, Yue," I called. "I'm here to talk about the Trial. We could join forces and form a faction."

Yue lifted her gaze, calm and unreadable, but she didn't respond. So, I kept talking.

"I know that, like me, no one's approached you." Alright, I could see why no crane Emberkin would ever bond me. That sounded much harsher than it had in my mind. "I just meant—none of the others have tried. That I've heard of." *Smooth*.

Yue tilted her head. "That's not true."

My brows furrowed.

"You've had offers?" I asked, not exactly concealing my confusion. Which, in hindsight, could have easily been misconstrued as condescension.

"No. I meant … you've approached me once." Yue tilted her head, a slow, almost nostalgic smile rising. "Years ago. Before you learned not to approach anyone."

No matter how much I tried preparing for conversations, they always seemed to end up diverting from what I'd anticipated.

"Once, you found me crying behind the training halls. Three mean boys had stolen my fireleaves and shoved my face into the mortar bowl. You came over with Shan and told them you would flay them with a brush dipped in Smokeacid. Then you sat beside me and said I smelled like Moonroot, making me laugh." Yue chuckled lightly.

I looked away, startled by the memory. It came back slowly, like water seeping through cracks. I hadn't expected to take a trip down memory lane.

"That was a long time ago," I said flatly. A time I'd been trying not to think about.

"Still," Yue said softly, "beneath it all, I don't think you've changed."

Should I be concerned about this girl's judgment? I found myself thinking.

"I want to form an alliance," I repeated, trying to steer us back to firmer ground. "But not a soft one. Not one of those back-patting groups where everyone pretends to be useful."

If my disregard for Yue's sentiments had displeased her, she showed no sign of it.

She only nodded once, her face brightening. "I'd love that. Have you thought of what next?"

"We'll divide and conquer. You work the poison angle. Some nobles like that sort of thing, discreet power and all. Offer me as collateral, a royal name in your back pocket. Meanwhile, I want to get first pick of the Generals before anyone else starts looking."

She hesitated then, fingers curling over her mortar. The nod came slower this time, as if she was weighing it seriously. Uncertainty, yes, but also resolve.

Satisfied, I was just about to turn to leave when Yue's voice caught me.

"Wait. Why me?"

A fair question—one I should have expected. I considered giving her the honest answer. That it was mostly instinct, fueled by observation and desperation, but I owed her better.

"Because you say what you mean," I said. "And because we both know how to vanish in plain sight. How to wield underestimation as a weapon."

And with that, the smoke of strategy began to rise. The Concordance Trial had begun. For now, it was just two girls standing at the edge of a game we didn't design, but trying anyway.

This time, however, the girl with no allies had already made her first move.

Reigning Fire

When I arrived at the training grounds of the Martial Academy, the sun was still hanging high in the sky. I squinted for a better view as I watched the student Warriors' training. Like the student Weavers, some came from noble families known for their martial prowess—many of whom had naturally inherited an affinity for Smokecraft and bonded Emberkin after their Binding Rites.

Here, their education focused on martial combat and military adroitness, but those with Weaving powers were also trained in select disciplines of Smokecraft. With that added advantage, they often rose through the ranks and became Generals after they were officially commissioned into the imperial forces.

Most student Warriors, however, were from commoner families without any Weaving gifts. They'd had to pass grueling trials before the best of them were selected to enter the Imperial Martial Academy. An achievement that was considered a great honor for not only their families, but also their villages and provinces.

I was just about to tap into the Smokeveil to weave an Obscurant glyph through Mo. The glyph would help me blend into the background rather than become fully invisible, which was only achievable with a Smokeveil Cloak. But then I heard it— a voice that froze the blood in my veins.

I located its source, and there he was. Strutting along the training perimeter like a General inspecting his troops before a battle. Laughing too loudly. Gesturing too broadly. A shameless thirty-year-old acting as if he owned this place, even when he probably hadn't landed a clean strike in years. But no one here would challenge him. Not yet.

Before the bitter poison exuded by his presence could be purged from my system, freeing my frozen limbs, a spear came barreling toward me. My eyes widened, and my survival instincts kicked in before I could think. One sharp swerve into a defensive stance—just like in the Dream Realm, sparring with Xiao.

Time seemed to slow once I started thinking like a fighter. I was quickly hit with the realization that the spear wasn't aimed to kill. It would have missed, even if I hadn't moved at all. But Princess Yan Xun from the Weavers' Academy wasn't supposed to *know* how to move like this. I was standing on the razor's edge of revealing everything.

Changing course mid-motion, I dropped into an ungraceful fall, feigning utter, paralyzing shock. That part wasn't challenging, considering how much real-life experience I'd accumulated in falling flat on my face. A few bruises I could survive.

My plan was working, until a hand shot out of nowhere to grab my arm. I turned just in time to see

Reigning Fire

a stranger's wide eyes before we both crashed to the ground in a dull thud. Unaccounted-for weight slammed into my dominant shoulder. Groaning, I moved my limbs gingerly to check for damage. Nothing broken. Good. Mildly concussed? Possibly.

"Your Highness, I'm so sorry—I was going to pull you back up, but you're heavier than I thought, and I was caught off guard ..." the stranger started rambling on, his ears turning scarlet.

Ah, I'd completely forgotten about all the hidden weight panels strapped onto my limbs.

"Just Yan Xun will do," I said firmly. "We don't pull ranks at the Academies. And don't worry, I know you meant well."

The boy looked as if he was about my age, tall and stocky, with a rugged strength about him. His eyes were open and sincere, and his smile reached all the way to his eyes. A body forged by training and a soul untouched by court politics. The kind of innocence a sixteen-year-old should still have. The kind of young man a royal would either envy or despise.

"Yan Xun! Oh heavens, are you alright?" The sound cut through me like a poisoned whip.

Fu Kai.

This was the first time in two years that he'd shown his face within these palace walls.

"I'm *so* sorry," he said, jogging over. "I was just demonstrating an effective spearing technique to the juniors. I didn't realize you were there!"

Mo flared bright under my sleeve, alarmed. Good. I needed the reminder. I was no longer a child. This was not then, and Mo was with me now. I channeled my fury to her. All of it. Every drop. Mo grew hot against my skin.

By the time Kai reached us, my expression was placid and neutral.

"Fu Kai." I nodded curtly. "I see you're back. No harm done. No cause for concern."

I held up my good arm just in time to block his attempt to check me over for injury, as if I was blessed with precognition powers. Another thing I was well practiced at.

My eyes flicked to the spear he'd thrown, now embedded in the wall ten feet behind me. Kai's gaze locked on mine, smiling almost imperceptibly. The smile of someone trying very hard not to smile and failing.

Innocence stepped in between us.

"Yan Xun, you should probably rest in the court-yard before heading back," he offered kindly. "I'll take you. It's just over there."

I turned and followed him. But unlike Xiao, every ounce of my attention remained behind me. If only

Emberkin could watch our backs. As far as I knew, mine couldn't. Not reliably.

Innocence—still bubbling with energy—turned mid-walk and gave me a quick bow.

"It's Jin Yang," he announced.

"What?"

"My name!"

"Oh."

At the courtyard, Jin Yang pulled out a bamboo stool from under a table by an old lacebark pine.

"Have a seat," he said. "I'll grab tea and sweets to settle your nerves." He grinned before jogging off.

He was barely out of earshot when I heard the rustle behind me. Kai emerged from the shadows with the unhurried gait of someone who'd already decided how the day would end. Of a man well acquainted with power. Not the kind forged in battle, or the kind that came with one's birthright. But the more insidious kind that slipped beneath the skin and stayed there.

"Well," he drawled in mock-affection, voice low, "if it isn't the darling of my fondest memories."

I didn't answer. My legs were leaden, but I refused to back away. He came closer, and for a moment, I could smell the trace of metal and pine on his uniform—the borderlands.

"You've grown," he purred. "But I'd know you anywhere. Same eyes. Same proud little chin." His smile didn't reach his eyes. "It's been two years, and yet … I always know you'd remember me and all the lessons I've taught you."

The air turned colder, though I knew it was just me, feeling as if I was being exsanguinated.

"Even without my little reminder," Kai continued softly, "you always know, don't you … that I could hurt you. Any time I choose to."

That was when the smile dropped. His gaze sharpened—predatory and practiced, like this was a script he'd rehearsed a thousand times.

Still, I was giving him nothing. From the moment I realized this nightmare was here to stay, I'd been channeling into Mo. Without her, I wouldn't have had the stomach for what I did next:

I stepped forward.

Toward Kai.

Said nothing and simply held his gaze.

This was something I'd been practicing daily since our last encounter. There was a certain technique to it. The trick was to avoid staring hard; that would make you blink. No—a firm gaze, eyes relaxed. Breaths even, so your emotions wouldn't be caught in your throat. No gulps, no dry swallows. You could channel all your emotions out to your Emberkin, but best to leave behind an unwavering veil of *cold* fury. That would show them you were still fully present.

Then, I smiled at Kai.

I noticed in that moment how much taller I'd grown over the last two years. I was now almost eye to eye with him, who, up to that point, had always felt like a troll towering over me.

At first, Kai seemed amused. Intrigued, even. But it didn't last. He was struggling not to blink, to keep up his act. His shoulders tensed as he was on the verge of losing the creepy staring game he'd invented. I could see him holding each breath longer. One beat too long.

And then, Kai took the tiniest backward step, just as Jin Yang's voice rang behind me.

"Yan Xun! I've found some dried lychee cakes!"

Kai. Saved by Innocence. How ironic.

I made a show of reassuring Kai I was fine, still holding my gaze steady. When I finally turned to face Jin Yang, Kai had left without another word. I could have imagined it … but I thought I saw Mo glow briefly in purple beneath my sleeve.

Have you seen that, Shan?

Chapter Five

梦魇

HELL OF A NIGHTMARE

Jin returned beaming, balancing a small plate in one hand and a teapot in the other, its lid capped by an upside-down chipped cup.

"Dried lychee cakes," he announced triumphantly, like he had just presented a peace offering to a war goddess. "And calming tea. You know, for nerves."

The scent hit before the plate even landed—that intense, oddly metallic sweetness that clung to the back of the throat. I blinked down at the cakes, their browned edges catching in the slant of sun. They looked drier than I remembered. Brittle and leathery all at once.

"Thanks," I said, because it was easier than explaining how the texture made my gums ache in anticipation.

I stared at them for a bit too long.

"You don't have to eat them," Jin Yang said quickly. "I just thought … my family used to get these once a year on the Ghost Festival. We'd split one between five kids. Tasted like treasure."

I slid the plate subtly toward him. "You eat them, then."

His brows lifted. "No way. I brought them for you."

"You sure? I wouldn't want to rob you of a sacred memory."

"You're not robbing anything," he said, grinning. "And I'm not letting you wiggle out of this."

I sighed and picked one up. *Here goes nothing.*

The chew was even worse than expected, like biting into pressed leather. My jaw clicked and I nearly winced. It jolted something loose in me—old memories of being forced to eat at palace banquets, even when the smell alone made my throat close.

But Jin Yang was still watching, hopeful. So, I swallowed reluctantly. Then blinked. I mean, I wouldn't say it tasted good, but it didn't taste awful, either. Just … real. Like something I'd tasted long before the world started tasting like ash.

"It's alright," I muttered, which was probably the highest praise I'd given anything I'd eaten all week.

Jin Yang beamed widely. "Told you."

I shook my head, a small huff of breath escaping me. Not quite a laugh, but close enough. I wasn't actually planning to head back after the tea and cakes. Kai's little stunt with the spear hadn't truly shaken me up. I had every intention of returning right to the training grounds after a sip of tea—and a bite of cake, at most—out of courtesy.

Scouting for a General was the whole point of rushing here today—so I would get the first pick. But I ended up eating the entire piece of the dried lychee cake Jin Yang had brought. Then another. Then the rest of the plate.

If there was an observable change in me since my nightly training with Xiao, it would be my appetite. I was still wary of most new foods, but these days, it seemed like I would eat almost anything and everything.

Jin Yang couldn't have looked prouder if he'd felled a beast with his bare hands. He continued talking animatedly—something about wrestling other student Warriors for the cakes. But I wasn't really listening. I downed all the tea, too—the cakes were so dry.

When I was done, out of nowhere, a wave of exhaustion washed over me. I wasn't a fan of surprises, but I didn't even have the strength to be properly perturbed by then. It felt like I was being lowered into a giant hammock, rocked gently by the pull of the tide. My body softened before I had time to resist.

I mumbled something that probably passed for a farewell and dragged myself back to my quarters before I could completely collapse. When I reached my bed, I dazedly brushed off the crumbs from the cakes still clinging to my sleeve. Mo gave a soft chime of reassurance, nosing at my hand before lowering herself onto the mattress.

Fine, just a few moments of shuteye, I told myself, *then I'll head back.*

I didn't remember lying down, just the cool kiss of fabric against my cheek and the familiar weight of Mo, tucked into the dip of my spine, as though protecting something fragile in me. And for the first time in over eighteen moons, the Dream Realm stayed quiet.

The next time I opened my eyes, I was fully enveloped in darkness, all disorientated. My body felt as if it'd grown roots, anchoring me to the bed.

Damn it, I'd slept through the afternoon. Unbelievable.

First pick of a General was the one advantage I'd had going for me. Parched, I poured myself some water and flopped back onto my bed in exasperation. The damage was done. By now, the rest of the student Weavers would have formed factions with one another *and* drawn up plans to recruit the strongest Generals.

If Wu and Lee had joined forces, they'd be an absolute menace. With two bonded Emberkin, their power would be hard to match. The strongest General candidate would probably be waiting for them at the Martial Academy's gates with a scroll of credentials, along with their Emberkin.

And honestly? It would make sense. Everyone at court could see Wu and Lee being primed for a political marriage a few years from now. Starting now would be strategic.

Then again, if Lee knew Councilor Wu at all, she would do better to form her own faction. And win, of course. Nothing impressed Councilor Wu more than a marvelous show of ruthless independence.

What was the point in speculating now, really? While everyone was out building alliances, the Princess had slept through the day. Just brilliant.

At least I might not be as fatigued as usual when training with Xiao in the Dream Realm tonight. A small consolation.

I didn't remember falling asleep again. But when I blinked, I recognized the familiar haze of a dream. Yet, this wasn't the Dream Realm. Not the snowed clearing where I'd always met with Xiao.

The night around me was uncannily quiet. No cicadas, no wind, no creaking of floorboards. Just a stillness that pressed against the skin like a damp cloth. I was standing—barefoot and weightless—in the corridor that led to my inner palace residence. I took a step forward, and the world breathed me in. A sudden force jerked me forward like a plaything, positioning me exactly where the nightmare always began.

It was *that night* again.

I knew where this would lead even before I saw the edge of the shadow lurking around the corner. Before I heard the give of the door that wasn't supposed to open. Before I heard Shan's voice, small and steady, saying, "You shouldn't be here."

I ran, but I didn't get to her in time. Because in memory, we never did.

He was already there, towering over her. Already seething with a rage that had nothing to do with her and everything to do with me. She was just a girl. A girl who'd seen too much and spoken too loudly. A girl with a lion's heart and a lamb's name.

And I—small, terrified, trembling, *useless*—had tried to pull him off. I remembered the pungent smell of blood. Not mine, but Shan's. I remembered screaming without sound. I remembered the thick hand around my throat. I remembered watching her disappear beneath his weight and hatred. I remembered the moment the world tipped into blackness.

When I came to, I was on Lady Linhua's lap, her hands gently stroking my hair, as if I'd just woken from a nap. Her touch was gentler than it had ever been, her voice soft as syrup.

"It has all been taken care of," she said. "You're safe now, thanks to Fu Kai warding off the intruder last night."

But Kai *was* the intruder.

The lie slid into me like a blade.

"Where's Shan?" I whispered, my voice barely surviving my throat.

Linhua didn't answer right away.

"She was just a servant," she said at last. "And a foolish one at that. Sticking her nose in the business of royals was going to get her killed sooner or later. Well … what's done is done."

I remembered shaking like my body had no longer belonged to me. Not out of pain from my injuries, but out of rage. Or grief. Or shame. I couldn't tell them apart anymore.

"Fu Kai has been protecting you your whole life," she went on, still smoothing hair out of my face, as though a head of messy hair was the greatest threat I faced, rather than a predator. "If anything … you should be grateful for him."

"I've told you," I said. "He hurt me. Has been for years. He—"

Linhua held up a hand, firmly. "Enough. You must never say that again. Never forget where we are. Words could easily have us all killed here. Besides, men have … needs. That's just the nature of things. What's important is that he's never ruined you completely."

She cupped my cheek in her hand, trying to reassure me. "He knows where to draw the line. I've spoken to him—he will do no such thing again."

I often wondered if it was possible to drown without being in the water. In that instant, that was exactly what it'd felt like.

"Your father must never know," Linhua stressed, her eyes boring into mine. "Do you understand? If he finds out, it will destroy him. And anyone related to Kai, including me, will be annihilated, according to the law. Is that what you want? To shame your father and have your mother's entire family detained and executed?"

I didn't answer. How could I, when what she was asking me was what I'd already been asking myself, over and over again?

Only difference was, looking at her in that moment, I failed to see a hint of the fragile woman who I'd believed wouldn't survive discovering this. The mother who needed my fierce protection.

I kept searching her face in desperation to find an inkling of the reality I'd been holding onto all that time, but all I could see was a reflection of my own childish delusion.

That night, I could feel something within me—whatever was left—curl into itself and die quietly and completely.

I woke with a gasp. Mo was already glowing, her wings stretched protectively across my chest like a smoke-born guardian. She didn't need any words from me to know I was hurting.

The whole room smelled like sandalwood, but I couldn't tell if it was incense or memory. I curled into Mo's embrace. Just for a while. Just until the morning. I didn't sleep again after that, just lay there, still as stone, clinging to Mo's warmth while the remnants of the memory sank their thorns into my flesh.

That had been Memory Looping. I'd only learned the name for it after it started happening to me, but

I recognized its effects from the first time it took hold. It was a form of intuitive Smokecraft that surfaced when the mind was fractured. When wounds of the heart bled so deeply into your being that nothing seemed able to hold it back.

In the early days, the Loop would drag me back to that night again and again. Without warning. Without mercy. Sometimes mid-sentence, sometimes mid-meal. I would vanish into smoke and bawl without sound. It was chaos, pure and absolute, and no one but Mo had seen it. Because I wouldn't allow anyone else to be close enough to see beyond the surface ever again.

After Shan's death, I was expected to carry on like nothing had happened. Court protocol didn't pause for grief. There was no funeral, no rites—not for a servant girl. Just a callous indifference. A new day, a new schedule, bringing the same heights of expectation, only heavier than before.

Shan … heavens, Shan. She was only twelve when she'd died. Two years younger than me, she was sold into palace service at the tender age of five. A tiny thing with fire in her eyes and scraped knees from running where she wasn't supposed to.

I'd chosen her for my quarters immediately, not out of kindness but necessity. She was too small to be useful to the other servants, and I could already see the bruises on her from being shoved around by the others. But she was so bright. She could see right through me—through the deference, the obedience, the pretty silence they all mistook for virtue.

She was the only one who'd seen the cracks and never flinched. I'd tried to protect her. Heavens, I'd tried. But she'd seen too much. And when she'd tried to intervene, to protect me when no one else would … she'd paid the price in my place.

Fu Kai. I could still taste the bile rising in my throat whenever I thought of him.

Fourteen years older, Kai was the only son of Fu Wan—Lady Linhua's adoptive brother and only kin, granted a noble name and residence in the outer palace as a boon to her. During the years Father and Lady Linhua had no children, Kai had become something like their surrogate son. He grew up within these walls. He knew every shadow, every blind spot.

And when I was born, Kai saw me not as kin, but as a threat. He'd made sure I knew it, right from the very beginning. Knew about his disillusionment that I was the only thing standing in his way of being a true royal. That if he could make me believe I was worthless, that was what I was going to become.

He wrapped cruelty in charisma, lies in silk. To the court, he was magnetic, charming, a true courtier. But behind the silks, behind closed doors, he'd made it his life's mission to break me. To make me fear him more than I feared disappointing my family.

Reigning Fire

And *I'd let him*. Because I believed I had to. Believed that if I'd exposed the truth, it would destroy everything I cared for. Starting with Lady Linhua … the vulnerable woman trapped within these gilded walls without a choice and a chance at freedom ever again. The devoted mother who'd sacrificed everything just to stay in the palace for her child's sake.

At least, that was the story I'd heard enough times to misconstrue as reality. I thought I had to protect her from the ugly reality that would shatter her.

And Father … as cold as he'd been, I knew how hard he'd worked to get to where he was now. For a man who prided himself on his shrewdness, how could he ever live with his monumental error in judgment about Fu Kai's character, I would ask myself.

So, I'd told myself I could bear the unbearable.

But Shan had seen the truth. No matter how much I'd tried to shut her out of it, to push her aside, to keep her safe, I'd failed. And ultimately, good intentions and desperate efforts meant nothing against the brutal finality of my failure.

After Shan's death, Lady Linhua had convinced Father to send Kai to the borderlands. To "cool things off a little," she'd said. A political reassignment. A temporary shift. But I knew better.

Since then, I'd refused to take on another personal attendant, even though royals were required to have at least one. Every time someone new was sent to my quarters, I would destroy the room, overturn furniture, smash heirloom vases, rip silk from walls. In time, they'd stopped trying. I became the only royal member without a personal attendant. Just a string connected to a bell.

I was well aware of the palace whispers calling me an aberrant lone wolf. Many hadn't even bothered whispering. But I was never exactly alone, even if no one knew that. The first time I saw Mo was the night after Shan had died.

I'd shattered everything in my quarters—porcelain, inkstones, the altar, even the legs of my own writing desk. I was bleeding from the palms and didn't even notice. Some said I was finally showing my true colors—a volatile, entitled royal unraveling at last.

I didn't bother correcting them. Let them believe what they wanted. It was easier than admitting the truth, which was that I'd been unraveling for years. I'd just never allowed the cracks to show. Some others said I was losing my mind.

Maybe I was.

But through the tears and wreckage, something flickered—ember-red, shaped like wings drawn in ash. She didn't do anything unusual, just hovered near me and stayed. I thought I'd imagined her. A fever dream. A grief hallucination.

She wasn't supposed to exist.

A phoenix was a celestial being, a myth. Emberkin weren't supposed to take on celestial forms—it was forbidden. Or, at the very least, feared. No one understood what it meant when they did, only that it had never ended well. No one would believe me if I said I'd seen a phoenix Emberkin. And without a doubt, no one would protect me if I admitted she was real.

But Mo didn't ask for acknowledgment. She had never tried to help, or heal, or make me understand anything. Rather, she was always just one breath away, a constant, unflinching presence even as I fell apart.

One night, long after the sobbing had stopped, long after I'd lost track of time, I asked her, "Are you here because he has finally broken me?"

I'd spent my young life thinking I had to learn how to be strong enough to protect those dear to me. I was fearful if it was already too late for me to start learning how to protect myself. Mo didn't pretend to have answers, just curled her wings a little closer to me and kept me company.

That was enough.

Eventually, I began noticing the way my Smokecraft had transformed since she'd come to me. Despite her mythic form, I realized she could be my conduit for the Smokeveil's powers to enhance my Smokecraft all the same, just like any other Emberkin.

When I'd tapped into the Smokeveil through Mo to push back against the Memory Looping, it … slowed. Then, one night, it'd stopped altogether.

Some scholars argued that Memory Looping was the mind's way of forcing us to process the impossible—to unearth truths we were too shattered to face directly. And I believed that. For a while, I'd clung to those loops like they held vital answers.

Why me? Why Shan? *Why?*

But there came a point where I knew that memory by heart. I could recount every detail of that night, every creak of floorboard, every breath I didn't take. There was nothing new left in it for me, and I'd never gotten the answers I sought. Some things in life didn't come with answers; no amount of obstinate insistence could change that.

And that was when the dreams changed. When I'd started crossing into the Dream Realm.

When I'd met Xiao.

That night, I lay in my bed until the sky began to shift. Until the darkness gave way to the beginnings of dawn. Until I could fold the memory back into its cage and face the day.

Because what else could I do? The Trial would wait for no one.

shàn

Kindness

Jasmine K. Y. Loo

Chapter Six

以爱之名

IN THE NAME OF LOVE

Lady Linhua

There were always at least eight rings on her fingers. No one ever dared to ask why. One was a gift from His Highness. Jade, custom-set. Bestowed the night he had first summoned her to his private study.

Another came from the late Empress herself. An offer of tolerance she'd cloaked in public displays of civility. Gilded silver, inlaid with green agate, presented during the Spring Festival as the court watched on in careful silence. The way she'd smiled at Linhua that day had told her everything she needed to know about her perspective. One that said:

You will never rise higher than this.

The rest were hers—earned, bought, hidden in a carved box until the time was right. She wore them now like a crown. The girl she used to be would never in her wildest dreams have believed she would slip even one of these onto her fingers. So, who cared if the Consort had an actual crown?

She admired her rings for a moment longer, then took them off one by one. Not with haste, but with quiet reverence. Each one nestled into its velvet-lined compartment inside a lacquered jewelry box intricately carved with floral motifs.

Then she stepped into the bath.

The wooden tub, fashioned from aged camphor wood and polished to a warm sheen, was large enough to stretch one's legs and soak away one's grief. Wisps of steam rose from the surface, scented with rose petals and citrus blossom oil.

Linhua leaned back slowly, letting the warmth swallow her limbs, the floral-sweet fragrance cocooning her in something almost like peace.

At the far end of the bath, etched into the baseboard, glowed a Heating glyph. She couldn't read it, of course. She'd never been trained in Smokecraft. But it kept her bath water at precisely the right temperature, maintained steadily by the soft pulses of Smokecraft fed into it by her personal Weaver.

Generally, Weavers were too valuable to be wasted on such menial things. House Yan had long decreed that only the Emperor and Empress were permitted to have personal attendants trained in Smokecraft. A concession made not for luxury, but for efficiency. Since His Highness had become the Prince Regent, he and the Princess Consort got to enjoy that luxury. But His Highness had granted Linhua an exception. He'd always doted on her. After all, she was the one who'd birthed his only child.

Linhua's Weaver had graduated from the Academy with barely passable Trial scores—high-born, yet far from remarkable. The sort of disappointment a noble clan could not disown but might quietly reassign. Attendants like her were still skilled, but not enough to serve in research divisions or war councils. Linhua sometimes watched her and thought, *My daughter will never end up heating anyone's bath water.*

The rising steam carried a scent that was pleasantly bittersweet, like old dreams that hadn't yet crumbled into dust. Closing her eyes, she let her fingers drift through the water. She'd come so far. But somehow, the weight of her past always found a way to float to the surface.

Linhua was five when she'd first stolen food. A cold and dirty orphan girl on the streets. A stringy mess of limbs with more soot than skin. Grabbing her by the back of her collar, the bun vendor didn't shout. Just slapped her once, hard, and told her to be smarter next time. So, she got smarter.

She didn't beg. Not often, anyway. Begging made people look at you, and pity was dangerous. She'd preferred to run errands—passing secret notes for lovers, delivering strange crates that smelled like wine and salt and guilt. The pay was better, and the rules were simple: don't look inside, don't get caught, don't talk.

Other kids hated her for it. A girl who could run fast and keep her mouth shut was competition. They'd tripped her when she was carrying parcels, trying to ruin her face with sharpened stones.

That was when she'd met Wan. Not Fu Wan—not yet at the time. Just Wan. Older by four years, he was already a seasoned thief, but with a strangely kind heart. At the time, he'd broken a boy's nose for insulting his friend. Linhua knew right then: having Wan close meant protection. So, she tagged along.

Since then, Wan had started to take her under his wing and save her scraps. Given her one of his old shoes when hers gave out. Called her "little fox" when she'd managed to talk an angry merchant into letting them go. He never asked her for anything in return.

There was a time, long before the palace, when Linhua had fallen in love with a hairpin. They were still street rats then, camping out beneath the east gate. A noblewoman had passed by on a palanquin, chin resting on its window as she was taking in the sights. Her hair, gleaming in the sun, was twisted into an elaborate coil and pinned with a gold phoenix that shimmered as it moved. Wan had noticed the way Linhua stared at it longingly. That night, he'd suggested they steal it. There was only one inn in town luxurious enough for nobles to stay in, so locating the woman wouldn't have been challenging.

She'd thought he was joking. But when she'd found him slipping out late at night with a torch and a grin that betrayed his spirit of devilry, she knew he wasn't. Impelled by his bravado, she'd followed along, but they didn't make it far. She'd frozen halfway climbing out of the inn room window when the guards had arrived.

Wan had pushed her out, whispering urgently, "Run, little fox." Then he'd stepped back in, arms raised, and taken the beating meant for both of them.

She'd run until her lungs had screamed for mercy. It had taken Wan three long moons to be released from the prison. When he'd finally returned, he'd lost two teeth, his nose had healed crooked, and his back was never quite straightened again. But he was still grinning at her the same way he used to. That was the day she'd decided: if she ever made it out of that cesspool, he was coming with her.

They'd survived that way for years. Wan was faster than anyone she knew; she was cleverer than anyone he knew. Together, they were ghosts. At least, until the day she'd vanished.

She was sixteen when they'd taken her. Said they needed more hands at the palace. Girls under eighteen were often absorbed discreetly into service this way, especially those with no family or legal standing. Someone had paid a bribe for her to be added to the registry. She'd never found out who. She could still feel a sliver of cold fury whenever she thought of this old grudge. But whoever it was, they'd ended up giving her the opportunity of a lifetime.

In the beginning, Linhua had been forced to scrub floors and wring out wet laundry until her fingers had bled. For moons on end, she'd only been eating scraps from the servants' hall. But she quickly learned how to read gestures and hierarchies, how to fade into the background until it was time to be noticed.

Prince Yan Yun had noticed her at twenty. He was taciturn, watchful, and almost gentle, in his own way. He'd only asked her name once. After that, he'd been calling her "Linhua." Said it suited her better than the name she'd had before.

When he'd taken her in, she'd only had one request, which was for Wan to be found. The Prince had obliged. Wan had arrived two moons later, all clean-shaven, eyes still sharp, wearing the uniform of an entry-level palace guard. Though he was too awed to smile at her, his eyes said he was proud of the life she'd made for herself. She'd thought that would be the end of all their suffering, but life in the inner palace was anything but easy.

Brought back to the present, Linhua stepped out and dried herself, slipping into robes of twilight blue silk. She sat at her vanity table and pulled out a worn, unremarkable comb from a drawer. Wan had given it to her years ago, just after he'd served his sentence for stealing the noblewoman's hairpin. Despite being barely recognizable, the first thing he'd said to her was, "Still dreaming about that phoenix pin?"

Then he gave her a wooden comb with roughly etched feathers along its spine. "This one won't get me killed," he'd reassured her with a haunted smile.

She never used it, but she'd always kept it. Wan had been her brother before she'd known what the word meant. Her accomplice before her ambition had truly awakened. And her shield, since long before she'd learned someone like her could have one. Tucking the comb back into the drawer, she smoothed down the sleeves of her robes and gazed into the mirror. Then daintily reapplied a thin layer of rouge with a finger, tilting her head slightly. One never knew when someone might come knocking.

There were rules in the House of Yan. While polygamy wasn't technically illegal in the Empire, it was absolutely frowned upon. It was considered crude and peasant-like. So, when Prince Yan Yun took only one concubine—Linhua—it was speculated that she must have had something worth keeping.

But the late Empress had made sure that Linhua would never forget her origins. Once, at a banquet, she'd said loudly enough for the senior ministers' wives to hear, "The roots of the foxglove are poisonous, but its petals are pretty, I suppose."

Linhua wasn't going to fall for her trap. She'd made sure to always maintain an appearance of reverence. But the following day, Linhua had replaced every flower in her quarters with foxgloves.

The maids called her terrifying behind her back. Not because she shouted. Why in heavens' name would she ever have to? Shouting was for unrefined simpletons. She simply watched them, closely, thoroughly, especially the pretty ones. Especially when His Highness visited. Being secretly feared beat being replaced.

She told herself she was only watching for his sake. For the dignity and stability of the royal family. But there were nights when she lay awake, wondering if *that* other household was filled with more laughter. If the Consort smiled more easily. If she was ever insecure, like Linhua was.

The Consort had never acknowledged her directly, at least not with words. But Linhua noticed how she sent her servants over for "caring check-ins," how her eyes lingered longer on His Highness whenever he'd stayed too long at Linhua's quarters.

Linhua liked to imagine they had an understanding, a silent truce. But more often, she told herself a different story. One where the Consort had forced Linhua's hand to make up for her own inability to produce an heir. She rehearsed the narrative that she'd never wanted this life, that she'd been coerced, cornered, made to stay. That she'd chosen humble servitude over freedom for the sake of her daughter.

In truth, even Linhua no longer knew how much of it was true. It was simply the version that hurt less. What she remembered vividly was how she used to scrub the Consort's chambers herself. Terrified servants from both houses had begged her to stop, crying that it was unseemly conduct for a royal concubine. But she was proud of that story—a dignified illustration of her part and commitment in maintaining peaceful dynamics between sister-wives.

Yet she wasn't truly a wife, was she? Not in name. Not in the Shrine. The Empire had no use for concubines beyond their utility. And when that use ended, so did their story. Even in death, concubines were forbidden from ever entering the Ancestral Shrine—left unhonored, unrecorded, as though they had never existed. Linhua often wondered if that was the real punishment. Not shame or pain, but erasure.

As the years passed, and she, too, had failed to bear a child, the palace began to whisper. His Highness's loyalty had become a spectacle. Ministers made jokes behind lacquered fans. One had even asked her after a few drinks at a banquet, half in jest, if His Highness had forgotten how to produce an heir altogether. Losing her composure wouldn't have been regal, so she'd worn her silence like an armor. Gritting her teeth, she'd smiled and bided her time, until an opportunity presented itself for her to remind the minister of the consequences of offending someone sharing a bedspread with a royal Prince.

That was when Kai began to rise.

Fu Wan's only son. Technically no royal blood, but raised just beyond the inner palace walls—close enough to be useful, near enough to be seen. And in the absence of an heir, people began to look his way, including His Highness. At first, it was as a courtesy to Linhua. Then it became habit.

Kai was clever and charismatic, brazen in the ways Linhua never could be. He could just as easily make people laugh as he could make them listen. Quick with praise and even quicker with blame, he spoke boldly, moved confidently, as if the palace was his birthright. She used to admire him for it. Used to feel a strange flicker of pride, even.

His own mother had died giving birth to him, and the poor boy had never felt a mother's love until Wan had brought him into the palace. Linhua often reminded herself that she wasn't his mother, but it was difficult not to feel as if she'd shaped some part of him. She'd been the one to select his tutors and sew the lining into his festival robes. She'd praised him in front of ministers and corrected his tone when he'd overstepped. She'd watched him grow.

Whenever young Kai had visited, it felt as though she'd given His Highness a family that was complete.

She used to tell herself men had needs; it was nothing personal. That boys raised without mothers could easily lose their way. That servants were sometimes chosen for such things—not ever spoken of but understood. Unfortunate, perhaps, but not uncommon. But a Princess? A child? *Her* child?

That night, when Yan Xun had woken in her arms trembling and covered in bruises, she'd said nothing for the longest time. Just held her shoulders, then tried getting her back to sleep. The next morning, she'd summoned Kai. She didn't scream or slap him. Just reminded him, coldly, that this was no tavern girl he was trifling with. That the honor of House Yan wasn't a toy. That if he ever touched the Princess again, she would see to it that he would spend the rest of his days scrubbing latrines in exile. He'd bowed low, his eyes cast down. He hadn't argued.

She'd thought that was the end of it. She told herself that sternness was protection. That endurance was strength. That her daughter would be safer if they never spoke of it again.

What could she have done otherwise? Raise an alarm? Let the court rip their family apart? Let people question how a mother could *let* this happen in her own household? And worst of all, it was someone *she* had invited into her child's life.

What kind of a mother would that make her to the rest of the world?

You don't survive the palace by bleeding where people can see, she thought. *You rise, or you sink. And if you don't rise far enough, they'll drown you.*

She understood the game of survival better than anyone. If you didn't rise, you became prey. And the higher you climbed, the more brutal the fall. The world would never stop feeding on the vulnerable. She'd taught Yan Xun to endure, to keep her eyes on the ultimate victory. Because it was the only lesson she'd ever learned that worked.

If Yan Xun was as tough as her *real* mother, she would move past all this nonsense with grace, as if it'd never happened. After all, no one could rise if their feet were weighed down by ghosts.

And yet, when it came to her daughter, that lesson had never felt quite enough. Yan Xun was born more than a decade after Linhua was taken into House Yan. Her brightest gem, her hope, her absolution.

Alas, Yan Xun had only inherited His Highness's appearance, not his exceptionality. His blood, but not the legitimacy of an heir born of a legal wife. By the time she'd arrived, the gossips had long curdled into an undercurrent of mockery.

The lavish celebrations during Yan Xun's birth had been overlaid with a thick layer of silent skepticism. Had she come too late? Would she ever be enough? Could she ever prove herself against all those who'd called her mother a wild card that had sullied the royal bloodline with mediocrity?

So, she'd taught Yan Xun how to walk with her back straight, how to speak with soft certainty, how to lower her lashes when questioned. Taught her not to scream—for screaming was useless—but instead, to be tough enough to withstand whatever life might throw at her. Pushed her to work harder than anyone else to be worthy of her name.

Even when Yan Xun had to call another woman Mother, she was *her* daughter, after all. And her father was Prince Yan Yun. So, anything short of all-round brilliance was out of the question.

When Yan Xun used to cry at night, Linhua would tell her, "We're women of the court. We do not break. We bend."

She'd meant every word. She still did.

Others scorned that she'd lived a charmed life, that she'd never had to climb the ladder—just leapt from the streets into silk.

Let them talk.

They didn't know what it took to stay. They didn't know her rings were earned.

They didn't know she was doing this all—

for Yan Xun.

林

lín

嬅

hùa

Chapter Seven

无火成烟

SMOKE WITHOUT FIRE

By the time I arrived back at the Martial Academy the next afternoon, the place had transformed. And not in a good way.

The courtyard was now swarmed with performative strategists—groups of student Weavers flitting between the student Warriors like polished emissaries, dropping carefully rehearsed lines about honor, legacy, and victory. Smokecraft shimmered in the air, glyphs cast mid-conversation to demonstrate skill or flash prestige. If I'd waited another hour, someone would probably offer their General a floral tribute.

Too late. Way too late.

The student Warriors with bonded Emberkin were already gone—claimed and sealed into factions that'd solidified overnight. Most of them didn't even glance at me. A few did, but only with faint amusement or wariness, as if I might still be dangerous enough to inconvenience their plans. I wasn't. Not today.

Then again, it wasn't as if I believed that having an Emberkin guaranteed superiority. I still stood by that sentiment. What I wanted was a chance to observe without others' preferences being waved in my face, clouding my judgment. To *know* what I was choosing, what I was risking. But now every path had already been paved by someone else.

I exhaled through my nose and glanced sideways. The contrast between the two Academies had never been clearer than during Concordance season. The Weavers' Academy was a gallery of brocade and bravado—most students from noble lines, wearing high-collared robes in jewel-toned gradients, embroidered with clan sigils and stylized glyphs that shimmered when touched by light. Even those without Emberkin walked with inherited pride.

The Martial Academy, by comparison, was forged on grit. The vast majority of student Warriors came from commoner families—villagers, tradesfolk, and laborers whose children had passed a brutal series of entrance trials to earn their place. Their uniforms were standard-issue dark linen and leather, minimal but practical. Only a sparse handful of nobles trained among them, and their finery was muted here. Pride came from performance, not pedigree.

Yue wasn't with me today. She'd agreed to focus on her recruitment angle quietly, weaving her poisons and deals in the shadows like she did everything else. Our alliance still technically held, but we'd barely begun to look like a faction. By the Trial's standards, a faction required at least three student Weavers and one General. So, we needed to find one more Weaver, or at least try to.

Though students across the two Academies generally had little to do with one another before this, my standing at court and within the Weavers' Academy wasn't exactly a secret. It wouldn't be hard for these student Warriors to know I wasn't popular, not even close. I was royal, yes, but being royal wasn't the same as being accepted. While I was the only child of the current Regent, I was also illegitimate. And in this Empire, that meant a great deal.

On the surface, I was respected as a Princess. But beyond shallow niceties, I was mocked for being born of a lowly concubine without any backing from a powerful clan. A shadow child, whispered about all my life, but especially since my Binding Rites a few moons ago. Now, there was officially a deadline to when they could see me fail. Nobles, especially the old families, loved their lineages neat and pure.

To the rest of the world, I hadn't bonded an Emberkin, either. And no matter how hard I'd been training, how many extra hours I put in, the ratio between effort and results remained wildly disproportionate. While generally competent and precise in most disciplines, I was inconceivably hopeless in Connate Charisma. Perhaps because there was hardly anyone for me to practice with.

The palace attendants were always polite and would go along with anything I said, and the other student Weavers preferred talking *about* me much more than *to* me. Most students quietly dispersed once I approached. As lovely as Shan had been, I couldn't have practiced with her, either. She'd understood me so well that I didn't have to be any different to be appealing to her.

But even taking the lack of practice opportunity out of the equation, I wasn't sure it would make a difference. Connate Charisma relied on a kind of subtle emotional choreography I could never quite master. I struggled with modulating my tone of voice—always either too flat or too sharp. When I tried to look people in the eye, I had to be conscious of reminding myself which eye, how long to look, and whether I seemed to be trying too hard. It was like weaving with smoke and mirrors, when all I'd ever known were straight lines and anchor points.

There were those like Kai, who oozed a kind of effortless charm—the kind that twisted words like blades without needing Smokecraft, and knew just when to smile to disarm. But Connate Charisma was different. It wasn't just about being likeable. It was a Smokecraft discipline honed through resonance training—weaving intent and emotional charge into your words and body language to compel, influence, or command.

Done well, it bypassed others' defenses entirely. But done poorly, it could backfire, turning awe into fear, or persuasion into revulsion. That was why it was considered one of the most difficult and danger-ous forms of Smokecraft to master.

In principle, I was expected to become next in line to the throne, just after Father. But the rumors were already rising like a tide—louder with every passing term—that my younger cousin, Prince Yan Lu, would make a much stronger candidate. At only thirteen, he was already brilliant and polished. A prodigy in multiple Smokecraft disciplines, espe-cially in Tradeweaving, like my father. The same of-ficials who bowed to me in the palace had children referring to Lu as "the Empire's future" in the Academy. They weren't subtle about it, either. They weren't meant to be.

This wasn't just academic competition, but suc-cession theater. And the court's favorite act was the slow public dismantling of a candidate who didn't measure up. So no, I wasn't exactly drowning in allies.

Still, I tried. First thing in the morning, I ap-proached Li Cheng to start—a phlegmatic, observant

Sealbinding student who sat two rows behind me. He was strong in logic, sharp in debate, and terrible at making friends. Which, of course, made me think he would be perfect. Like Lady Linhua always lectured, *"Make allies, not friends."*

"Already pledged," he said curtly before I'd even finished my first sentence.

"To whom?"

He blinked slowly, as if he wasn't sure if I was seriously asking. "Wu."

Of course.

I tried two more. A girl whose name had slipped my mind mid-conversation—that was on me—and another who stared at me like I was offering her a curse.

"You aren't close to having a General yet," she said softly, like she was sorry for me. "And honestly? People say you're a gamble."

I smiled. "That's fair. You're not wrong."

She blinked several times in rapid succession before walking away, looking confused by my response. I let her.

There weren't many left. Most students who hadn't already formed or joined a faction were either hopelessly unskilled or so conceited that no one wanted to work with them. Or both. One had already tried to negotiate a leadership trade for their sister at court before I'd even started speaking.

I sat on the edge of the training terrace, arms folded, watching the final flurry of movement as faction rosters were scribbled and sealed, names locked in. I wasn't panicking. Not yet.

I couldn't help but notice that Jin Yang was still unpledged. He was talking cordially to a few people—student Warriors and Weavers alike—but no one seemed to hold his attention for long. No scrolls exchanged. No Sealbinding drawn up.

Interesting.

He caught me watching and gave me a small wave. By the time I waved back, he'd already looked away.

They began drills soon after midday, when the sun climbed high enough to turn the courtyard into a furnace. Student Weavers were politely asked to observe from the shaded perimeter, but I didn't bother pretending I would stay in the shadows. I stepped closer, arms crossed, letting the heat sting the back of my neck.

Other factions' Generals took their places in the sparring lanes—some with fanfare, others with silent confidence. I scanned the field automatically, tension crawling up the back of my spine, until I was sure of what I was looking for.

Fu Kai wasn't here. Thank heavens.

Rumor had it he'd been reassigned to palace duty after two years of supposedly excellent service at the borders. "Commended for great work," they said. I didn't need to guess whose merits he'd claimed to earn that praise. He was always good at shining with stolen light. Regardless, for now, this place was clear of him. And that made it easier to breathe.

I turned my attention to the lines of student Warriors. Fast and disciplined, they'd clearly been drilled hard throughout their six years of Academy training, just like we'd been on the other side. Other factions' Generals demonstrated coordination and flair, moving seamlessly between formation drills and paired sparring, drawing glyphs midair to amplify their footwork or disrupt an opponent's balance.

My attention lingered on Jin Yang. He didn't flash glyphs or raise his voice. But he *moved* with grounded precision, like every muscle had been taught not just to strike, but to endure. He didn't posture or seek attention, which I thought made him stand out even more. Yet, in the face of opponents with an obvious advantage—their Emberkin—he never shrank either.

His uniform looked older than most, and his boots had clearly seen more than one repair stitch. But nothing about him gave off lack. Only lived-in certainty, like he knew exactly what he was capable of, and didn't need a birthright to say so.

One of the instructors barked a correction at him, something about his posture. Jin adjusted and nodded once without flinching or arguing, just took on the feedback. I noticed the way his stance absorbed the impact of each clash. The way he quickly recovered and recalibrated, adapting his next move to exploit the smallest gaps in his opponent's form. The way he tracked movement without needing to dominate it.

Interesting.

I leaned further against the edge of the banister, just enough to feel the Cooling glyph etched into its stone base. The other Generals were being cheered on by their factions, applauded after every demonstration. Jin Yang had no one cheering, but he didn't seem to need it. I stayed for longer than I'd meant to.

I caught up with him near the south gate, just as the training session ended.

"Jin Yang," I called.

He turned, wiping sweat from his brow.

"Your Highness," he said with a grin, before catching himself. "Sorry. Yan Xun."

I narrowed my eyes. "Were you just about to bow?" I asked.

"I was considering it. Then I remembered you don't like pomp."

"And yet you smiled like you were about to present me with a fruit basket."

"Next time, I'll bring dried lychee cakes."

He was teasing, but only gently. Like he was testing the waters for something.

"I'm forming a faction," I said plainly. No sense in pretending I was good at small talk. "And I need a General."

He tilted his head. "Do you now?"

"You were sizing me up during drills. That tells me you're interested."

He shrugged. "I was observing *everyone*."

I raised a brow. "But you looked a little longer at me."

He smiled. "Maybe I just liked the view."

I blinked. He wasn't winking or smirking, just standing there, that open grin still hovering like it wasn't doing anything suspicious. I brushed off whatever that was and didn't let it fluster me.

"Your stance was decent."

"Oh. That. Yeah, it's decent. Could use a little polish." He squinted, holding up his fingers just a sliver apart, as if measuring how close it was to perfection.

I sighed and rolled my eyes. "So, will you be joining me or not?" I asked, cutting to the chase.

He scratched the back of his neck. "Well … you're not exactly the most popular choice right now. Not the safest bet."

"I'm not offering safe. I'm offering real. Besides, safe is boring. And you don't strike me as boring."

He was quiet for a beat, before observing, "You talk like someone with something to prove. And like someone who's already lost too much to care what others think."

Pfft, I wish. But I didn't correct him.

"I don't have an Emberkin," I reminded him, trying to keep steady eye contact. According to Shan, my tell had always been my darting gaze when I lied.

"Neither do I. Never will have a chance to, in fact. That's never stopped me," he replied.

Another pause ensued before he held out his hand. "Alright, Yan Xun. Let's cause a little trouble."

I clapped it hard, and we clasped wrists—firm, grounded, the way Warriors did when words weren't enough. There was definitely an element of luck involved here, but perhaps being first wasn't always the point. Jin was the General we needed; I just knew it in my heart.

By the time evening rolled in, Yue reappeared with a girl I'd never spoken to before—a round-eyed student Weaver with ink-stained fingertips and a flat, unreadable expression. She didn't speak much, just gave a curt nod when Yue introduced her as Ruo.

"She's good," Yue said. "People just didn't bother looking."

According to Yue, Ruo specialized in casting silent glyphs, a precise and elusive technique that took the standard finger-glyphing that final-year students had to master and stripped it down to its quietest, cleanest form. No shimmer, no hum. Just intent, drawn with air and will. It was, strictly speaking, a more advanced skill that required restraint, precision, and control. Sadly, these qualities were not often celebrated at the Academy, where louder, flashier displays of skill earned louder, flashier praise.

Just like Yue, Ruo was one of the few sponsored students in the Imperial Weavers' Academy who didn't come from a noble or royal line. While not always the case, that in itself spoke volumes about her potential.

Narrow-shouldered and willowy, her sable-dark hair was held together by a wooden pin that looked unevenly shaved. Like she'd fashioned it herself with a dull blade. Her robes were standard issue but looked worn in, mended seams and sleeves stained faintly with the ghost of old ink. Not the mess of someone careless, but a sign of someone who worked in the shadows, not limelight.

As we were facing each other properly for the first time despite having spent six years together in the same class, Ruo wasn't trying to impress me or convince me that she was the right choice for our faction. She just stood there, posture open and steady, meeting my eyes squarely. Her gaze carried neither reverence nor wariness. Neither disdain nor opportunism.

A recognition of us as equals, that was what it was.

Now we were three. Well, four, if you counted the General.

Chapter Eight

首选兵刃

WEAPON OF CHOICE

Jin Yang

The Grand Courtyard of the Martial Academy had been cleared and polished to a sheen, flanked by carved stone torches that burned with bluish smoke. The student factions stood in six tight formations before the raised stage—each with a faction leader at the front and a General at the back, flanking their fellow Weavers.

Jin's boots rang against the stones as they assembled. Even the air felt sharper, as if holding its breath. The stage had been erected especially for today's event with ceremonial precision—elevated lacquered wood panels inlaid with silver glyph borders that shimmered in the sun. At the center of the stage stood Master Dan from the Weavers' Academy in high-collared robes, his Emberkin by his side. Some kind of a pelican, perhaps?

Deep violet banners hung along the edges, each embroidered with the official crest of the Concordance Trial: a flame encircled by stylized smoke. With the whole setup, Jin was half-expecting a cleric to appear out of nowhere to begin a ceremony. Then again, what would he know about noble customs and grandeur?

Standing toward the back of the platform was Grandmaster Shao of the Martial Academy, a stark contrast to Master Dan in both presence and attire. Dressed in charcoal-gray battle robes reinforced with leather pads, arms folded across his chest, he watched the students with the heavy stillness of someone who'd once smashed a man's nose without so much as a word uttered. He had.

A lacquered urn gleamed beside Master Dan—blackened wood trimmed with silver, with a lid sealed with three layers of glyphs. Next to it was a row of ceremonial blades, spears, and staves—each weapon lined neatly on a long brocade-draped table.

"Today, you will each draw a plaque that determines your General's arms," Master Dan announced, his voice echoing across the courtyard. "There are six plaques—sword, spear, dagger, staff, shield, and one that is blank."

A ripple of unease moved through the rows at the reminder.

Blank.

"The only person who may draw a plaque is the faction leader. The draw will be public. Only the faction leader will see the plaque's contents, and it is up to them whether they reveal it or not. What you do with that information afterward is your choice."

His gaze scanned the crowd. "Over the next week, you may trade plaques, attempt to acquire more, or deceive your opponents into giving up theirs. But know this: on the day of the duel, your General will only be granted whichever arms correspond to the plaque they're in possession of when they step onto the field. No plaque, no arms."

"If a General enters the duel with more than one plaque," Master Dan elaborated, "they may either choose one of the plaques, or request for all of them—but only what they're able to carry on their person at once. No arms may be placed aside or held in reserve."

He let the words settle like fog.

"You may not present a plaque that has already been used by another faction. All arms will only be issued once. No duplicates." He gave a tight nod. "Step forward when your name is called."

One by one, the names of the faction leaders rang out. Wu went early. He was the kind of person who would make an impression on you—for better or worse—even when you'd barely just met. Striding up with that smug confidence he wore like a shield, he reached into the urn and decisively pulled a plaque. He only stared at it briefly, then gave a satisfied nod and turned back to his faction.

Wu didn't show his plaque. But by the time he stepped off the stage, the word was already out.

"Wu got a spear," someone whispered, loud enough to be heard. Meant to be heard.

Lee stepped up next, graceful and unhurried. When she returned to her faction, her expression was blank. Nothing to give away, which, in some ways, gave away everything.

Then Yan Xun stepped forward. Jin watched her closely—because everyone was watching her, yes, but also because he wanted to. There was always something brittle but deliberate in her movements, like someone picking their way across a frozen lake. She didn't hesitate. Like Wu, she reached right into the urn and pulled a plaque.

For a breath, he thought he saw something flicker across her face. A flash of alarm. Stunned terror, maybe. Then it was gone. Her expression settled into neutrality so fast that Jin wasn't sure he'd really seen anything at all. She returned to their formation with the plaque tucked somewhere within her robes. Said nothing, gave away nothing more, not even to him.

Once all six plaques had been drawn, Master Dan raised his hand again. "You will now have three weeks to prepare. During this time, you must decide which faction you wish to challenge in the first round of the Trial. A week before the duels, each leader will submit a slip of parchment with the name of your chosen opponent. Only if two factions select each other will a match be sealed."

A few murmurs passed through the crowd.

"If your chosen opponent does not select you in return, no duel will be arranged. You will resubmit until all factions are paired into three matched duels." He paused. "You're not allowed to see the other slips. All names will be submitted folded in this urn. Choose wisely. If you challenge someone much stronger, or someone with superior arms—"

"—you bleed," Wu said, under his breath. Loud enough.

Master Dan ignored him. "If you challenge someone who appears to be far weaker, they may not challenge you back. In which case, you would have simply showed your hand."

Jin caught Yue glancing sideways at Yan Xun, who remained impassive, as always.

Master Dan looked over the six formations. "Use this week to plan, watch, listen. But remember, your strategy only lasts as long as your secrets hold."

He stepped down from the platform.

"As a reminder," Grandmaster Shao's voice cut through the noise that was already beginning to rise, "only one faction will emerge victorious from the Concordance Trial. But this year, after the initial round of three duels, instead of entering the next rounds of duels, the winning factions will all face one another in a final convergence battle."

His words sparked an uproar.

Yet another surprise sprung on them at the last moment. Of course, now the part where a relic will be offered as a reward made more sense to Jin.

Grandmaster Shao held up a hand to signal for the students to settle down.

"In the deciding round, each faction must send their General and their faction leader into a single, shared battlefield. A second Weaver may offer support from the observation tower via Signal glyphs. Strategy, cohesion, and adaptability will determine your final standing. All candidates within the arena will be fair targets, Weavers and Warriors alike. The convergence battlefield is no place for spectators. Anyone entering it must be prepared to defend and attack—because your opponents will not be sparing their strikes."

Master Dan gave a nod of approval but said nothing further. And the scramble began.

In the days that followed, alliances blurred into suspicion. Jin tried to keep calm, but even he couldn't ignore the knot of unease in his gut. It would be precarious if he had no Emberkin and no arms—at least none he knew of yet. And the weight of the silence Yan Xun carried made every plan feel like it could crack if he leaned too hard on it.

Other factions began testing them—from casual sparring invitations, to sudden interests in Jin's stance, Yue's herbaceous work, or Ruo's coordination with glyphs. The scrutiny wasn't overt, but it wasn't subtle, either. They were being weighed up.

What unsettled Jin more, though, was the complete absence of negotiations. Not a single faction had approached them to propose a plaque exchange. No deals, no threats, no small talk that might be a prelude to something else. Jin could only come up with three possible explanations for this.

One: others somehow already knew they were fucked. His worst fear confirmed—Yan Xun had drawn a blank plaque.

Two: they were being underestimated. An unpopular royal, two underdogs, and a common General who was a non-Weaver. It stung, but he would take that over the first.

And three: no one bothered negotiating because they were planning to cut all pretense and go straight for stealing their plaque. That would put the plaque holder at risk. Overt maiming was against the rules, sure, but Smokecraft had a way of making things look like accidents.

And if someone *did* end up hurt "by accident" … who would defend a faction like theirs?

Some factions immediately began dropping hints about what they'd drawn—casual comments about reach, weight, and preferred fighting range. Others stayed entirely silent, which somehow made them more suspicious.

Wu's faction, true to form, leaned into theatrics. One of their Weavers, a sharp-tongued girl with beady eyes, casually mentioned in pure admiration that Wu had drawn a spear about every other day. As if fate just liked him long and pointy. Everyone knew it was a performance, but the question remained: was it a bluff or a double bluff?

One thing was certain—only two of the six factions had Generals with bonded Emberkin. Lee's General was one: a tall, broad-shouldered noble named Qiao, with a hawk-like Emberkin that shimmered with bronze smoke. Not Jin's favorite person.

The second was Wu's faction, who was already a crowd favorite. His General was a formidable girl named Wen—arguably the best in Jin's year—who rarely spoke but moved like she knew the ground would *obey* her. Her tiger Emberkin was a magnificent creature who could knock half a dozen student

Warriors over, which only deepened everyone else's dread.

Jin initially tried to find loopholes in the whole arms lottery system. Would it be possible for one of their Weavers to secretly draw a glyph on his arm before the duel to help draw his weapon of choice to him mid-duel? Forcefully disarm his opponent and claim their arms?

He wasn't sure what he was asking, what with his limited knowledge of Smokecraft and the Smokeveil. It was like trying to plan a duel with half a map and not knowing which way was up. So much to learn, so little time. His new Weaver friends patiently explained as best they could. All arms issued during the Trial would be Smokebound. Coded to the plaque bearer through a glyph woven by the Trial officiants right before the initial duels.

Once the duel began, their arms would be locked to their hands alone. If disarmed, they would either return like breath being pulled back into lungs, or collapse into smoke entirely, if they were flung out of the arena. No one else could pick them up, not even another bonded General. Which was technically good news … if you were armed.

If someone entered the arena unarmed, there would be no second chances. No on-the-spot quick steals, no improvisation. Just your bare hands, and whatever ghosts you could conjure to fight alongside you.

Jin tried not to let his dread show. A scared General wasn't exactly great for morale. But within their own faction, Ruo and Yue never stopped pushing for answers, gently at first, but increasingly insistent.

"Yan Xun," Yue said, keeping her voice low but tone firm, "we can plan much better if we know what we're working with."

"We do," Yan Xun replied, not unkindly. "The plan is: you and Ruo are to focus solely on laying claim to at least one other plaque. Two, if possible. Even better still? Find out who has what. Use discretion. Don't be caught."

Ruo opened her mouth to protest. "But—"

"If Jin ever enters that arena empty-handed," Yan Xun said, "we lose. That's all you need to know for now."

Her tone was calm and measured, but firm enough that neither pushed any further.

Reigning Fire

Jin, being the General, had been given a different mission during a private meeting with Yan Xun.

"You want to what?" he asked.

"Test your instincts," Yan Xun said, already drawing her fingers through the air. "See what kind of opponent you are, especially when it's not flesh and blood in front of you."

She cast fast-moving, erratic smoke illusions that shifted form, mimicking other factions' likely styles and reach with different arms. As Jin traded strikes with the illusions, his surprise grew. The smoke-opponents moved with distinct martial forms—every stance, guard, and counter-strike was terrifyingly accurate, even though they were cast by someone untrained in combat.

He lost sight of Yan Xun more than once in the smoke, until her voice cut through the illusions like a guiding star. It grounded him in a strange way, focused him more than his instructors' yelling ever had.

As the exercise went on, she alternated the arms in his hands—first a dagger, then a staff, then bare hands against a spear. It was equally brutal and purposeful, like she was simulating what the duel and battle might throw at him, one combination at a time.

It was a strange novelty, but Jin forced himself to focus on his mission, slipping back into his usual momentum without overthinking. Just gave it his best each time.

"You fight like someone who listens to his body more than his mind under pressure," she remarked afterward.

"Will I ever feel certain if you're actually complimenting or mocking me?" he asked half-jokingly. "Well, I find that if I lean too much into my thoughts, I end up hesitating. And mid-combat, even a moment's hesitation could be costly."

If she approved, she didn't let on. But she didn't look disenchanted, either. And sometimes, when she watched him with her full concentration, her brows furrowed, he found it hard to remember that this was all just part of a test.

Why was he even obsessing over what she thought of him, anyway? Especially when what he *should* be worrying about was whether she was about to get him skewered—sent into a battle against Emberkin-bonded opponents with nothing but his bare fists and crossed fingers. He shook his head hard to clear his mind. He was *not* going there.

Still … something else about those smoke illusions she'd cast kept tugging at him. As far as Jin knew from his recent Smokeveil crash course, Smokecraft didn't allow you to create something out of nothing. Weavers could enhance, distort, or diminish—alter what already existed, whether tangible or intangible—but not conjure what wasn't there. They could even manipulate someone's emotions by either dialing them up or down but not manufacture an emotion that wasn't already there.

This was why even bonded Generals wouldn't be able to fashion weapons out of thin air during the duel and battle, if they hadn't secured plaques with their arms of choice by then. While bonded Emberkin, being smoke creatures, could produce smoke that a Weaver could shape into images or tricks, even that had its limits.

But Yan Xun wasn't supposed to be bonded with an Emberkin, yet. And there had definitely been no smoke present during their session. They'd even sealed off the indoor training grounds—doors locked, windows shut—to keep out prying eyes. So, how had she done it?

He tried to tell himself it didn't matter. That strategy came first, answers later. They all had more pressing issues at hand. Besides, it wasn't as if he believed Yan Xun would offer a candid response if he'd simply asked, anyway. But something in his gut remained unsettled, like he'd glimpsed the edge of a rule no one had told him was allowed to be broken.

Every evening, their campfire turned into a circle of half-truths and careful glances.

"You're really not going to tell us what we're working with?" Ruo asked again on the fourth night.

Yan Xun looked up from where she was drawing glyphs—or doodling, Jin couldn't tell—in the dirt.

"We're working against time, based on an understanding that we each have our own part, our own important objectives to accomplish."

It was infuriating, but Jin could see what she was doing. The secrecy wasn't about ego or a lack of trust in them. It was about making everyone lean on their instincts and focus whole-mindedly onto their own missions.

Besides, if they failed—if her faction suffered a humiliating defeat under her lead—it wouldn't just be bruises and missed glory. All eyes would be on her. The royal daughter who dared to lead but couldn't deliver.

After spending just a few days around the student Weavers, Jin had already heard more tittle-tattle about her than anyone else. Even more than Wu, who seemed extremely keen to be the center of attention.

Yan Xun had the most to lose, and she, of all people, should be the most painfully aware of that.

And despite everything, Jin couldn't help but suspect that she was playing a longer game than anyone else here by choosing not to disclose their weapon to another soul. But even long games had weak flanks. And he wasn't sure how many risks she could stack before an enemy spotted the opening.

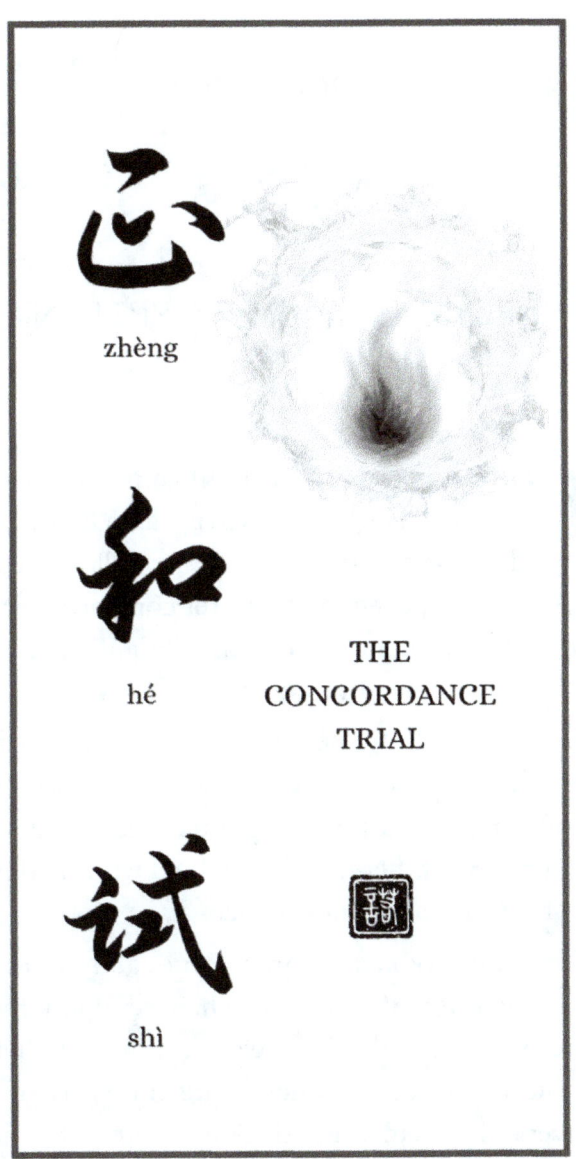

正
zhèng

和
hé

试
shì

THE
CONCORDANCE
TRIAL

Jasmine K. Y. Loo

Chapter Nine

烟雨濛濛

SECRETS AND DECEPTION

The plaque was no bigger than my palm, yet it weighed almost as heavily as a sword. I'd thought of hiding it under my pillow, behind the scroll racks, even in the secret compartment beneath my bed. But none of them felt right. Either too easy, too obvious, or too vulnerable.

In the end, I'd gone with the one place that allowed me to be sure I would always have it on me: my silk wraps used for strength training. I had more than a dozen of them, each weighted with sand panels for performance and balance.

The wraps looked decorative enough to not raise much suspicion if someone chanced upon them. Some were hand-dyed in seasonal tones with fine metallic embroidery. Others bore the sigils of the Weavers' Academy: interlocking rings of smoke stitched in a pattern only visible at certain angles, like

Reigning Fire

the glyphs themselves. A nod to tradition, they would assume. Or vanity.

I emptied out a single sand panel from a dusk-blue wrap, slid the plaque in, then stitched it back up by hand, slow and seamless. Now, the only time I would be parted from it would be when I was bathing. So, I made sure my bath times were rotated. And I always secured the doors, even when my bathing chamber was within my private quarters.

By our year level, most student Weavers were more than capable of drawing a basic Heating glyph to keep the bathwater warm. I traced mine by memory along the inner rim of the tub before stepping in, each curve flickering under my fingertip. The glyph shimmered to life like pressed embers beneath lacquered wood, its light soft and pulsing, like the breath of something in repose.

When I sank into the bath, the heat it emitted was coaxing, like the kind of warmth that seeped into your bones and reminded you of safety. Without the need for servants bringing extra buckets of hot water, the added privacy had been a rare kind of bliss. It was one of the few comforts I'd allowed myself.

That night, only moments after I'd stepped into my bath, something inside me tensed. A barely perceptible shuffle from the other side of the wooden screen, a distant echo of muted footfalls from slow, creeping movements outside my chambers.

Mo's glow flickered when she picked up on my sudden wariness. Swiftly slipping on my inner robes as I exited the tub, I inched soundlessly toward the door just as it cracked open.

A figure in black stepped in, face partially covered. But he was tall and broad. Very much so. Not built like a student. And even with half his face obscured, there was no mistaking the hostile energy he carried.

Fucking Fu Kai. He didn't move like someone trying to steal, but like someone who was simply making his rightful claim to something in my possession. *Over me.*

My fingers twitched. I could have struck first, and it would have been fast. But unless I could kill him now *and* get away with it—that was a dangerous *if*—it would mean handing my mortal enemy one of my biggest secrets: my martial training with Xiao. A secret that, once revealed, would topple the rest like falling dominoes.

Possible repercussions on Lady Linhua flashed through my mind, and I hesitated. Still paralyzed by my own internal debate behind the door, I met the Kai's gaze as he turned—his eyes burning with that wild, zealous glint I knew too well. My hesitation could've cost me. It might have, had another shadow not stepped into the room just in time.

Jin.

Without raising an alarm, he simply planted himself between the trespasser and me, one hand resting casually across his torso where his belt met his hip. From that position, he was poised to strike swiftly, if necessary.

"Strange time for cleaning duty," Jin said to the intruder, tone light.

Kai froze. Then turned, smooth and calm, slipping back out the same way he'd entered before another word could be said. Right before disappearing, his eyes caught mine, gleaming with a silent promise: *This isn't over.*

Jin didn't look toward me right away, just continued staring at the now closed door.

"Big guy," he said. "Didn't walk like a student."

The blood in my veins was still fizzling wildly, as though undecided if it was getting close to a boiling or freezing point.

"Must've been one of the staff," I said, absently tugging on an outer robe that was draped over a lounge nearby, bath water still dripping. "Probably looking for something he'd dropped in the day."

I focused on channeling my emotions to Mo and didn't work too hard on coming up with something seamless in logic.

"Sure. Didn't realize that the Weavers' Academy staff was assigned black uniforms, complete with a face veil," he replied tartly. "Funny, though. Back in the courtyard on the day we first met, when you were talking to that palace man … you had a genteel manner about you. But you were also emanating this energy. Cold. Focused. Almost … lethal." He gave a small shrug. "Thought I saw a flicker of that again just then."

When I didn't answer, he finally turned around, looking at me with a somber expression. "I'm not asking what you're hiding. But if you ever need backup, don't wait until you're outnumbered. You know you only have to ask."

This time, I wanted to say something. But a lump lodged in my throat, thick and sudden, stopping me from speaking. We stood there, eyes boring into each other's for what felt like an eternity, until Jin turned around and left.

Since then, I found out from Mo that Jin had been sleeping on my roof every night. Emberkin couldn't speak, but that didn't mean she wouldn't find ways to communicate with me. Her focus lingered above us, toward the direction of the roof for the longest time. Then she shaped a puff of smoke into a plate of lychee cakes, resting it gently midair between us. I found it interesting that Mo now recognized Jin's energy well enough to know when he was around.

I was aware that I should've said something to Jin. Assured him that this was unnecessary. That I'd always had myself covered. I should've but I didn't. Heavens knew why. Maybe I was selfish, which was not an uncommon trait amongst royals.

At least the cool seasons won't come until after the Trial, I told myself. And I wondered, fleetingly, what it would feel like to sleep beneath the vast sky, under a blanket of stars pulled straight from the heavens.

The next day, we sat together as a group around our campfire, waiting for Yue to return from her mission. Ruo and Jin started exchanging old Academy tales to pass the time. As a light drizzle began to fall, I pretended to focus on maintaining the strength of the Flame glyph for our little campfire, even though it wasn't necessary during the warm season.

Truth was, I never knew what to say about myself. From the little snippets I caught of their conversation— stories about communal dorm pranks, late-night snack raids, and awkward crushes—there was really nothing I could offer without sounding like I was dropping a horror story into a bowl of nostalgia.

So, I sat without joining in the chatter, my eyes on the fire, constantly fine-tuning the glyph just enough to stay occupied without seeming disengaged or rude. I kept replaying the memory of standing behind my chamber's door—of Kai's wild, diabolical eyes catching mine just before he'd fled. I wasn't dissecting the incident out of fear, but rather because I needed to understand his motives.

He didn't come to inflict any physical harm on me last night, especially not since his last attempt had brought him two years in the borderlands. But there were more ways to destroy a person than in the flesh and blood. And he'd since learned to hone much more insidious weapons against me.

Given the timing, this had to be about the Trial. If Kai could get his hands on our plaque, he wouldn't keep it. He would find a way to leak its contents—anonymously, of course—to every faction leader. Let them spread the word and plan accordingly. No one would trace it back to him.

He wouldn't win anything from it directly, but that was beside the point. He would do it to humiliate me, to remind me that no matter how carefully I played this game, he could tilt the board at any time. But if his little trespassing stunt managed to shake me enough to falter before the Trial—well, that would be an added bonus.

At one point, I noticed Jin had caught me deep in thought, his eyes raking my face. But he didn't say anything. And, more importantly, he hadn't said a word about what had happened with Kai to the others.

Yue returned just before dusk, her long braid trailing over her shoulder, still damp from the rain. Ignoring Jin and Ruo's flood of questions, she laid three slips of parchment by the fire. When I picked one up for closer inspection, I caught a subtle whiff of valeroot and bitter plum. Yue still had the habit of reusing the parchment she'd used for wrapping herbs for notetaking.

I gave her a look. "Spill-leaf?"

Yue inclined her head and fixed her gaze on me, before saying, "Barely enough to loosen a tongue. No one's noticed I mixed them into one of the incense coils in their quarters, instead of their tea."

I thought that was clever. The scent of sandalwood would've masked the spill-leaf's.

Then Yue tapped on the first parchment. "Wu's faction. They're still parading that 'spear' story, but their General, a girl named Wen, has been secretly drilling with both a shield and a dagger. Totally out of rhythm with the rest of the group."

Ruo chuckled. "Already stolen something, huh? That's fast. At least we now know who to focus on stealing from."

Jin nodded. "Would explain why Wen has been focusing on her close-quarter deflection. But it's also possible that they've gone for the big bluff from the start. Drawn a blank but later stolen a shield.

Practicing with a dagger may be yet another smoke screen," he mused.

Yue moved on to the second slip. "Lee's faction. I managed to find out from one of their Weavers that their General, Qiao, used to despise spears. Called them unwieldy. But now? He's suddenly calling them noble. And he's been mocking the General from Mu's faction for scrambling to train for upper body strength when it's already too late to start."

"What, as in Rin?" Jin asked, stunned and looking almost sympathetic.

Yue nodded. "Yes, or *that tiny thing*, as he called Rin. My guess is that either Lee's drawn a spear or sweet-talked another faction into a swap. Regardless, they've most likely called Wu's bluff without even needing to infiltrate their inner workings."

I kept my expression still, listening and mapping.

Yue tapped on the last slip. "Luo's faction. Officially, they're claiming the sword, but one of their own let slip that their General's best asset is improvisation. When I asked her, directly, which arms they were training for, she said, 'Whichever we can get our hands on *again*.'"

Ruo frowned. "So, they're the unlucky bastards who've lost their plaque to Wu's faction?"

"Or got tricked and traded it," Yue said. "Could be part of their deception. Didn't sound like a lie, though."

Jin leaned forward, arms braced across his knees. "That makes things interesting …"

I could see his cogs turning as he was weighing the odds, analyzing the patterns and intentions behind everything we'd learned so far. And wondering if maybe, just maybe, we'd caught a break.

The following afternoon, Jin caught up to me after our group had dispersed. He walked beside me in silence for a few steps before speaking.

"Meet me at the East Training Hall tonight? Nothing weird, I promise."

Glancing sidelong at him, I asked, "Why?"

He scratched the back of his neck. "Just … something I thought that might help. You'll see."

The training hall had long been emptied when we arrived. Only the faintest lamplight flickered through the narrow slats of the closed shutters. Jin carefully lifted the wooden latch on the sparring chamber's door, before nudging it open for us to slip through.

"So, why did you want to meet?" I asked as he was bolting the door behind us, unsure what to expect.

"I know you're trained in Smokecraft and all, but after what happened in your quarters the other night …" He paused. "I thought learning some basic self-defense would help you feel safer."

"I'm not rattled," I said, perhaps a bit too quickly.

"You've done a terrible job at pretending not to be," he pointed out. "You've totally been in your own head in the past two days."

I arched a brow in challenge. "And how would you know that?"

He answered without hesitating, "'Cause I've been watching you." His eyes darted away abruptly, as though he hadn't meant to reveal that. "Just humor me, alright? Let me teach you something."

Lost for words, I didn't argue.

Jin walked over to the rack along the wall and pulled down two short wooden batons. "These are light. Good for learning grip, blocks, angles. No sharp edges, so I can't accidentally maim you."

"How reassuring," I said drily.

He smiled a little and handed one to me, grip-end first. The weight and texture of the baton felt familiar in my hand, but I was worried about exposing myself.

For nearly two years now, I'd been clandestinely training in Swordcraft—a specialized form of Smokecraft practiced by Weavers who channeled intent into their weapons, stripping away all superfluous moves. It was about directing emotion, purpose, and instinct into each movement. Those adept in Swordcraft could anticipate the arc of an opponent's strike before it happened, sensing intention in the air.

Strictly speaking, two years in combat training wasn't long. But as a Smokeveil Weaver, that time had given me an edge in gaining skill that many non-Weavers would spend a decade earning. Because of that, I would already be almost holding even with Jin, who'd been training at the Martial Academy for six years. That was the unfair advantage of our kind.

But no one knew of my combat training, owing to the fact that the nightly realm-crossing to train with Xiao was only made possible by my mythic Emberkin. Withholding truth was always easier for me than blatantly lying and pretending, which was the real reason why I'd been taciturn. The more others knew about you, the more they would have to use against you. Such was the way of the court.

"Let's start simple," Jin said, snapping me out of my thoughts. "Raise it like this—elbow slightly bent, baton angled outward. Defensive stance."

I mirrored him, too stiff on purpose.

His brows creased. "Loosen your grip a little. You'll drop it like that if someone knocks it too hard."

He stepped closer, reaching to adjust my hands. My breath caught when his fingers brushed mine, steady and warm.

He cleared his throat. "OK, good. Now, let's try a slow swing, just across the middle like this."

Once again, I under-rotated deliberately when mimicking him. Pretending to learn something I already knew felt strange, to say the least. But there was something different about this. For once, someone was paying attention to what I might actually need, rather than assigning me lessons they believed were important. Teaching me something so I could protect myself, instead of their interests. The gesture was unfamiliar … and quietly touching.

We cycled through a few sequences—strikes, blocks, and kicks. Jin taught me how to circle round to an opponent's blind spot, where to hit for maximum impact, offering patient corrections.

"Better," he said eventually, after I let a block land a touch too late. "But you're holding back."

I blinked. "What makes you think that?"

He tilted his head. "I don't know. Just a feeling. Like you already kind of know what you're doing but pretending not to."

I tried not to let my guilty conscience show. "Maybe I'm just a fast learner."

He gave a half-laugh, dabbing his forehead with his sleeve. "Right. Or maybe I'm just being a busybody forcing something you don't need on you."

"You're not," I said, before I could stop myself.

His lips quirked. "Well … just remember, even if you're good at looking fine, it doesn't mean you always need to keep up a strong front."

I wanted to tell him that falling apart was never an option for someone like me. That my discretion wasn't merely about withholding trust, but protection for those I cared for.

Reigning Fire

But instead, I stepped back and raised the baton again. "One more round?"

He gave a small nod, stepping lightly into position.

We practiced late into the evening—just focusing on the rhythm of wood meeting wood and the shuffle of feet across the floor, breath catching on effort. I let myself ease into it, just enough to match his pace without drawing suspicion.

On the last block, he fumbled slightly, and my hand shot out to grab his wrist instead of the baton. He locked gazes with me, a flicker of surprise flashing across his face, now inches away from mine.

"Maybe you're a bit more dangerous than you let on," he teased, his breath grazing my cheek.

"Or maybe you're just easy to disarm," I offered, releasing his wrist and taking a step back.

He chuckled. "Alright, enough of bruising my ego for one night."

When I was just about to return my baton to the weapons' rack, Jin stopped me. "Keep it. Just in case."

I hesitated briefly, wary about someone finding a weapon in my quarters and raising questions. But nodded in the end and tucked it beneath my arm.

Outside, the only sounds were the piercing screeches of cicadas. We didn't speak as he was locking up. But just before we left, he glanced over his shoulder and said, "I'm glad you came."

I felt a smile playing on my lips. "Thank you, Jin." *Thank you, from the deepest part of my heart.*

Despite having tried every trick up their sleeve, Yue and Ruo hadn't been able to secure a second plaque. Which meant we now knew with high confidence that, of the six factions, at least two were in serious trouble. We unanimously agreed that they were functionally unarmed. One had already lost their plaque.

Another—Mu's faction—had a General known for his speed, not brute strength. But it appeared they'd traded away their original arms for a staff, likely being misguided in thinking it was going to be a weapon that could offer them better odds, like a sword or a dagger. In theory, they could use Smokecraft to lighten the staff so Rin could wield it more easily. But doing so would more or less defeat the purpose of the weapon. A staff without the weight was just an overlong cane. The very thing that gave it lethality would have been stripped.

"Which leaves the final mysterious faction with a blank, a sword, or whichever remains between the dagger and the shield, if Wu's bluffing," Yue inferred.

All of them glanced toward me in poorly shrouded, expectant looks. But this time, no one explicitly asked me about our plaque anymore.

Focusing on something more practical, Ruo asked, "Do you know much about their General, Jin?"

Jin considered for a moment before offering his honest outlook. "Yeah. We're from the same year. She has no Weaving powers, like the most of us, but is a seasoned fighter. I'd say she's on par with me, all things considered. Better at reading the broader field during combat, but sometimes that slows her down when a situation calls for split-moment decisions."

This, in theory, should've left us with a clear choice of which faction's name to submit and challenge for a duel: to either go after the team that had lost their plaque, or poor General Rin. But after much conferring, we all agreed that even if we did, it wouldn't likely be a match. The smartest play for the factions with a known disadvantage in the arms department was to challenge the faction they were certain could beat them in the initial duel, simply because its rules were "winner draws first blood."

The duels weren't meant to carry fatality risks. Even if it meant losing early, it would give the vulnerable factions a safe way out of the final round, where survival wasn't guaranteed. It was better to lose early—gracefully, strategically—than to dance with death later on.

And if the two known stronger factions were thinking ahead, they would be working with the same logic. Secure quick and easy victories from factions they knew to be in an unfavorable position, thanks to them.

In other words, Wu's faction would go after the one they'd stolen the dagger from. Meanwhile, Lee's faction would challenge Mu's, the faction they'd tricked into that staff swap. And they would most likely all get a match from the deprived factions who would do well to bow out of the final convergence battle. Which left us with only one option: the last faction that was still unaccounted for.

Jin now openly surveyed me with a quizzing look. I didn't blame him. After all, he might be entering the duel armed, fighting an unarmed opponent. Or … he could be the one standing bare-handed against someone armed. The tension settled over us like a dust cloud. I understood their exasperation with my secrecy. Yet I also knew knowledge could just as easily translate to power as court peril. And to lead a faction—to one day rule the Empire—I must first master the art of evoking an unquestioning faith in my acumen. That much had always been made clear to me, whether I believed that was something I was capable of or not.

Finally, with a great exhale, Jin slapped both of his thighs, hard, as if he'd decided that, if worse came to worst, he would simply accept an early defeat. Avoid the pure chaos that the final convergence battle promised, just like the other two Generals.

When I went to submit the name of the faction we were challenging, exactly a week before the deciding day, Master Dan informed me that other duels had already been mutually agreed upon. Wu and Lee's choices had been logged and were a match with their intended opponent's. That left only one faction unchallenged, just like we'd deduced.

That night, I crossed over to the Dream Realm the way I'd been doing over the last few weeks. I used to be drawn into the Dream Realm without conscious volition. I'd just come to expect it at some point in my sleep. But after much trial and error, I'd learned to deliberately enter the Dream Realm by closing my eyes in meditation, until the waking world blurred and softened, giving way to snow.

I opened my eyes to Xiao's familiar and comforting silhouette in the distance. They stood at the center of the snow clearing, sword in hand, their long robes billowing out around them in the gentle breeze. I joined them, drawing my own blade from memory. We bowed in unison, and the sparring began. But I was slow, sluggish. Each time I struck, I struck late. Each parry was an echo of what it should have been.

My eyes were on Xiao, but my mind wasn't. It was still spinning through a dozen possible futures—

each one a branching path depending on whether Jin won or lost his duel. And if he *won* …

Going against two faction leaders with bonded Emberkin would already put us in a precarious situation. But to concurrently engage two bonded Generals head on? The odds were stacked against us.

Xiao stopped mid-motion, blade still raised. They never spoke, but I knew that disengagement meant we were done for the night. So, I'd expected them to vanish into the snowy horizon and expel me from the Dream Realm. Instead, they sheathed their sword and gestured for me to follow.

We walked past the trees that bordered the clearing, past the place where I'd first bled, first broken down before rising back up again. Eventually, we emerged not into another training ground, but onto palace grounds. The stone paths, the moonlit gardens, the glint of lacquered wood—everything was identical to its counterpart in the Mortal Realm, despite being shrouded in an inexplicable surreality.

Without warning, Xiao circled behind me, gripping my waist and launching us both into the air. The Dream Realm obeyed will more than gravity. Before I could protest, we landed atop the Grand Pavilion's sloping tiled roof, the wind stirring the hem of my robes. Beneath my feet was where I'd undergone my Binding five moons ago, when the deadline to prove myself as the Empire's future Empress was set in stone. More than ever, every pair of eyes around me had been eagerly watching if I would sink or swim.

I waited for Xiao's lesson, but none came. They only stayed by me, looking into the distance. At this height, the palace grounds stretched in miniature: the twin Academies lay abreast in perfect symmetry, the magnificent Lifeng Pagoda stood on the far end, my old annex's dusky outline tucked in the folds of the inner palace. And finally, the Imperial Arena—desolate now, but no less hungry for blood. This was where it would all soon take place.

A question kept circling in my mind like ash caught in a downdraft: *What would Father have done in my place?* Would he choose to exercise absoluteness, even if it cost him the trust of his allies? Or would he sacrifice a pawn to protect the game?

Most likely both of the above, considering my uncles' Emberkin confined within Lifeng after Father's takeover. But I was not Father. I could never be.

So, this line of thought was futile, like most things I'd been turning over in my mind, lately.

I tried not to think of Lady Linhua's expression in the event of our inglorious defeat, if I should fail to "show the world what we both were really made of." Tried not to picture the look on Father's face—the confirmation of every doubt he'd ever held about me, the proof that I would never be enough. Not for the Empire, not for him.

And what about Jin? What if his life was put in jeopardy because we failed? What would I say to *his* parents? Heavens, to think that all this time, I'd been consumed by the fear of disappointing my parents. All while the possibility of having to one day inform other parents of their child's death loomed.

I *was* self-serving, after all.

Leaning forward, I pressed my palms into the cool tile, gasping for air. The fear I'd been carrying, usually kept buried deep within me or channeled to Mo whenever it threatened to overflow, now wrapped its roots around me in a death-bind. The sheer weight of duty, expectations, stakes, and secrets felt like it would send me crashing right through this rooftop in a free fall. The heaviness was so palpable, as if it'd defied even the physics of the Dream Realm.

There was an old saying among royals: *Ten thousand skeletons paving the way to a victor's legacy.*

At that thought, a renewed resolve anchored me against the pulling tide of my fear.

"No one else will die for me," I declared aloud to no one in particular.

In that moment, it was as if Mo's heat had touched my core and spread to the rest of my body, even when she couldn't physically be in the Dream Realm.

Over my very own dead body, I promised myself.

xiāo

Chapter Ten

坐埃未定

BEFORE THE DUST SETTLES

That night, I was in black from collar to boots, my face veiled. Entry to the Archives of Imperfect Artifacts wasn't forbidden, but I didn't want curious eyes from other factions trailing after me. This had to be done discreetly and precisely.

I was slipping through the open training grounds of the Martial Academy when I saw Jin, standing shirtless under the summer moon. Chest heaving, arms tense from repeated strikes, he moved like a creature made for motion—fluid, sharp, and unrelenting. Each pivot carved through the air with focused aggression. Sweat clung to his skin, glinting like molten silver in the lantern haze.

I should've kept moving, but I didn't. A memory surfaced, sudden and uninvited, of Jin's voice saying, *Maybe I just liked the view.* Clapping a hand across my mouth, I barely silenced a gasp in time.

That was *completely* out of context. *Entirely* the wrong moment to be recalling. And yet, it stuck.

There wasn't a chance to figure out what in heavens' name that was about because I caught a blur of movement behind Jin then. Another figure in black, masked and armed. Whoever they were, they would have to be tapping into Smokeveil powers to be moving so soundlessly.

With no time to warn Jin and no weapon in reach, I moved on instinct, driven only by reflex and rage. Disrupting the attacker's aim with a Flash-Burst glyph, I struck them mid-lunge, followed by a sharp thrust of my elbow into their solar plexus. When they staggered, I twisted low and swept out their legs, aiming a punch at their face.

The attacker slumped just as Jin spun around with his half-drawn blade, blinking rapidly, his eyes still reeling from the flash of my glyph.

"Who—"

But I was already backing into shadow.

"Watch your back, Academy boy," I murmured, my voice lowered by several octaves with the glyph over my throat. "Not everyone fights fair."

I continued my journey without waiting for his reaction. When I reached the Archives, a great exhale of relief escaped me upon finding the stones I was looking for still sitting there, untouched. I gathered them into a cloth bundle and slung the pack over my shoulder. *One last trick to master.*

It would all come down to whether I could execute Smokeshifting across the entire arena's perimeter, all at the exact same time. It was a much larger spread than anything I'd tried moving before. I'd been practicing drawing and redrawing the glyph for days. But no matter how precise I tried to be, I couldn't execute it cleanly beyond even half the circumference of what was needed.

I'd even tried spinning my body at speed to cover all directions, hoping to achieve a broader cast. Even when I started seeing stars, it still didn't work. The glyphs would ripple, fray, or collapse entirely, failing before the illusion could even take shape.

The phantasm wouldn't harm anyone physically. It didn't need to. Belief, once seeded, could bend the world more surely than force. It didn't matter what was real, only what was *believed* to be. And the rest would unravel on its own … so long as I could pull this off.

I tugged on the string connected to my bell to summon an inner palace attendant to my quarters under the pretense of requesting a top-up of my quarter's supply of incense coils.

Each core royal member had a unique incense specially crafted by the Imperial Fragrance Artisan just for us. A glimpse into the profligacies of life as a royal. And the supply of such rare items had to come directly from the inner palace. Ironically, I'd never fancied my assigned scent—a rich, inky redolence. But it was mine, and I was to use it. I'd gotten accustomed to it, much like everything else I abhorred but had to accept with grace.

When the knock came, I opened the door guilelessly. A man with graying hair stepped in with his head bowed, never raising his eyes beyond the polished floor. He didn't ask why I was making such a request, or what sort of trouble he might get into if someone caught him doing what I asked. He simply waited for my orders.

"Twelve," I said, pressing a piece of parchment into his palm. "No more, no less, placed as indicated on the sketch. Each five miles apart, buried at a finger's depth, encircling the edge in silent rhythm."

The man bowed deferentially.

Years ago, I'd helped his wife procure a duty re-assignment when her Lung-Shielding glyphs began collapsing from long hours of working with Smoke-acid. She wouldn't have lasted another year if she'd remained in her post. I hadn't expected anything in return, but the memory of my favor had lingered with him, like how smoke always left a trace. He tucked the linen bundle I handed him into his supply cart, between bundles of incense coils and braziers. By dusk, its contents would be exactly where they needed to be.

Deceivingly ordinary in appearance, Smokemirrors were thousand-year-old flat river stones amassed from the base of the Great Smoke Falls, etched with layered glyphs and polished smooth until they gleamed. However, they weren't officially catalogued as relics or even considered useful, let alone threatening in any sense.

The Great Smoke Falls plunged from a mountain so tall its apex was said to touch the Smokeveil itself. The river stones found at its base were believed to carry a trace of its powers—wild and onerous to harness. The glyphs sealed the powers within the stones before they could dissipate, allowing Weavers to activate them under the right conditions.

The Empire Weavers had once tried to refine them, eons ago. But the illusions casted from Smokemirrors were still considered too weak, too unstable, and nowhere nearly as convincing as what a bonded Weaver could achieve, rendering them redundant. So, they'd been shelved since, rejected and forgotten.

As a young child, I'd gone through a period of obsessive delving into Smokeveil artifacts. I would spend hours being tucked away in the Archives of Imperfect Artifacts—a dumping ground for Smokeveil projects deemed unworthy of ceremony—for no other reason than its ease of access. Its collections were no different from broken toys that'd been left to gather dust, abandoned by the court's scholars and Weavers alike.

But to Shan and me, it was a cave of wonders. I was barely nine when we'd claimed it as our secret base. A narrow hallway hidden behind the east wing's old herb storerooms, marked only by a splintered plaque and an ever-drifting scent of old parchment, dust, and … potential.

There was always something fascinating about the light in that space. In the way the sun slipped through the parchment-lined lattice windows, casting square-paned shadows onto the messy shelves. Dust particles would catch the light like flecks of mica, suspended midair, turning every breath into a spell.

We would dig through half-studied relics and neglected scrolls, two girls racing through ruin, breathless with the possibility of finding something forgotten but magical. Something only we would recognize for what it was: a secret worth keeping.

That was how I'd stumbled upon what looked like ordinary river stones with pretty etchings in a shabby wooden box. And buried under them was a torn piece of parchment, folded up carelessly. A note from one of the lesser Ministry scribes—just a single line scrawled in haste, barely legible. It said: *When twelve breathe as one, their ring unbroken, the veil between thought and form begins to thin.*

That was all it took, yet ... no one else knew. Otherwise, they would have ended up in the highly secured Vault of Relics instead.

Once, long ago, I'd activated the Smokemirrors for something else entirely. A projection of a dinner table next to a hearth, my mother humming in the background, my father smiling for a change. A reposeful home where no one raised their voices, where I could be nothing more than a girl with two parents who didn't need her to be a miracle. It was a tremendous source of solace, but I'd never activated them again. I knew myself too well. I would've watched it again and again, until the illusion became more substantial than memory, more enticing than reality.

After Shan's death, the idea of seeing her once more using Smokemirrors had crossed my mind. But as soon as the thought had formed, an excruciating pain had shot through me, like lightning threading through nerves. I would never go there.

So, I'd left the rest of the stones hidden at the back of the Archives of Imperfect Artifacts, beneath some loose floorboards behind an unlabeled shelf. A private reassurance that I *could* activate them again if I ever chose to.

Now, they would serve another purpose entirely. Not to soothe, but to unsettle. Not to comfort, but to confuse.

I watched as the old servant gave me another deep bow before rolling his cart, loaded with more than its usual burdens, back out of my quarters and disappearing into the hallway. It'd always baffled me how someone made of flesh and breath could become so invisible to the world, simply by being born into the wrong circumstances. No glyphs or relics were needed to bind a soul into a lifetime of being overlooked. Status alone was a heavy enough curse.

On the day before the Trial, I stopped by the Weavers' Academy kitchens in the late afternoon. Most students, being nobles, had never known its location. There was no need for them to.

When I entered, the servants immediately stopped what they were doing, looking perturbed. Bowing deeply, they all veered wordlessly out of my way, forming a wall of lowered heads.

I raised a hand. "Rise. I need this space to myself. I won't be long, just need a stick of incense-burning time."

They hesitated only briefly, stealing glances at one another, before obliging with another bow and filing out in silence. While I didn't care for power the way Father did, I certainly appreciated it on the rare occasion when the only response I required from others was "Your wish is my command," with no questions asked. Especially since I didn't particularly fancy explaining myself.

After I was done in the kitchens, I walked the perimeter of the Imperial Arena, just to feel the scale of it one last time under moonlight. The arena always felt different in the evenings, when its striking grandeur in the day gave way to solemn quietude. The space would soon be sealed off for the palace attendants to work on the final preparations for tomorrow.

The glyph towers stood handsomely across the back, their frames etched with ceremonial glyphs. Somewhere beyond, Jin was probably still practicing his footwork, Yue double-checking battle salves, and Ruo refining her Signal glyphing.

One way or another, by this time tomorrow, the dust would have settled.

It happened just as I returned from my little stroll to regroup with the rest. Ruo was pacing frantically

Reigning Fire

along the far end of the classroom we'd occupied for our final walkthrough, hair still damp from washing, sleeves rolled high. The usual chatter among them was completely absent. The moment I crossed the threshold, I could sense the tension.

"Where were you?" Ruo demanded curtly.

"Out," I said, shutting the door behind me. "It's the night before the Trial. We all have our rituals."

Ruo let out a scathing laugh. "Oh, I forgot. You get to keep secrets and call it ritual."

I held back a response and just inhaled slowly through my nose, but Ruo was stalking toward me.

"You've been planning something. And I don't need the details. I've decided that I can live without those. But what I can't live with is going into the Trial tomorrow with nothing but faith in someone who never gives us anything back."

Behind her, Yue's hands froze mid-sorting, hovering uncertainly over her assortment of herbs.

Ruo's voice grew louder. "You've got your own chambers, your own resources, a father who's the *Regent*. But the rest of us?" She gestured at herself, Jin, and Yue. "We had to *claw* our way here. Sponsorships don't come easy to kids like us. Our families had to sacrifice everything just for us to be here. If we fail, we don't just lose a game. Six years of working tirelessly could just go straight into the sewers!"

Jin stepped forward, looking like he was trying to conciliate the dispute, but she wasn't done.

"You're not the only one with something to prove, Yan Xun. And if this whole thing goes up in smoke tomorrow because you thought secrecy works better than trust, then I hope you're ready to watch your strategy bury our prospects, too." Ruo turned sharply, her boots thudding across the floor as she stormed out.

Yue looked flustered, as if uncertain if she should say something to me or go after Ruo.

"Let her go," I said, feeling tears starting to prick my eyes.

Nothing a few quick blinks and a gentle channel to Mo couldn't solve. Perched on my left shoulder, Mo draped a wing over me, as if to shield my heart. Being the only one who could see Mo was really helpful for moments like this, when I needed to keep my heart safely tucked away.

When I went to shut the door after Ruo, I caught a glimpse of a passing faction who appeared to have overheard our row but chose to feign ignorance.

Well, everyone had a different way of handling pressure. I should know better than anyone that it was better to let it all out than to keep it in. It didn't necessarily mean we were falling apart. Though deep down, the fear that we truly might be lurked in the shadows.

Later, Yue offered to flay Ruo with a brush dipped in Smokeacid to return my favor from when we were children, if I so wished. We both smiled at the memory. She gifted me some calming tea leaves before we were all finally ready to retire to our own quarters. Or to my roof, for Jin. I still hadn't let on that I was aware of his recent sleeping arrangements.

I asked for Jin's help to carry some scrolls back to my quarters. Ruo had previously borrowed them from my personal library to read up on silent glyphing but had left them scattered across the preparation bench when she'd stormed off.

Once he stepped into my chamber, I closed the door behind us and fastened the wooden latch.

Jin glanced back at me, one brow raised. "Everything alright?"

"Take off your robe," I said, fixing my eyes on the tea table as I was making my way toward it, hoping my voice wouldn't betray my nerves.

Now, both his brows were raised. "You want me to what?"

"I need to draw something on your back," I explained calmly, reaching for the inkstone.

"You're going to draw a glyph now?"

"It needs to be done tonight."

"But won't it fade by dawn?" he asked.

"It's not a timed glyph but a tether," I murmured, grinding a stick of smokeink on the inkstone. "It won't activate until I say so."

Jin blinked once before settling on a stool beside me. Then he tentatively removed his robe, the linen shifting down his shoulders with a whisper, baring the planes of his back in the low glyphlight. In that instant, it hit me—how much he must have trusted me. Enough to let me weave Smokecraft on him, especially when it wasn't something he could really understand.

Dipping two fingers into the cool ink, I began drawing, hand steady. First a line, then a loop, using careful pressure and fluid strokes. This wasn't just any smokeink. Darker and slower to dry, it was made of ground Smokemirror fragments bound in camphor resin. Tether glyphs needed weight to be able to cling.

"You might see something tomorrow," I said softly. "Something massive … that shouldn't exist."

He tilted his head slightly. "And you're telling me this now?"

"I'm telling you not to panic if I'm not panicking."

Jin let out something between a scoff and a laugh but kept still. "Is there a point in asking what that is?"

"Not tonight." At the final stroke, I pressed my palm over the glyph to seal it and felt a subtle shudder pass through him. The ink shimmered under my touch before fading to a dull gray.

"Trust me," I added with earnest conviction. "I won't let you burn, Jin."

A brief silence ensued. Then he said, "You know, Ruo wasn't wrong. We did have to claw our way here. Every step. Every day." He looked over his shoulder. "But she was wrong about you. I don't think you keep secrets because you're selfish or cynical, but because you're terrified of what it might cost not to."

That lump in my throat had returned once more, and a strange thought came to me. I wondered if this was how it would feel for a ghost to finally encounter someone who could see them, after an eternity of being invisible.

"And for the record, I do," he added as he turned his body toward me, snapping me out of my thoughts. "Trust you, I mean. For what it's worth."

His robes still hung low around his arms as we locked eyes. Then he slowly nodded, his lips pressed tightly together, gaze flicking away as he pulled his robes back on.

"Get some rest," I said, busying myself with the clean-up. "Tomorrow will be a long day."

He nodded again and left without another word.

Standing alone in my room, I unconsciously pressed a hand over my heart, where I'd drawn my

Tether glyph—a twin to the one on Jin's back. In my world, loyalty and care were the nemeses of ambition. Yet, I couldn't help but hope they could coexist to carry us through fire tomorrow.

That night, a nightmare severed the Dream Realm's call to me. It came without warning. No edges or entrance signaling the domain I was wrenched into, just jagged, shifting fragments of fear in its purest form.

Jin stepped into the arena without looking back, not even when I called out for him. Not even when I ran after him. The arena started dissolving into ash, rising like mist, and I found myself standing alone in a circle of mute, faceless drummers who were completely immobilized. Xiao was nowhere to be seen.

The Tether glyph I'd drawn on Jin's back hovered in the air before me, pulsing feebly, before it began to dim. *No, that's not where you're supposed to be*, I thought. When I tried reaching for it, my fingers went right through it, as if it was only a phantom that was baiting me.

A scorching wave of grief surged through me, forcing me to confront memories entombed in my mausoleum of a soul. Then, the Tether burst into flames, twisting, curling, and vanishing before my eyes.

Jin fell as the ground caved into a sinkhole.

I screamed, just as a blizzard of ash swallowed everything around me, my voice included.

Somewhere in the distance, Lady Linhua's voice echoed, *"He's just a servant."*

But Jin wasn't a servant. He never was.

Shan's face appeared before me then. Telling me in her soft but distorted voice that she promised to look after Jin. I tried to tell Shan that Jin couldn't go with her. To plead with her to stay with me. But I couldn't make a sound, no matter how hard I tried.

I woke with a start, mouth wide open, as if in a soundless scream, fingers clawing at my throat. My sheets tangled around my legs like a net, entwining me as I sank to the ocean floor.

Drenched in cold sweat, I couldn't even tell what exactly had gone wrong, just consumed by the visceral certainty that I was about to lose everything.

Outside, the chimes were already sounding.

Dawn had come.

Chapter Eleven

灰飞烟舞

A Dance Before the Ashes

We gathered in the Martial Academy court-yard under a dull morning sky, low clouds hanging heavy above our heads, mirroring the tension that pervaded the space. Even though the morning duels were only open to a small audi-ence of School Masters and members of the six factions, the air was charged with equal parts antici-pation and shrouded dread. Soon, every faction's weapons would be openly known to all.

We were dressed in combat robes for the day—sleeves tailored close and secured just beneath the el-bows by linen wraps, offering the practicality and ef-ficiency that our usual flowing attire lacked. It lent a sense of solemnity to the day, each Warrior poised and ready, each Weaver primed and alert. All except for Ruo, who was trying not to shake, her eyes wide and panicked, voice laced with desperation as she darted between other factions, pleading for any scraps of information they would offer.

"Please, just tell me what weapon your faction ended up with! At least let me know if we even stand a chance! I can't afford to lose. Please ..."

Some of the students were snickering openly, their sneers cutting like shards of jade. Ruo's distress, raw and unfiltered, only made them look down on us even more. To them, we were already defeated.

Others regarded Ruo with pity, as the Weaver from a faction of underdogs who wasn't even privy to key details of her team's strategy. I stood slightly apart from the others, looking unperturbed by neither Ruo's behavior nor the others' reactions. But inside, my heart raced.

Glancing over at Jin, I could see that he was trying to maintain a composed façade, but his distant eyes betrayed a mind that was miles away. I wished I could reach out to him. To do what, I wasn't sure. Any reassurance at this point would seem empty of meaning. The memory of my hand on his skin, along with the burning glyph in my nightmare came floating back.

Before getting dressed that morning, I'd cut our arms plaque free from the silk wrap it'd been hidden in all these weeks. Then, winding a stiff layer of linen binding around my chest, I secured it firmly under my robes, right up to the very last moment. Now, as the glowing ember of the incense stick was reaching all the way down to its bare bamboo core, marking the start of the duels, I discreetly reached under my robes and extricated our plaque. Mercifully, no one caught my eye during the process.

I held Jin's gaze as I handed him the plaque, wrong side up. He gulped, his hands trembling lightly as he took it, carefully keeping it faced down. He seemed to have decided not to look at it, or to even have a quick feel of the word engraved on it.

"Guess we'll see," he murmured, forcing a tight smile.

I nodded, hoping my eyes conveyed the reassurance I couldn't seem to utter.

"Just remember," I whispered, bringing my lips close to his ear, my voice quivering against my will. "I'll be right there with you. We're tethered. To the very end."

His smile softened into something more genuine, albeit faint. "I remember."

Next to Master Dan, Grandmaster Shao's voice rose sharply from the dais, naming the first combatants. "First duel—General Jin Yang of House Yan and General Chen of the House Situ."

Half-cheers and scattered, polite applause sounded briefly from the audience as Jin squared his shoulders and stepped forward. Even as he was presenting our plaque to Master Dan, still facing down, he was already turning his head sideways, as if bracing for Master Dan to simply wave him into position without offering any of the arms at all.

Master Dan surveyed Jin's face silently for a moment, unsure what to make of his strange behavior. Jin didn't even seem to notice when Master Dan briefly turned away. Only looked up in disbelief when Master Dan extended a sword to him, hilt-first.

A sword.

A wave of surprised whispers and murmurs rippled through the crowd. Jin accepted the blade and watched on with a surreal expression as Master Dan drew a Smokebinding glyph on his dominant arm, identical to the one etched on his weapon.

When his eyes found mine, his fingers tightening around the sword's hilt, I let out the breath I hadn't realized I'd been holding. Jin and his weapon were now Smokebound.

We'd made it.

My lips curled into a smile watching Jin mount the stage with his newly awakened confidence.

As both student Warriors bowed to each other, I could see that Jin regarded the bare-handed General Chen with sincere respect. Chen, in return, carried herself in a way that suggested her trust in Jin to have a fair fight, despite finding themselves in wildly unfair circumstances that were out of their control.

The crowd's whispers faded into a taut silence when both combatants settled into their starting forms. Then Grandmaster Shao's voice rang out once again, clear and commanding.

"Begin!"

Jin moved first, blade angled defensively, advancing with controlled, fluid steps that mirrored his internal composure. Chen, on the other hand, adopted a poised martial stance, her open palms ready, eyes sharp and watchful.

Chen struck swiftly, a measured yet assertive attempt to seize control. Her precise movements blended agile footwork with calculated, short blitzes, proving her tactical mastery. But Jin met her advances with equal precision, matching her tempo with graceful parries and deft sidesteps, never once fully pressing the advantage that his sword provided.

It was clear to everyone watching that Jin could have ended the duel in moments, yet he was holding back as a way of acknowledging Chen's strength and the inequitable power distribution. Still, he maintained a constant, subtle pressure—just enough to challenge her skill without overwhelming her.

The crowd, exuding disinterest at first, began watching on with rapt attention as the match unfolded. In time, Chen's movements began to show strain, each strike fractionally slower than the last, each deflection increasingly labored. Finally, Jin executed a swift maneuver, his blade flashing. Chen froze, eyes wide, as a thin red line appeared on the sleeve over her non-dominant upper arm.

Grandmaster Shao's sonorous voice broke the stillness that now hung in the space. "First blood to General Jin Yang."

Jin lowered his sword immediately, clasping his hands together before him and stepping back into a bow. Chen mirrored him, accepting her defeat with quiet dignity. As Jin was descending the stage, his eyes flicked toward me once more, his face painted in relief imbued with sorrow. The cost of that victory had weighed heavily on him. The court had always had a way of crushing the spirits of those with a code of honor. My heart ached for Jin at the inevitability of it.

The second duel was announced swiftly after, this time between General Wen from Wu's faction and General Pang from Luo's faction. Eyeing Wen's dagger bitterly, Pang looked as if he was trying to swallow the humiliation at something that was his being used against him. Wen stepped forward, formidable and unabashed. If she had a second arms plaque, she decided against using it in this duel. After all, a shield was hardly necessary against a bare-handed opponent. The tiger Emberkin paced behind her with sharp, vicious amber eyes.

From the very beginning, the disparity was clear. Hailed as unparalleled in her year, Wen moved with an ease that suggested she was well-acquainted with her excellence. She attacked decisively and wasn't invested in extending the fight for spectacle or decorum. Fierce and unrelenting, she switched seamlessly between offensive and defensive stances without breaking a sweat. Drawing from Smokeveil through her Emberkin magnified the potency of her strikes.

Pang was putting up a commendable effort, all things considered. He tried to redirect the impact of Wen's strikes with a series of deft dodges, using her own momentum against her, before executing his counterstrike along the new trajectory. Even then, it was merely delaying the preordained. In hardly any time at all, a deep gash ran down the length of Pang's forearm, and Wen was declared the victor.

The final duel was between House Lee's General Qiao, a broad-shouldered and imposing boy, and House Mu's General Rin. His smaller frame was already visibly strained under the unwieldy staff he was forced to use after Lee's cunning manipulation.

Qiao, armed with a spear and flanked by his ferocious hawk Emberkin circling high above, mounted the stage confidently, eyes fixed upon Rin in thinly veiled disdain. Radiating the arrogance of a Warrior who knew he held every advantage, Qiao's fluid movements created a near-perfect momentum, powered by a combination of low sweeps and high strikes. His hawk Emberkin insistently swished around Rin to expose openings and weaknesses in his stance, bolstering Qiao's aggressive assault.

Rin put up his best fight, his speed admirable, but was hampered by the cumbersome weight of his staff. His struggles bled through each frantic block and strained counterstrike. Qiao showed no mercy, pushing relentlessly until Rin finally faltered. Once Rin was flat on his back, it became clear it was the start of the end. With a decisive thrust of his spear into Rin's shoulder, Qiao claimed his victory. Jin, Chen, and Pang immediately rushed to Rin's aid.

The stabbing was both unnecessary and despicable. Though I categorically shunned the Consort's ties, I wasn't expecting to see such ruthlessness—clearly bred by Qiao's royal proximity. Even so, it wouldn't be prudent for the Consort to try to end me during a public spectacle like the final convergence battle.

As the winners stepped forward, a wave of cheers erupted from the audience. Wen and Qiao exchanged a piercing glance, grinning smugly, as if acknowledging only each other as real competition. They'd delivered exactly what their factions had expected of them—a swift demonstration of power and superiority.

Despite Jin's victory, our faction stayed awkwardly on the periphery. Yue and Ruo both looked dazed, as if still processing everything that had just happened. I gave Jin a small, rueful smile, feeling a kind of wordless understanding pass between us.

Amidst the overlapping congratulatory voices and slaps on the back from the main group, barely anyone paid attention to the losing factions who were silently departing. Rin had to be supported by Chen as they left with Pang to tend to their wounds. The Weavers whom they'd spent all moon with simply departed without bidding them farewell, now that their use to the factions had ended.

"Make allies, not friends," indeed. Often, as I observed others, I couldn't help but keep noticing all the other much better suited candidates for Lady Linhua's daughter. Yet through it all, my mind kept getting drawn back to Jin's conflicted gaze, as if he couldn't decide which was more brutal: victories built on others' pain, or the world's extolment of them.

There was a brief recess before the final convergence battle. School Masters dispersed to prepare for the event's transition to the Imperial Arena. Student Weavers and Generals split off to recover, both mentally and physically, from the morning's duels.

Yue and Ruo decided to return to their shared dormitory for a rest, both still looking hollowed out. I watched them walk off, leaving just Jin and me.

We awkwardly turned toward each other at the same time, both of us holding a small linen-wrapped parcel in our hands.

A beat passed before either of us spoke.

"… For you," we said to each other, almost in unison.

I blinked; so did he. Clearly, neither of us had expected something from the other.

As we silently exchanged the parcels and untied the knots holding them closed, I felt heat creeping up my cheeks. I was almost afraid to open mine, unsure what it would mean to see something tender in the middle of all this.

But when the contents came into view, I stopped short. Inside mine were two dried lychee cakes—slightly crumbled from the journey but intact. The scent hit me first. Light, sweet, and achingly familiar.

Stealing a glance at Jin, I caught him staring down at his cakes in disbelief. We'd brought each other the same thing. Except I'd prepared a dozen, having seen his appetite. There was also a small sun motif branded onto the middle of each of his cakes. I thought the pattern matched his name.

"You made these?" he asked, his eyes darting up with a mix of confusion and something else that made it hard for me to look away.

The memory of me kneading the dough in the Academy kitchens and watching the fire yesterday surfaced. I told myself the most sensible way to keep Jin from being poisoned right before our battle was to remove the possibility entirely. To personally make and deliver the cakes. It was the least that any faction leader could do for someone putting their life on the line for them. It was also why I'd been furtively monitoring his food since he'd agreed to become our General.

"I figured it'd take less effort than sending someone to track down the same market vendor," I said mildly, barely remembering the speech I'd been rehearsing in my mind.

A quiet huff escaped him. "Still ... that's very—" He halted mid-sentence, then shook his head and said, "Thank you."

We enjoyed our cakes in a companionable silence at the Martial Academy courtyard, just like the day we'd first met.

Not long after, the Imperial Arena was filled with a sea of restless spectators—royals, nobles, School Masters, and students across all year levels from both Academies. Thrilled chatter cascaded from the stands, tension building rapidly like a gathering storm.

It hardly required any effort to locate Father among the spectators, seated on his throne, between the Consort and Lady Linhua. Even from this distance, I could feel his penetrating stare, cold and heavy with judgment. Unlike the Consort's carefully neutral demeanor, Lady Linhua was fanning furiously at herself, betraying her nerves.

Oh, Mom, I thought, *do you want me to succeed, or for us to shine?*

Tearing my gaze away from my parents, I looked instead at what was grounding me, at Mo clinging protectively onto my front. If the rest of the world could see her, it would probably look as if I was carrying a red-feathered infant. She slowly blinked up at me, assuring me that it would all be alright. I sincerely hoped she was right.

Beside me, Jin had once again withdrawn into his own mind. Within the vast arena, our presence felt inconsequential compared to the energy from the other factions. Wu and Wen stood poised near the opposite edge, their fox and tiger Emberkin emanating barely contained ferocity, fur bristling. Across from them, Lee and Qiao waited with an equally pugnacious intensity, the wings of both their Emberkin fanning wide. It was a clash of land against sky, fur against feathers.

Ruo was already positioned high on our faction's designated watchtower, eyes sharp, poised to relay strategic commands through silent Signal glyphs so as to avoid giving away our battle strategies. She was looking calmer since returning from her break, entering the battle with us with strengthened resolve.

Wu and Lee nodded to their Weavers stationed on their respective watchtowers as Grandmaster Shao began to ascend the stage. A hush befell the space. Using an Augmentation glyph, the Grand-master's voice reverberated across the arena.

"The final convergence battle begins!"

Instantly, the air erupted with a blinding chaos.

Wen lunged forward at full speed before ducking low, sliding with one leg outstretched toward Qiao, her newly acquired shield held high in one hand, dagger flashing in arcs of silver in the other. Her tiger Emberkin roared, shaking the very ground, as she closed in on Qiao. In response, Qiao spun his spear deftly before him to block her advance, so it looked like a whirl of steel. His hawk Emberkin dove at full speed from above, his talons extended, beak aiming straight for the crown of Wen's head.

Dropping into a forward roll in the nick of time, Wen raised her shield to deflect a deadly strike from Qiao's spear that closely followed his Emberkin's advancing talons. At the same time, her tiger lunged forward, clashing mid-air with the hawk in a fury of sharp claws and curved beaks.

On the other side, Wu faced Lee with the same ruthless precision, glyphs flashing urgently between them as they manipulated the air and earth, drawing power through their Emberkin. Their fox and crane Emberkin engaged head-on in a battle of flair and deception. Wisps of smoke and sparks erupted from colliding air currents as the two Weavers countered each other's strikes and recalibrated in real time.

As the battle stretched on, the space became increasingly shrouded by clouds of dust, dirt, and smoke, causing a drop in visibility. All four of them started relying on their Weavers from the watchtowers to help them navigate.

It was clear to everyone present that the two factions were focusing solely on each other—neither had paid Jin and me any attention at all. They never saw us as real competition, just a mild nuisance to be finished off after they'd taken care of their biggest rival. Exactly as I'd expected.

Standing dumbly on the sidelines, Jin and I became fellow spectators of their deadly dance of martial arts and Smokecraft, blended seamlessly into a dizzying choreography of agility and lethal precision.

To the crowd, it might seem as though we'd frozen in hesitation, overwhelmed by the consummate adroitness of our rivals. But Jin's unwavering alertness wasn't lost on me. Carefully monitoring the unfolding battle, his sword angled defensively before us, he kept a fluid stance, ready to jump into either offense or defense as the situation demanded.

Kneeling down, I pressed a palm to the ground, my eyes closed as if in quiet reflection. In truth, I was sending my consciousness outward through Mo to check on the locations of the Smokemirrors one last time. A smile tugged at the corners of my mouth when I confirmed they were buried and waiting.

But I made the mistake of looking back toward the audience. My heart clenched at the sight of Father's face turning a vivid shade of red, bordering on purple, jaw clenched tight in a rare, overt display of fury. To him, we were standing disgracefully idle, an utter embarrassment before the gathered highborns.

For a beat, Father looked as if he might burst into flames right then and there from sheer outrage. Lady Linhua was now fanning him anxiously while whispering urgently in his ear. But there was no soothing his fury. I forced myself to return my focus to the battle.

Any moment now ...

Wu and Lee's factions were still fully absorbed in defeating each other, dismissing us. But their arrogance was playing precisely to our advantage. With a decisive final strike, Wen drove her dagger into Qiao's shoulder, before twisting it sharply and kicking him out of the arena, effectively disqualifying Lee's faction. Cheers erupted from the crowd.

That was my cue.

But as I took a step forward, the world suddenly tilted violently. My vision spun wildly, as though I were caught in a tornado spiral, making it impossible to find my bearings. Panic seized my chest when the realization sank in—I'd been poisoned, somehow.

I desperately wanted to discern what I'd missed, but my mind was a spiraling chaos, my thoughts fragmented and barely coherent. Swaying danger-ously on my feet, I would have collapsed had Jin not reached out and steadied me around the waist.

"Yan Xun?" His voice sounded distant and echoing, drowned by the roaring confusion in my mind.

Catching their breaths, Wu and Wen slowly turned their attention toward us.

Time was running out.

That was when Mo's vivid red feathers came into sight. Instinct took over, and with desperate focus, I began channeling the overwhelming mental confu-sion to Mo, just as I'd always done with my emotions.

I knew the poison itself couldn't be transferred—not that I would ever wish it upon her—but the men-tal turmoil could be redirected, at least temporarily. Mo could carry the chaos, not the injury. And she would bear it for me, if it kept me standing. I couldn't let myself be incapacitated. Not now.

To my relief, the world around me sharpened into focus once more, clarity finally returning.

"Now," I whispered to myself, swiftly tracing the glyph I'd been rehearsing countless times in the air as I stepped onto the dead center of the arena.

Then I slammed my palm as forcefully as I could onto the ground, catching the glyph I'd just drawn along the way.

Please work, I pleaded in my heart.

A ripple, barely visible, surged outward from my hand, shifting the topsoil to reveal each carefully hidden Smokemirror along the perimeter. The air distorted—fractured—before the arena ignited into a brilliant, blazing illusion. I clung to that mental image, breathing life into it. Roaring fire climbed higher and higher, encircling the entire arena and blocking the sky from view, forging a giant cage of flame that trapped us all within.

Sheer terror swept across Wu and Wen's faces, bleeding into the bonds with their Emberkin. The fox started backing away, his fur bristling, eyes wide. The tiger recoiled with a low growl, hissing in fear. I allowed myself a fleeting, grim satisfaction. After all, no real-world creature was immune to fire, be it Emberkin, beast, or human.

Beside me, Jin faltered for a heartbeat, but his training quickly reasserted itself. He glanced my way, looking for direction. When he saw I was remaining steady, he inhaled sharply and composed himself.

"Go. NOW!" I shouted at him.

Jin surged forward, swift and decisive. Wen managed to steel herself enough to mount a shaky defense, but in that moment, she wasn't just fighting Jin, but also her own fear closing in on her. And Jin was relentless—each strike measured, efficient, and purposeful. Before long, he found an opening and struck, driving Wen to her knees and knocking her out with the hilt of his sword.

Wu, paralyzed by panic and overwhelmed by the illusion, had collapsed onto the arena floor, scrambling backward the moment the illusion took hold. I was grateful for not having to deal with him while maintaining this monstrous illusion. Satisfied Wen had been incapacitated, Jin charged Wu. Pivoting sharply, he drove a devastating kick across Wu's midsection, sending him crashing off the stage and plunging through a wall of flames.

It was over.

The strain of sustaining the illusion was too much. So, I let go. In an instant, the inferno vanished as if it'd never existed. Though that was technically true, no one knew it. The crowd broke into a deafening, astonished applause, but my heartbeat was thundering louder in my chest.

Jin was shouting in a mix of disbelief and sheer exhilaration. Even Mo radiated something like triumph, despite having absorbed the mental chaos from the poison.

Of course, she was born of fire.

Feeling completely spent, I stopped channeling to Mo, and the full force of the poison slammed back into my body. I caught one last flicker of the blue sky above us before darkness consumed me whole.

燕尋

yān xún

Reigning Fire

Chapter Twelve

梦幻泡影

THE ILLUSION OF YOU

Jin

Jin didn't know what he'd expected after Wen drove her dagger into Qiao's shoulder, sending him flying from the stage. But it sure as hell wasn't this.

His heart pounded as a sweat-slicked Wu and Wen started turning toward them. Wu's eyes widened in wild certainty that they'd had Xun and Jin nailed, whereas Wen's narrowed in concentration. Both of their Emberkin were bristling with restless energy. Wen raised her blade again, and her tiger growled at them. Feeling the familiar pull in his gut, the readiness before a fight, Jin adjusted his grip on his sword and braced himself.

Then, beside him, Yan Xun began to sway. He caught it in the smallest movement: the flutter of her robes, the subtle shift in her posture before she righted herself. It wasn't dramatic, perhaps not even obvious to anyone who hadn't spent the past weeks memorizing her every move.

Jin stepped closer, reaching instinctively to steady her. The timing couldn't have been worse, but he was ready to hold the line for them both if he had to. He should've been focusing on the threat in front of them. On Wen. On Wu. But all he could think about was how much Xun was putting on the line just being here with him. Not just the outcome of the Trial, but also her name, her place at court, in an Empire that didn't know what to do with girls like her.

And him? He couldn't afford to lose either—not the Trial, not her. If he failed, there would be nowhere to go but down from here. He knew what happened to student Warriors who didn't make the cut. You didn't get a second shot; you would just disappear into service as a foot soldier on the frontlines.

But she'd said to him, *Trust me.* And he did.

To his surprise, she seemed to recover quickly from whatever that was. Then, moving far more swiftly than he'd expected, she stalked toward the middle of the arena, sketching a massive glyph in the air. Floating, shimmering, and alive, it preceded her like a reverse shadow as she moved.

What the hell is she doing? he thought as he started to run after her. That was when the world exploded into fire. It didn't *feel* like just an illusion, but it got him to question his reality. Flames erupted from the edges of the arena in a perfect ring, climbing high and curling inward, caging the four of them.

The battlefield was bathed in gold-and-orange light, dancing flames threatening to lick their skin. It should've been unbearably hot. Jin's sword hand should've burned. His lungs should've seized. But none of that was happening. He didn't feel a damn thing—not heat, nor pain. Only the prickling awareness that the world had been turned upside down, yet he was somehow untouched. It was like being trapped in a bizarre dream.

His first thought was that he'd gone into shock, that something had blown up and he was just too injured to register it. Then he looked over at Wu and Wen—and their Emberkin. The tiger shrieked and stumbled backward, tail low, all her former bravado dissipating into smoke. The fox bared his teeth and scrabbled frantically at the floor like he was trying to dig his way out of there. Wu had dropped to his knees. Wen's blade trembled.

His gaze snapped back to Yan Xun. She wasn't panicking. Her breathing was shallow, her posture was off, but her face hadn't changed. She still had that uncanny stolidity she always carried when the stakes were highest. Her words from the night before drifted into his mind:

Stay calm. If I'm not panicking, don't panic.

So, Jin didn't panic.

"NOW!" her voice rang in his ears.

Gritting his teeth, Jin tightened his grip around his sword's hilt and launched forward. The rest unfolded in a blur. Training took over; muscle memory did the rest. Wen tried to raise her shield, but her rhythm was off. He disarmed her in two clean strikes and knocked her out. Wu was still frozen, too far gone to react. He could've knock him out too, but chose to send him flying out of the arena with a kick.

There was a deafening silence before the flames vanished as though they'd never been real. He turned back just in time to see Yan Xun's eyes rolling back, her legs giving out. Jin caught her before she hit the ground, but this time, she stayed completely motionless, not even a flutter of her eyelids.

The crowd was roaring, but all he could hear was his own heartbeat, booming like war drums. Then the Imperial Guards were there, lifting her onto a stretcher. Jin tried to follow, but they shut him out. Wen and Wu's schoolmates scrambled over to pull them to their feet and get away from all the chaos. Most likely, also trying to rescue them before their disgruntled parents could reach them, if anything.

Jin looked around for Ruo and Yue in a frenzy—anyone who might have a clue about what the hell was going on. But Yue was nowhere to be found, and Master Dan told him Ruo was being treated for heatstroke and would soon recover.

Heatstroke? Sure, it was the tail end of the warm season, but Ruo had been up in the shade of the watchtower. It didn't make sense.

"All contenders of the Trial are given two days off. Then we'll formally announce the winning faction. Catch some rest," Master Dan said before waving him off.

With no answers and nowhere else to go, his chest still tight with a sense of helplessness, Jin returned to the Martial Academy. The image of Xun collapsing haunted him, looping through his mind like a broken Signal glyph. If something had gone wrong—if he'd missed a sign, he needed to know. He needed to understand.

Before Jin even crossed the threshold of the Martial Academy gates, he was being welcomed back like a newly crowned feudal lord. Everyone wanted a word, a shoulder slam, a retelling. But Jin wasn't in the mood. Not when Xun was somewhere behind closed doors and Yue had vanished.

So, he did what he always did—he escaped. Made a quick trip to the bathhouse, where he was disheartened to find the Tether glyph on his back had already vanished. Had a meal he barely tasted. Then he climbed back onto the only place that'd felt like peace these past weeks: on the roof of her quarters.

The rules of the Martial Academy were strict when it came to their training—harsh, even—but after hours, they turned a blind eye to minor rule-breaking. He'd been sleeping up here ever since the bath chamber incident. It was uncomfortable, but it felt like a territory he'd claimed. Yet tonight, it just wasn't enough. Because she wasn't there, beneath the roof tiles. That quiet sense of her presence was missing. Staring up at the night sky, he thought, *That's right, it's emptiness stacked on emptiness.*

Eventually, he made a plan. Not a great one, but a plan regardless. First thing tomorrow, he would find Ruo and Yue again, or at least try to. Then he would figure out how to request permission to visit the inner palace. Because wherever she'd gone, that was where he would be heading next.

The next morning, Jin was up before the sun. He hadn't meant to stay awake all night, but rest had never really come—not when his thoughts kept spiraling back to her collapsing form, to the inferno that felt too surreal, to the way her body had gone limp in his arms. The helplessness sat like a boulder in his chest, growing heavier by the hour.

So, he made his way down early, washed up, and went looking. No one had seen Yue since the convergence battle, but at least Ruo hadn't vanished. He found her sitting alone behind the stables, knees drawn up, playing with a stalk of reed in her mouth. Her shoulders stiffened when she saw him.

Spitting out the reed, she muttered, "I'm fine."

"Didn't ask."

"Suit yourself."

Jin settled next to her. After a long silence, he glanced sideways and asked, "So … heatstroke?"

Ruo let out a wry laugh. "Yeah, sure. That's what it was." Then she asked, "Is Yan Xun OK?"

"She's still unconscious. Or at least she was, last I saw her. The guards wouldn't let me through."

Ruo nodded slowly before reaching into her robe to pull out a folded slip of parchment.

"I'm not supposed to be showing you this," she said, handing it to him. "But I figured you've earned it."

Jin frowned as he studied the parchment, unsure what to make of it. It was full of glyph lines layered in ways he couldn't begin to decipher.

"She told you about the illusions?" Ruo asked.

"I thought that's what it was! Well, she didn't, really. Only that there was going to be something massive. And not to panic if she wasn't panicking."

"Even I'm not entirely sure what they were. Some sort of mirror she's found for casting illusions. But they didn't work on their own," Ruo explained. "At least, not well enough. She came to me and asked if there was a way to make an illusion that's purely visual feel convincing enough. Even if just for less than half a stick of incense-burning time." She pointed at the symbols. "So, I drew these glyphs right before the duels. On Wu, Wen, Qiao, and Lee."

"You what? How?!" he asked, incredulous.

A somewhat cheeky smile slowly spread across Ruo's face. "I made it look like I was losing it. That row we had the night before? It was staged. Yan Xun's idea, so that we were already planting the seed in the others' minds that I was falling apart under pressure. Then, that morning, I was begging them to tell me what weapons they'd drawn. Made a scene so no one would think twice about me running around like a headless chicken."

Until then, Jin hadn't considered Ruo working with Xun on another angle.

"I went to everyone so it wouldn't look suspicious," Ruo continued, "but those were the only four people I'd marked when I got close enough to them. Casting silent glyphs through their robes to lower their mental resistance and increase sensory suggestibility."

Jin's jaw dropped. "You drugged them with glyphs?"

"Kind of. More like … made them more likely to believe what they saw. So … that meant when it was all happening, Lee, watching from the outside, would've thought her future betrothed was actually getting roasted in a pit." She flashed an evil smirk.

Jin figured there was some bad blood there. Probably enough to fuel an entire banquet's gossip. Then it hit him—

"You're telling me you've known all along that we hadn't drawn a blank?" he asked, scandalized.

Grinning apologetically, Ruo confessed, "Well, Yan Xun has never explicitly said it, but I figured if she was planning ahead for the convergence battle, she must've been confident you would win your duel. But your natural reactions would help with our strategy. Hope you didn't lose too much sleep over it."

Leaning back, Jin could still scarcely believe what he was hearing. "So ... none of that was real."

"That's the whole point of an illusion, asshead," Ruo teased, rolling her eyes. "The mirrors created a powerful visual illusion. Their minds filled in what they expected to feel. With a little nudge from me, of course. And while Emberkin have their own consciousness, they don't have the physical mechanisms that allow for human sensory experiences. They simply respond to the sensory world based on their Weavers' perceptions through their bonds."

Jin stared at the glyph slip, then back at her again, perplexed by what she'd pulled off. "You've done this before?"

"Never at this scale. But when you've been overlooked your whole life, you get good at thinking sideways." Ruo gave him a crooked grin. "I knew that I wouldn't be of use to either of you up in the watchtower, not when you actually needed it, anyway. It's not as if anyone could see through that fire cave. But I still had to go up there so no one would grow suspicious, risking exposure to my real mission."

Jin thought about Wu's terror and Wen's hesitation. About the way their Emberkin were backing away, as if the illusion had teeth.

"The mirrors created the visuals of that massive fire on their own?" he asked.

Ruo shook her head. "Nah, Yan Xun first had to activate them by uncovering them. She's somehow managed to get them buried around the arena without drawing attention. Then she had to keep that mental image alive, for as long as it went on."

"Is that what caused her to go unconscious after?"

Ruo considered briefly. "I've been thinking about that, too. I know that she'd never pulled something like that off at this scale, either. I went into a small burnout afterward, but nothing a bit of tonic, rest, and food couldn't fix. Maybe what she had to do drained her more than mine did?"

Jin tilted his head as he deliberated it. "No, something was off even before she started doing anything. I had to steady her briefly. Then it passed, like it'd

never happened. She was fine … until she wasn't."
He was about tell Ruo about the Tether glyph Xun
drew on his back but held his tongue in the end.

The memory felt … personal. He couldn't help
but think about her touch on his back, grounding
and comforting. When his eyes fluttered shut at the
remembrance, he felt a tingle run up his spine.
Clamping down a shudder, he told himself it wasn't
as if there was anything secretive about the
memory—*no*—but it wasn't crucial for Ruo to know
about it, anyway.

Ruo shrugged and inhaled sharply, nudging him
out of his reverie. "Well, you know she never tells
any one person everything. Have you spoken to Yue?"

Now, she had his full attention. Looking up at her
in surprise, Jin asked, "Wait, you haven't seen her,
either? I've been trying to look for you both once
I managed to wrestle through the crowd of students.
Master Dan told me you were with the healers, but
no one knew where Yue was."

"That's strange. I hope she's alright."

"We should divide and conquer," he muttered.
"You look for Yue. I need to find Xun."

But he'd barely left the Weavers' Academy com-
pound when an attendant from the inner palace
stepped in front of him and gave a curtsy. "Greetings,
student Warrior. I've been ordered by Princess Yan
Xun to guide you to her inner palace residence."

Xun's orders. *Thank fucking goodness.*

The halls leading to Xun's annex were paved in the soft gleam of white stone tiles, sunlight catching in the polished surfaces like water made solid. Latticed windows cast patterned shadows across the floor.

Every corner was sumptuously decorated, from tall blue-and-white porcelain vases, to large, embroidered silk tapestries that shimmered with gold thread. The scent of sandalwood lingered in the air, the kind that didn't just come from incense, but from wealth passed down across generations.

Jin tried not to gawk; it was hard not to feel the stark contrast press into his skin. At the Academy, Xun's quarters had been spacious, yes, but almost bare. Functional. It hadn't matched any of this.

The attendant led him to wait in a smaller chamber that was clearly designed for receiving guests. The carved wooden chairs were cushioned with patterned brocade. A low table was set with a steaming tea service, untouched.

To one side, an elaborate folding screen with mountain scenes pieced together using inlaid mother-of-pearl glowed under the daylight filtering through reinforced paper windows. Even the dust motes here floated with grace. His gaze lingered on a gold phoenix motif on one of the wooden beams. The whole room looked as though it belonged in a painting. It was quiet, save for the muffled trickle of water from a fountain out in her courtyard.

And suddenly, the memories came, uninvited: Jin's childhood bed pushed into the corner of a single-room house, with him squeezed in between four other siblings. The thin blanket he'd had to share with one of his brothers in winter. The sweltering heat of being sardined together in summer. The endless scrape of noise and mess in the shared dorm he was living in at the Martial Academy—ten students to a room, all snoring, sweating, laughing.

This … wasn't that. He swallowed hard, not with envy, but with something else he didn't have a name for yet. She was born into a life most others couldn't even have dreamed of. Not in their wildest of dreams.

Jin hadn't seen his family in years—travel was expensive, and poor students didn't go home unless someone had died, or if the Academy made them. The world mocked that poverty was bad karma accumulated from one's past life. His feelings of wonder were tinged with sorrow at that thought. He recalled his exchanges with his squadmates when he'd returned to the Academy after the battle.

"Look who's back."

"Must be nice. Win a single duel, and now he's palace bound."

"Break a leg in your next battle, they'll probably give you a noble title and a manor."

The words didn't necessarily carry malice. They were accompanied by a grin, half-friendly, half-sharp. Jin remembered laughing it off, but something had twisted in his chest. It wasn't hard to notice the shift in the way people were looking at him, as if his worth had doubled overnight. Not entirely because of skill, but because the Princess had taken notice.

He didn't belong here, not really. But she'd opened this world to him, anyway. And that meant more than she could ever know. Drawing a deep breath, he thought, *Well, if poverty is bad karma, Xun must have accumulated the best of karma through all of her past lives.*

Good. She deserves every bit of it.

Footsteps approached, soft as snowfall on stone. He stood just as Xun entered the room, wearing robes of ivory and sage. Her long, flowing sleeves hung under her arms as she lightly held her hands together before her waist. It wasn't the grandeur of formal court attire, but it was far from plain, either. The silk shimmered in the light, an unspoken reminder of who she was.

Jin thought she still looked a little pale, feeling a strange compulsion to cup her cheek in his hand.

Reigning Fire

The sunlight caught in her silken hair, casting her in a glow that made him forget, for a moment, that she was still supposed to be convalescing.

It took him some time to notice the palace attendants around them, still bowed, were openly staring up at him, staring at Xun. His first thought was, *Oh no, everyone caught me gaping at her.*

Eventually, it clicked. And then it was: *Oh wait, am I supposed to bow to the Princess?*

They were no longer in the Academy, after all.

But Xun lifted a hand, looking straight ahead. Immediately, the attendants in the room and out in the corridor withdrew wordlessly, leaving them alone. It was a movement so fluid, so habitual, Jin wondered if she'd even registered doing it.

Jin blinked several times in succession when he realized he should be saying something. Something thoughtful. Or caring. Anything.

"Y-you're feeling better?" he stammered, followed by a dry swallow. He wanted to kick himself.

She nodded and took a seat, gesturing for him to do the same.

"I was poisoned," she said equably, as if she was just explaining the material of her robes to Jin.

Jin's heart skipped. "What?!" he exclaimed.

"The palace attendants review the meal logs daily. Every bite that a royal takes must be recorded, but I hadn't eaten anything that day. Not officially."

His stomach dropped. The image of her eating the dried lychee cakes he'd given her flashed across his mind like a dagger.

"Xun, I swear I would never—"

"I know," she said, cutting him off. "If I was incapacitated mid-battle, you would be in trouble, too. I know you're not an idiot."

But something about that answer had rubbed him the wrong way. So, if it would only have affected her, then what? She could imagine Jin poisoning her? Was that all he was in her eyes—*not an idiot*? Still, he bit down on a retort as the realization hit him.

"I got the cakes from Yue," he said, perplexed. "She handed them to me right after the duels. Said it'd be a nice gesture for me to give them to you before entering the battle together."

Xun's expression remained phlegmatic. "I've been suspecting Yue for some time now. The night before the Trial, she left me some calming tea leaves … I didn't use them. And weeks ago, before she shared with us about using spill-leaves on the other factions, I thought I'd caught a whiff of fragrance that didn't belong in my incense coils. I threw the entire batch out, to be safe. I've been keeping an eye on her since, though I'd hoped I was wrong."

Jin frowned. "Why not poison me, too?"

"Because I've been watching your food since you joined us." Her gaze flicked up in surprise, as if the answer had slipped out before she'd thought it through.

"You—*what?*" He gaped.

"Just in case," she replied hastily.

In that moment, Jin was torn between joy at her attentiveness and exasperation at his own naivety. But somehow, knowing she'd been looking out for him—silently, methodically—made his heart swell. He'd never had anyone caring for him in that way. His parents were wonderful, but with five mouths to feed, Jin was always used to fending for himself.

"So, how did you … how the hell did you manage to do all that Smokecraft if you were poisoned?"

She looked down at her hands. "I found out just in time. Took an antidote. It wasn't meant to cause any lasting harm, anyway, only temporary confusion. I was fine until the battle was over. Casting the illusion just took more out of me than I'd expected."

Jin said nothing, but something told him this either wasn't the truth or wasn't the whole truth.

He wanted to stay a bit mad at her. For thinking that the only reason he wouldn't betray her was for self-preservation. For not believing that she could trust him with the plain truth.

He tried staying mad and failed. All he could think of was how he'd been guarding her sleep, while she'd been guarding his food. Like they'd been protecting parts of each other that no one else ever thought to.

The next day, Jin was once again intercepted by a palace attendant, except this time, it was to summon him to the Hall of Honor. The leaders and Generals of the final contending factions in the convergence battle had been requested to present themselves for a final review and deliberation. When Jin arrived, the tension in the room snapped taut.

Wu and Wen stood together on one side, their arms crossed, postures stiff. But Jin's gaze was immediately drawn to someone he hadn't expected to see there. Having scoured through the Academies for Yue the past two days, this was the last place he thought he would find her. To make things even more interesting, she was standing with Wu's faction. Jin felt a ball of fury scorching through him at the thought of what she'd done to Xun. *Using him* to, no less. But he swallowed his anger—this wasn't the time and place to sort this out.

On the other side of the room, Xun had already arrived and was standing alone. And at the head of the room, seated beside Master Dan was Prince Yan Yun himself. His intimidating Emberkin coiled around his left trouser leg, under his robes, so that only parts of his long body were visible at an angle.

Seeing the Prince Regent up close for the first time, Jin marveled at the resemblance between Xun and her father, though he didn't seem too pleased with her right now.

With a quick bow, Jin stepped forward to stand beside Xun. Her face had betrayed nothing, but Jin noticed a line of tension in her shoulders. It seemed like a discussion had already begun before Jin had got there.

Without any acknowledgment of Jin's arrival, Prince Yan Yun's eyes continued boring into Xun's, his voice cutting through the silence like a blade.

"You didn't have your faction sign any Sealbinding agreements?"

"No, I didn't," Xun answered matter-of-factly, her back straight.

The Prince's eyes narrowed just a fraction, a dangerous glint flashing past them.

"Why?" he asked curtly.

Even Jin picked up on what a loaded question that was. He found himself adjusting his posture, standing straighter, though he wasn't the one being asked.

But Xun only offered another candid reply.

"I've never seen a point in forcing allegiance. They'd stay if they wanted to."

The serpent Emberkin abruptly tightened his coil around the Prince's leg, just as a scoff came from Wu's direction. Meanwhile, Yue kept her gaze firmly fixed on the floor.

The Prince's tone sent the room plunging into sub-zero temperatures on a summer's day.

"Idealism is a dangerous luxury, especially for someone in your position. I'd expected you to know better than that."

Master Dan cleared his throat and unrolled a scroll. "Yue has presented an active Sealbinding agreement with Wu's faction, signed almost three weeks before the day of the Trial. Which effectively leaves Princess Yan Xun's faction with only two student Weavers, below the Trial's requirements."

At those words, Wen's lips curled into a smile, and Wu tilted his head up, smugly.

"However," Master Dan continued, "in light of extraordinary sabotage, as well as documentation of combat performances and witness accounts—including reports submitted by Grandmaster Shao—the High Council has ruled that the minimum composition requirement will be waived in this instance. The victory stands."

The smile was wiped clean off Wen's face.

Wu stepped forward, indignant. "What about the artifacts she used during the battle?" he demanded. "Smokeveil relics aren't permitted in the Trial. No one else but a royal has access to palace artifacts."

Master Dan raised a brow, warningly.

"Your concern was duly noted. Upon review, it's been found that the items employed during the convergence battle are not classified as relics or Vault-guarded artifacts. Smokemirrors were dismissed as failed constructs from a long-defunct experiment—wrongly so, as we now know. The illusion cast was no doubt remarkable, but the tools themselves are not of restricted classification. Thus, no rule has been broken."

Wu looked ready to argue further, but Prince Yan Yun's expression had turned distinctly unimpressed. The silent pressure of his presence made Wu reconsider. He kept his mouth shut, looking as if he'd been publicly kicked in the guts a second time.

"You may go," Master Dan said, dismissing Wu, Wen, and Yue with a wave of hand in their direction.

Yue's head dipped lower, and she left without a word. Wen simply bowed and left in false dignity. Wu, on the other hand, threw Jin a dirty look before turning around sharply with huff and an angry fling of his robe. Jin got the unspoken message: this wasn't over, and Wu would eventually make him pay for that unceremonious ejection.

Oh well, that would be a future-Jin problem. Right now, almost nothing could compete with how he was feeling.

Until Master Dan started speaking again. "This year, as a token of the Empire's recognition for young talent and strategy, the winning faction will be permitted to select not one but *three* relics from the Vault. One per surviving faction member."

Xun's eyes flared with surprise before her features were quickly schooled into neutrality again.

Just as she and Jin were about to bow in gratitude for the Empire's generosity, Master Dan added offhandedly, "As for Princess Yan Xun's request for private annexes for her remaining faction members during the remainder of their studies—it has been approved. Preparations are already underway."

Jin almost barked a laugh and had to clamp a hand over his mouth, trying not to grin like an idiot. To him, this was much more exhilarating than being allowed to pick a Vault souvenir. Untrained in Smokecraft and barred from the Smokeveil, he doubted there was anything of use for him in there.

Prince Yan Yun remained in a venomous silence as they displayed their reverence and took their leave. Through it all, he simply sat there, still as a blade, eyes fixed on his daughter, as if calling onto the heavens for patience he didn't have.

Chapter Thirteen

万丈深渊

GRAVEYARD OF TRUTHS

The Imperial Healers cleared me with a clean bill of health upon my return from the Hall of Honor, where Master Dan had affirmed the legitimacy of our victory. I hadn't allowed myself to hope for triumph, not when my all-consuming fear of the corollaries of losing loomed. But as victory became a real possibility … hope bloomed fast, closely followed by a zealous desire. Not for the title itself, but for the reward that awaited: a relic of choice. Something that could finally offer the breakthrough in my research that I so desperately needed.

Even for bonded Weavers, Smokecraft wasn't without its limits. It allowed us to manipulate the world around us, but only within the bounds of the extant. It was like managing the sluice gates—we could open them wide or narrow to channel the water faster or slower, even twist and redirect the flow, but not conjure a stream from a dry bed. The over-arching laws of the realm still held firm.

But Smokeveil relics were different.

Though each relic only served a singular purpose, they defied the natural limits of Smokecraft in that specific manner. Relics didn't just amplify a Weaver's abilities. They let us *transcend*, imbued with powers that allowed for pushing past the edges of what would otherwise have been impossible. And in a world bound by stringent rules, even the smallest transcendence in reality was priceless.

I'd spent last night tossing and turning, wondering what I could possibly offer Jin and Ruo in exchange for total liberty in my choice of relic. But nothing had even come close. After all, how could anyone agree to walk away from *that?*

Yet to my astonishment, Father had granted all three of us to select a relic from the Vault. The order had almost certainly come from him. Barring the ailing Emperor, he was the sole figure across the Empire with the authority to grant something of this caliber.

I mulled over what could have spurred such a decision. Sure, Father always recognized talent where it was due. He was the first to accede to the acceptance of select sponsored students into the Weavers' Academy. Until then, Smokecraft education was the prerogative of nobles and royals—the only ones who could access Smokeveil's powers. But three Smokeveil relics were hardly comparable with a few sponsored entries to the Academy.

Then again, Father didn't just tolerate secrecy and cunning—he glorified them when flawlessly executed. No notable ruler would ever come to be without myriads of secrets and ghosts, he would contend. *Well, good to know I would meet at least one of his standards for a fitting successor*, I thought bitterly.

So ... maybe this was his way of rewarding that?

Or maybe I was just projecting again, hoping for meaning where there was none. Who really knew what he was thinking?

Now, as I was getting ready to return to the Weavers' Academy, Mo nosed at my wrist, clearly more than ready to leave. She still abhorred the inner palace— too many eyes, too many shadows. I scratched beneath her beak, and she leaned in like she always did.

Upon waking, the sight of Mo instantly released me from my maelstrom of guilt. It was a calculated risk. But since mythic Emberkin were still an enigma, there was no guaranteeing my actions would do her no harm. Mercifully, the poison's grip on her had broken once I'd ceased channeling. I couldn't fathom losing my little familiar, though she wasn't so little anymore. Over the last two years, she'd been growing intermittently in size.

On our way back to the Academy, I couldn't help but pause before the monumental bronze doors of the Lifeng Pagoda. The magnificent structure was the source of inspiration for my fire illusion. Or rather, the enchanted glass prison on its top floor for outlawed Emberkin was.

That night, sitting on Grand Pavilion's roof with Xiao, overlooking the palace grounds, an idea had sparked in my mind. For a while, I'd been fixated on formulating a plan to procure some Lifeng glass. But that had proven an unattainable goal. Not only was Lifeng glass one of the most intractable materials in the Empire, I would also need to bypass the twenty-four layers—or however many there were meant to be—of palace security guarding it.

Eventually, it'd dawned on me that I'd been boxing myself in—"imprisoned" by the idea of Lifeng glass. My secret gambit in the convergence battle required no literal prison for the opponents' Emberkin. Even if I could incapacitate them that way, there was still the matter of defeating their bonded humans. Instead, my best hope was to entrench the belief that they'd all become trapped in their grimmest terrors.

Who would've thought … the girl who'd been haunted by her own ghosts would become someone else's worst nightmare, for once? Smiling wryly to myself, I walked on. But before returning to my quarters, there was someone I needed to see.

When Yue arrived at the Academy courtyard, her hood half-drawn, I was already there, waiting. Clutching my note in one hand, her gait was a contradiction: steady, focused, yet with a forced, rhythmic tension that exposed her inner conflict.

"Yan Xun," she called, a tinge of dread coloring her voice.

I nodded without moving closer. "Yue."

A long silence stretched between us, one neither of us seemed inclined to fill. I knew perfidy was a possible, natural consequence of my reluctance to compel loyalty—a fact that Father was all too happy to remind me of. But I would be lying if I claimed to be impervious to betrayal when it finally happened.

Yue broke the stillness first. "It was only meant to dull your reflexes. Weaken your focus," she blurted. "Not … kill you."

My voice sounded flat when I spoke. "You couldn't have guaranteed that."

"You were right," she admitted. "Anything could've happened once you were out of action mid-battle. I'd just convinced myself that Wu would never take it that far. That was on me."

"I just want to know why."

Yue and I had never beaten around the bush with each other. Perhaps I should've directly asked her about it when my doubts started emerging. But perhaps I'd wanted to trust her. That was on me.

Looking down at her feet, Yue said, "Wu promised my family something we've never had. An official herb license and a storefront in the Capital meant security for us. A future."

When I didn't respond, she continued in a softer voice, "His clan dominates the licenses for medicinal trade across the Empire. It'd change our family's destiny forever. I thought—" She faltered, before continuing, "It was a price I had to pay. We don't have a choice when it comes to family."

I wished I had a comeback to that final sentiment.

Yue's mouth tightened. "I still owe you one, I know. From back then."

"You don't owe me anything," I said to her, and I meant it. "You never did."

She bit her lip. "Still ... I remember."

I'd gotten what I wanted; there was nothing left to be said. So, I turned and left. While I might be learning to emulate Father on the outside, deep within me, something had loosened. An insidious kind of hurt, like a clean cut that didn't bleed right away.

All things considered, I was thankful to have done a neat job with Jin's tether that night, even if I was worried about ... not fully concentrating. If I'd made even a slight mess of it, the symptoms of poisoning could have bled into our tethered bond and incapacitated him, too.

The Vault of Smokeveil Relics lay hidden beneath the palace grounds—a labyrinthine network of sealed chambers etched into mountain stone, forbidden to all but the Imperial Custodian of Relics and the select few who were granted clearances. For just today, that included us.

Our footsteps echoed along the narrow corridor as we walked in abreast. I kept barely ahead, my eyes relentlessly tracking each glyph-marked turn. Regardless, Ruo's searching eyes weren't lost on me. She appeared just as ardent as I was in making our selections today.

Trailing along like an awestruck, lost puppy who'd stumbled into a celestial garden, Jin had no idea what he was looking at, or what he should be looking for.

"Anything I should avoid?" he muttered.

I didn't slow my pace. "Since you're not a Weaver, you need something that doesn't require channeling Smokeveil powers or glyphcasting."

"Right, so … like a stick to hit people with?"

I glanced over at him, my jaw tight as I fought the traitorous upward curve of my lips. "That's not off the table. But some artifacts are suitable for non-Weavers—preset tools with specific functions that don't require further Smokecraft activation to work. You'll want one of those."

"And you already know what you're looking for?" Jin asked.

"I have … a direction. Of sorts."

Ruo raised an eyebrow at me. "A direction, huh?"

Before I could render more prevarication, I recognized where we were and picked up my pace, only stopping when I reached a pair of thick bronze doors. Jin and Ruo quickly caught up with me. Sensing the glyphs that Master Dan had drawn onto our arms just prior, the doors' Locking glyphs flared. They unbolted on their own, groaning as they swung forward to reveal the monumental Vault that stretched beyond.

Countless artifacts were suspended midair in rows from floor to ceiling, floating on Smokecrafted shelves of mist. The room thrummed with power emanating from objects that might seem unassuming to the untrained eye—some as old as the Empire itself, others enigmatic with long-forgotten purpose.

Jin had barely registered anything before something caught his eye. Displayed on a black nephrite stand near the entrance was a piece of long, inky fabric that rippled like water—a cloak darker than night but lighter than smoke. He drifted toward it, as if the relic was calling to him.

"Try it," I nudged him on.

When his hand brushed the surface of the cloak, it shimmered for the briefest moment, its weight settling slowly around his shoulders. A grin was spreading across Jin's face, until he looked down, where his body was supposed to be under the cloak.

"I'm—"

"Invisible," I confirmed. "Not just to the eye. This one's laced with Suppressing glyphs. It blocks most forms of detection, including ones using Smokecraft. From a series of espionage artifacts fashioned during the old Ember Wars."

"I want this one," Jin declared, beaming.

"Sneaky bastard." Ruo gave a faux clap. "Alright, I'm off. I need to concentrate on my own treasure hunt without the distraction."

She playfully gave Jin a head-to-toe glance before vanishing between the mist-made shelves.

They were both in high spirits today, but I maintained a lightning-sharp focus on my mission. As Jin continued admiring his new cloak, I moved toward the far shelves, my fingers brushing against the laconic descriptions etched in dimly glowing ink.

Jin trotted after me, still bouncing on the balls of his feet in excitement. Not unlike a five-year-old who'd chanced upon a jar of candy. Or dried lychee cakes.

"What about you?" he asked.

I held my breath when my gaze landed on a jade pendant in the shape of a crescent moon, its tips on both ends encased in white gold. With layers of glyphs etched onto it, the white and green of the jade looked as if they were swirling within, not unlike the movements of smoke.

"I'm looking for something that allows for instant translocation. For moving through wards undetected," I said, still transfixed by the pendant. "Not sneak past but *fully bypass*."

"Like teleportation?"

That was close enough. But more than just distance, I needed precision. Racking my brains through every detail I'd read about the relic I'd been coveting, I wondered if the God of Fortune could really have noticed me today.

"This might be it," I whispered without further explanation, looping the chain on the pendant over my neck.

Might as well give it a test.

Grabbing onto Jin's arm, I weaved my fingers through the air to sketch the glyph I'd spent all night practicing, concentrating hard. My worries about whether I'd done it right never got to take shape be-cause instantly, it felt as if I'd been turned into smoke and siphoned into the abyss. Yet, before my mind could register the discomfort, we found ourselves back where Jin had discovered his cloak.

Stumbling as we rematerialized, Jin's wide-eyed gaze darted back and forth between where we'd vanished from and where we were now standing.

"OK …" he said, regaining his composure. "That was like … being yanked through smoke by the ribs."

Then, spinning toward me, he asked, "Is that what it feels like, being a Weaver?"

"I'd never tried doing this before," I said. "But this relic is *exactly* what I need." To slip through the cracks, find what I need …

Jin looked at me, expectant, but I hesitated.

I'd never divulged any of this to anyone; it was always meant to be a solo mission. Too much was at stake. Yet, how could I pass on this opportunity?

"There's something I have to look into. Quietly," I explained, perhaps against my better judgment. "No one can know, not even Ruo. Not yet."

He didn't interrupt, so I continued, barely keeping the frenzy out of my voice. "This relic gets me into places. Yours keeps you hidden. Used together, it'll almost be an unparalleled power."

Finally meeting his gaze, I forced the question out of my mouth before I could change my mind. "Would you want in?"

He tilted his head, his gaze settling on the pendant. "So, that's how we're going to do this? Just slip in and out before anyone even notices we're there?"

"If everything goes right," I said.

A pause ensued. Perhaps he was less impulsive than I'd thought. After all, even I had no idea what I could be getting us into.

Then his lips curled slowly into a lopsided grin. "I hate how thrilled I am. This is probably a terrible idea." He jabbed an elbow friskily into my side. "You're bad news, Xun."

This time, I was no longer able to suppress the smile blooming across my face.

I was still beaming when we regrouped with Ruo later on. Lips pursed, she raised both brows but held back from making any remarks, offering me an un-spoken agreement: *I won't ask if you don't.*

We'd all earned our relics. But more than that, we'd earned an expedient—a way in. And somewhere, deep inside the belly of the palace, were more secrets. Ones that we were going to need every trick up our sleeve, every ounce of luck, and every shred of trust between us to uncover.

It was already past curfew when I activated the relic pendant in my quarters. I'd been experimenting discreetly for days to ensure it wouldn't malfunction when I needed to travel longer distances.

I replayed the memory from earlier in the day when Jin and I had made a pact with each other, hoping I'd covered all angles. If such a thing was even possible.

"No questions asked," I said.

Jin raised a brow. "None?"

"Not unless it's life and death. And even then, ask fast."

He looked like he wanted to argue. But in the end, he just leaned back with a sigh, perhaps wondering what he was getting himself into.

"Alright. What are we looking for, then?"

"Historical records of unregistered Emberkin," I said, my tone neutral. "Mythic ones. Any anomalies that have never made it into the official royal archives."

Jin's eyes raked my face. "You've seen one before," he said.

An observation, not a question.

I sighed inconspicuously. He wasn't an idiot—of course he wasn't. I couldn't pinpoint when it'd begun, but more and more, I'd been struggling to meet his gaze. Not without feeling thoroughly convinced that he'd seen right through me. Through all the layers I'd been carefully wrapping myself in over the years.

Through all the masks and secrets. It was petrifying in an inexplicable way.

I'd only exhaled when Jin had stopped pressing on and simply said, "Two readers are faster than one."

However, it had taken some convincing before he'd agreed to my second request. In the end, he'd begrudgingly given me his word that if we were ever separated, he would focus on leaving posthaste without searching for me and wait at our rendezvous.

Our meeting place sat on the western fringe of the inner palace grounds—a secluded, abandoned cottage with an algae-ridden pond, said to once house a royal concubine who'd died under suspicious circumstances. No one dared go near it for generations now; not even Emberkin would have anything to do with the place. Some said her unquiet spirit still lingered.

Perfect.

The roof tiles were crumbling at the edges, and a single unlit lantern oscillated from a rusted chain above the warped doorway. I didn't knock. She oughtn't care for feigned civilities, I wouldn't think.

Inside, dust was clinging onto moth-eaten tapestries and curling brocade scrolls. Rotting dressing screens leaned against the wall precariously, their wooden frames bowing under time and neglect. According to palace lore, anyone who initiated entry into this place would be cursed. But I was fairly certain I'd already been cursed, long before I could step foot in here.

Once, a Weaver was said to re-emerge from here days after entering, raving and incoherent. They'd screamed at mirrors and shadows alike, unable to distinguish phantoms from reality. And their Emberkin wouldn't stop flickering uncontrollably, as if they'd both been trapped in a perpetual hell no one else could see. They'd apparently vanished into thin air soon after. No one ever saw them since.

Another story claimed that a junior archivist sent to map out the cottage's interior had later been found cowering in a dried-out fountain basin, scribbling pages upon pages of someone else's memories. There were no eyewitness accounts of resulting fatalities, but there were worse things in life than death.

So, just to be safe, I announced to the empty space around me, enunciating each word clearly, "I'm Princess Xun of House Yan, heir to the Empire. I'm the one who's initiated entry into your space. He's only ever going to be here under my orders."

It was strange. I should be feeling frightened, or at least some unease. Especially since I was most likely a direct descendent of the very people who'd wronged her in life and sent her to the afterlife.

Instead, I felt a profound sense of calm that was foreign to me. Perhaps it was because all my ghosts had finally found a place that felt like home. Besides,

I'd never understood the compulsion to fear super-natural forces, not when humans were already perfectly capable of inflicting terror and destruction.

A shimmer disrupted the peace of the air near the periphery of my vision.

"… could've warned me it's haunted," Jin grumbled while pulling off his relic cloak and reappearing mid-step.

I tossed him a parcel. "Didn't say it's not."

Catching it with one hand like he wasn't even trying, he opened the linen wrap to reveal a still-steaming taro bun. I thought I should at least offer a tokenistic bribe, considering he was sticking his neck out for me without asking for anything in return.

"No lychees this time?" he teased lightly, smiling at the bun.

My mouth quirked up unconsciously as I watched him. I didn't tell him taro was my favorite.

There was something dazzling about the way the corners of his lips curled up in his usual puckish manner, catching a sliver of moonlight on the edges of his cheekbones.

When he caught me staring, I could feel the heat rising in my cheeks. Turning away hastily, I began to draw a glyph in the air.

"W-we'll start small," I stammered. "Somewhere I know."

Before I knew it, Jin had closed the distance between us and flung his cloak over us in one swift motion, the glyph shimmering between our chests. I held onto his arms as his cloak, light as mist, descended upon us in slow motion—a blanket of stars sealing us away into an exclusive universe.

Then, leaning over, he whispered into my ear, "Lead the way, Xun."

My breath caught just as we vanished into the pull of Smokedrift.

The world reassembled around us before I even had a chance to exhale. The musty chill of the Forbidden Archives settled over us the moment we landed. A muted creak sounded from our sudden weight on the floorboards, echoing faintly across the space, creating an ambience eerier than the haunted cottage. If my heart had been thrashing wildly a moment before, it was now for a different reason.

For a few moments, we stood as still as the insentient objects around us, listening for any signs of danger. But there was no other human in here. At least, none corporeal. Not this deep within. When Jin pulled the cloak off us, I swiftly casted several Silencing glyphs to deaden any noise we might make from moving scrolls around or accidentally knocking something over.

I gestured toward the far wall, where the old dossiers on Emberkin classes that frequently chose to remain unbonded were rumored to be kept. A section that hadn't been touched in decades. Jin nodded, his face lit softly by the glyphlight I'd drawn on the collar of his robes. And we began searching.

It might've been much safer for him to stay under his cloak, but that would impede his movements, since he needed both his hands to quickly unfurl and roll up the scrolls. So, he kept the cloak folded and tucked within his robes—ready to vanish at a moment's notice, with or without me.

I didn't know how long we'd been searching. Maybe a stick of incense-burning time. Maybe two. The silence blurred time into something shapeless. Understanding the weight of what we were doing, Jin worked with quiet diligence, his usual humor dimmed but not extinguished. I caught him mouthing silent curses when his fingers unknowingly touched a desiccated corpse of a once curious critter, or whenever a scroll turned out to be yet another miscategorized inventory record.

There were times when he had to check in with me or simply leave a scroll to me because none of it was making any sense to him. Most of what we'd found was irrelevant—misuse of Smokeveil relics, dangerous Smokecraft experimentations, attempted treason. A dossier on a Weaver who'd descended into insanity after bonding with a deformed sparrow

Emberkin, of all things. Jin snorted at that, but I didn't laugh.

Sometimes, madness held truths beyond human comprehension. Other times, it might be no more than a loud consensus, forged through sheer fanatic insistence. After all, what gave one the right to define madness—be they mere mortal or divinity?

Then I found it. A brittle scroll, tucked behind a register of discontinued teaching modules, its faded title peeking through: *Catalogue of Concordant Deviations (Restricted Mentions)*.

Sitting back on my heels, I unrolled it with slow care. Jin came closer, sensing the shift in my breath.

"What is it?" he signed with his hands.

Instead of answering, my eyes scanned the fragmented and laconic entries. A girl's smoke-familiar who resembled "neither beast nor fiend." A boy whose bond had allowed him to pass into "waking dream states" that weren't induced by any glyphwork.

Another case listed only a few phrases before the rest was redacted: *Form unverified. Removed from record. Believed mythic. Eliminated.*

No names, no elaborations. Though I couldn't help but notice these records had avoided calling the familiars "Emberkin," as if erasing them on account of their mythic status. But this was proof that Mo wasn't the only mythic Emberkin, that others existed.

Only they might have all been ... *eliminated*. My hands started trembling.

"This isn't an archive. It's a graveyard," I finally whispered.

Crouching beside me, Jin didn't push for an explanation. He skimmed through the scroll again, eyes narrowing. Then he pointed to a single word, barely visible beneath a smudge of old ink, written completely devoid of any context: *Chongming*.

Chongming was the name of a mythical bird said to be cognizant of symbols, shapes, and patterns that extant beings were oblivious to. A creature from the stories Shan used to tell me, only meant to belong in celestial legends. Just like Mo. Except it carried no fire, no fury—only clarity, the kind that saw through what others couldn't. Wouldn't.

Jin watched me anxiously, as though worried I might fall apart.

Inhaling shakily, I gingerly rolled the scroll back up, then signed to him, "We'll come back."

He nodded, already tucking the scroll behind the old teaching records, back where I'd found it.

One major clue, a hundred new questions. The Vault might have given us the tools, but what we found tonight was a key. And behind the door for it were ghosts, waiting to be named.

黎
lí

封
fēng

塔
tǎ

Chapter Fourteen

镜中人

WHAT THE MIRROR SAW

They said you couldn't see your own soul, but maybe the right kind of mirror could. Only sometimes, perhaps that mirror wasn't made of silver and glass, but smoke and fur.

It'd started with something small, little moments I'd brushed aside at first. Until the evening after the convergence battle, when I was still recovering in the inner palace. I'd wanted nothing more than to return to the Academy right away. But palace protocol demanded that I remained under the Imperial Healers' supervision for at least one full day. Though Father *was* protocol, there was no point in arguing with my parents.

Lady Linhua had stayed by me when I'd stirred awake. Her eyes were glassy with worry, but also with something else. That sharp tension she always held whenever she didn't know where to place me, as if she couldn't decide if I were her daughter, or an imperial asset too unpredictable to handle.

I remembered blinking up at her, parched and half-floating in a haze of lingering confusion.

She was dabbing at my forehead with a damp cloth, muttering rapidly, "… poisoned by bad influence, that's what this is. That Academy has done nothing but poison your mind. Got you thinking you can run amok with wild children who have no business forming alliances with a royal Princess. No wonder you've ended up like this."

At the time, I hadn't even flinched at her conjectures. Maybe I was still too disorientated. Or maybe, somewhere deeper, I still wanted to believe she knew what was best for me. That we were one and the same, as she always proclaimed. There was something profoundly comforting in having someone you could trust unconditionally to guide your way. Especially when you had no idea what you were doing, or where you were going.

But later, I would berate myself for not expressing my dissent. I could never stand behind what she'd said; Jin and Ruo were the main reasons I'd got through the Trial. Yet, something else from that evening had haunted me far longer than her words.

Mo was perched beside the open screen, perfectly still. Her eyes—often unreadable, even to me—had narrowed into a sharp, piercing stillness. Her attention was transfixed on Lady Linhua. Emberkin didn't "see," but they could sometimes pick up on certain energy and auras in ways that humans couldn't. Mo's expression reminded me of how mortals might look when we were straining to recall where and when we'd encountered something before. Like a look of unplaced recognition. Of what, I couldn't say yet.

That was why I was now standing outside Lady Linhua's residence, ten days later, well past dusk. My face veil, black robes, and the Smokeveil-reinforced Obscurant glyph on my collar still wouldn't have been anywhere nearly as secure as being under Jin's cloak, but this was something I needed to do alone. I was uncertain what I would find, or even what exactly I was looking for, just knew that I needed to try to settle my unease.

When I re-emerged within her private chambers in a whisper of Smokedrift without so much as a flutter on the silk drapes I was standing behind, there were no guards around, only her muffled shouting that wasn't unfamiliar to me.

"... never enough for you, is it? Nothing's ever enough! The Consort this, the Consort that—has it occurred to you that *I* am the one who has to live in her shadow, *every single day*—"

Then came a crash of porcelain. Followed by the heavy thud of her bronze brazier slamming into the hardwood floor, sending ash blooming up in a dry, choking cloud before settling like silt.

"Get out! All of you! OUT!" she yelled, poised to hurl something else at the servants scurrying away. One collided with another in her hurry to leave.

It didn't take long before the space fell silent, save for Lady Linhua's ragged breathing. That was when I saw it. Barely a flicker at first, then steadily gathering into form. Nine silken tails coiled upward in a graceful arc behind her, giving the illusion of a human body with tails of smoke. Then a fox's body—ethereal and white with streaks of gold along her spine—emerged from behind Lady Linhua. But she was more than a fox. Her eyes shimmered like mirrors, reflecting not just the room, but the storm within her.

Lady Linhua never directly acknowledged her Emberkin, as if she'd grown utterly accustomed to keeping her invisible, to denying her existence, even to herself. Instead, she only continued pacing in rage, muttering furiously under her breath. The Emberkin hovered behind her—elegant and patient, as if to remind her of both their beauty. Their dominance.

I held my breath, my mind immediately trying to convince me to wipe all this clean from my memory. *It's not real*, I caught that unwanted conviction trying to root itself in my mind. But I clung on tight to the raw facts of this night, refusing to let them be overwritten.

In time, Lady Linhua finally dropped onto her chair with a deep sigh, fanning herself maudlinly. And the nine-tailed fox Emberkin faded until it vanished from sight, as if it'd never been there.

I activated my pendant once more, slipping out the same way I'd entered, back to my own quarters. My mind was threatening to spin out of control. How could it be? Lady Linhua had grown up on the streets. No one from commoner bloodlines was supposed to be able to bond an Emberkin, let alone one that looked like *that*. Mythic, majestic, *terrifying*.

That was what we'd been indoctrinated with all our lives. Yet, what I'd witnessed tonight didn't fit with how our world was meant to work. In between my gasps for air, a memory resurfaced. It was during one of our recent nighttime escapades, when Jin had shown me a scroll he'd uncovered. One I'd previously considered irrelevant to my circumstances.

It detailed rare cases, scattered across centuries, of individuals without any formal Smokecraft training who'd bonded with Emberkin, often from unregistered and undocumented classes widely believed to be fabrications. Without knowledge of accessing Smokeveil's powers, their Emberkin acted instead as a conduit that amplified the most prominent aspect of their bearer's personality or talent to unnatural extremes. What resulted were powers that were volatile and hazardous.

All the mythical legends we'd read as children about the nine-tailed fox flashed through my mind. With each breath I took, every dot I connected, my dismay grew, like a cyclone that wouldn't cease gathering momentum. Then it all morphed into a blast of shattering clarity: manipulating others' emotions wasn't just a skill. Wasn't just Smokecraft. Not for Lady Linhua.

It was her *nature*.

Of course, that was the one thing she'd refined into mastery through her Emberkin.

I didn't know which moments we'd shared between us were truly free of scheming and interference from her powers beneath the surface. So, I started obsessively turning over memories of everything she'd ever fed me. Second-guessing every emotional response I'd ever had to her tragic life stories. Questioning every choice I'd made—to defend her, to please her, to make her proud.

And all the ones I *didn't* make.

So I could protect her—prioritizing her interests, her safety over mine. So I could keep *her* illusions alive, even if it'd meant slowly letting myself die. Gladly so.

I felt *foolish*. Violated. Broken.

My heart felt as if it was being wrung out like wet laundry. My head spun mercilessly, my lungs seizing with the effort to breathe, before the sobs finally broke out, violent and unstoppable.

Maybe Kai did break me. But I'd always known what to expect from him, even if it was stuff from the deepest of hell. This hurt differently. Like someone had carved my heart out while I was watching. And had still somehow gotten me to smile prettily, swearing my undying loyalty in the afterlife.

The fox's eyes hadn't gleamed with malice but with *certainty*, smug and unshakable. Like they'd both seen it all before. That no matter how tangled things got, Lady Linhua would always have those of consequence wrapped around her finger.

Perhaps it was the naivety of a child who would never doubt a parent—the *only* parent she'd thought she ever truly had. Or perhaps Lady Linhua's Emberkin was why, of all the people in this perilous palace, she was the last person I would ever imagine to be harboring a secret like this.

Jin

Jin didn't ask what happened. He didn't need to. Something in Xun had clearly been hollowed out. On the outside, she was still dressed in her fine robes,

Reigning Fire

her hair neatly bound and adorned with sundry be-jeweled hairpins, her back straight. But whatever used to be powering her inside … was gone.

The Weavers' Academy dormitories were now almost empty for the Mid-Autumn Festival celebrations. A time customarily spent with one's family, as per the Empire's culture. But Xun had somehow managed to avoid returning to the inner palace's lavish festivities. As if she didn't mind risking punishment or being without her family on a day of reunion.

Sneaking some tea into her quarters, he found her sequestered there without so much as a window cracked open to admire the full moon in its glory. She uttered her thanks mechanically, then slunk back into that vacuous silence, leaving her tea untouched.

So, Jin tried something else. "Let's do something stupid," he said, flashing her a devilish grin.

That got her attention.

He leaned forward on the tea table. "Not dangerously stupid but *spontaneous*. Let's use the relics for something *fun*. Something that doesn't involve smoke or fire or illusions. Not unless there's sugar involved."

A tiny tilt of her head. "What do you have in mind?" she asked, curious.

"You'll see," he said, grinning. "Meet me in an hour. Oh, and wear a disguise."

She rose a brow mildly. "A disguise?"

"You want to walk out of the palace in plain sight dressed like a Princess?"

Her lips twitched. That was almost a smile. Every time he made her smile, his heart fluttered. It was an unnerving sensation, feeling for a moment as if his heart was preparing to take flight, leaving his body behind. But he'd grown fond of feeling this way.

That night, they rendezvoused in the shadows of their haunted house. Jin smiled at the thought of a house that was theirs, haunted or not. When Xun turned up, he almost couldn't recognize her. She wore a plain ivory silk robe bound at the waist with a leather cord. Her hair was pulled back in a nape knot with a matching silk bandana, eschewing the coiled topknot hallmark of the aristocracy. In this ensemble, she looked more like a scholar's son. The silk was a giveaway, so she wouldn't fully blend in with the true commoners. But it would have to do.

"Where did you get the clothes from?" he asked.

She glanced at him sidelong. "Stole them from Wu's wardrobe chest. With the size of that thing, he won't even notice something's gone missing."

At the mention of Wu, something hot and indignant curled in Jin's gut. What he wouldn't give to kick that prick through a wall of flames one more time. But when he leaned in close to fix her bandana, her own scent still cut through the borrowed silk— vivid and unmistakably her. It was hard to describe, but he always thought she smelled like a mysterious blend of smokeink, jasmine blossoms, and … regret.

She must have caught his expression, since she asked with a look of mild apprehension, "What?"

He cleared his throat. "Nothing. Just … they fit." For a girl, Xun stood tall—her head almost reaching Jin's ear whenever they stood side by side. "Just make sure you never return them afterward. Burn them if you want." He clenched his fist at the thought of Wu smelling like her.

She raised a brow, as if she wasn't sure what to make of that. "Wasn't planning to."

Yeah … stupid of him to be worrying about Wu smelling like her when in a few years' time, she would be married off to some lordling with the right bloodline and an ambition the size of this Empire.

Oh, *now* he'd done it—let his mind slip into those prohibited lands he'd worked so hard to wall off. It hurt like he'd just cut out his own heart to be marinated in a jar of Smokeacid. He gave his mental compass a sharp jolt, veering his focus firmly back to the present.

No, not tonight, he told himself. Tonight was for her and her only. Holding out his cloak as she stepped closer, he draped it gingerly over them. Her shoulder brushed his, just barely, but it lit up something in him that he didn't want to name. In that closeness, she'd been carefully avoiding his eyes whenever they were Smokedrifting. But that'd only gotten him dangerously engrossed in the way her lashes fluttered softly on her downcast eyes. She activated the pendant based on the coordinates he'd given her, and the world shifted around them.

They landed in a deserted alley on the outskirts of the Capital, just before the old northern market square. They could already hear it from here—the music, the clattering, the buzz of laughter. The gentle breeze carried mouth-watering smells of grilled meats and sweet pastries to them in wafts.

Xun slowly pulled the cloak off, her eyes wide with wonder as they raked through the sight before her, taking it all in. The whole main street shimmered like a sparkle of fireflies, the glow of red lanterns painting her face in warmth. Doorways on both sides were decorated with couplets or riddles on red rice paper. Rows of stalls were covered in myriads of paper lanterns, with bamboo frames shaped like rabbits, fish, and dragons. Some even resembled miniature models of chariots and palanquins.

Then Xun's lips curled into a smile that reached her eyes, igniting the bobs of lantern light dancing within. That was when Jin realized why she'd almost never smiled. Not a real smile like this.

Because that was the kind of smile that could bring empires to their knees. Get a man to do the most demented of things—anything—for her. In that moment, he swore the whole world around them lit up a little more.

They wandered through the crowds pretending they weren't who they were. Just two teenagers, perhaps students visiting from a nearby town, wrapped in stolen moments and flickering lights.

At the ring-toss booth, Jin elbowed her forward for a game, handing her a ring. "Go on, see if your Smokecraft training counts for anything."

She raised a brow. "That's not how it works."

"You're just scared you'll lose."

She tossed the ring without looking. It landed squarely on a stick shaped like a frog's tongue.

Unfolding his arms in surprise, Jin blinked a few times in rapid succession. "D-did you just …?"

She shrugged. "Beginner's luck."

He muttered something profane under his breath and stepped up, only to miss *every single shot*. The vendor took pity on him and handed him a consolation prize: a rabbit lantern with absurdly long ears and googly eyes.

Holding it up to eye level, Xun regarded it in feigned solemnness. "It looks … dignified."

He snorted. "It looks like it regrets being born."

"I can relate to that."

He handed it to her. "All yours, then."

She accepted it with exaggerated reverence.

Later, toward the end of the street where the old artisans' stalls gathered, they stumbled on a weathered cart with paper lanterns hung all around, rustling like leaves. Some glowed with glyphed papers customarily handed out by palace Weavers during festivities. Others shimmered with fine golden threads flowing from their bases.

An old woman sat behind the stall, her gray hair pinned up in a simple bun. Her face was a map of soft lines, but her eyes twinkled. She said nothing when they approached—just smiled warmly at Xun, for perhaps longer than custom allowed.

Jin's jovial mood instantly turned guarded. After all, he was sneaking a Princess out of the palace. But Xun looked curious, not wary.

Then, reaching beneath the counter, the woman drew out a phoenix lantern made of intricately cut red paper, with gold-trimmed wings spread wide in flight. She gently pressed it into Xun's hands, gesturing for her to take it. Xun started to reach for her coin pouch, but the old woman closed her fingers over it and gave a small shake of the head.

Xun hesitated briefly, holding the lantern to her chest. Then, bowing low, she said, "Thank you."

The woman's smile deepened into a calming anchor amidst the hustle and bustle of the market. But what she did next baffled Jin. She raised a hand and softly patted the side of Xun's head, like she'd known her all her life, before quietly returning to her seat.

They walked on in silence for a while after that. Xun let the moment settle around her, tracing her fingers around the edge of the phoenix's wing.

"She reminded me of someone. Or … something. I don't know," she said eventually, trying to find the right words. "Is it possible to be reminded of something you've never had?"

Jin stole a glance at her, but she still seemed deep in thought.

"She felt like … home," Xun said.

He wanted to respond with something wise, something moving. But all he could think of was how the lantern lights made her look soft around the edges. Like something worth protecting, always.

You feel like home, he thought. *My home.*

The crowd thinned the farther they walked, until they reached a cobbled path winding up to a garden running along the riverbank. A soft current murmured beneath a stone arch bridge, the moon hanging low ahead and bathing everything in an ethereal glow.

Out of nowhere, Xun tilted her head toward the bridge with a look of mischief. "Race you."

Without waiting for an answer, she darted up the path with a suddenness that made Jin laugh. Though she was only a few moons younger than he was, he often thought she carried the aura of someone who'd lived too many lifetimes. Until now.

He chased after her without thinking, both of them running like they hadn't done in years. No Trials, no court, no illusions. Just limbs and breath and light.

She reached the crest of the bridge first, out of breath and doubling over in laughter. He caught up barely a moment later, and, without forethought, picked her up and spun her round lightly by the waist. A startled laugh escaped her as her lantern trailed gold ribbons in the air.

When her feet touched the ground again, it was as if time had stilled. The distant crowd, the river—everything quieted when she looked up at him, his hands still on her waist. Hers had landed on his chest. Neither moved while they were catching their breath.

He hesitantly reached up with one hand and cupped her cheek, his thumb gently brushing just beneath her eye. Her breath hitched almost imperceptibly as her eyes fluttered close. She didn't lean in, but she didn't pull away either.

Until then, Jin had never thought it possible to hold the entire realm in his own two hands. Immobilized by duty, he didn't kiss her. But heavens, he wanted to—so badly it hurt. When she slowly opened her eyes again, they were moistened.

"Thank you," she whispered, gazing into his eyes.

He swallowed. "Always."

A dull ache slammed into his chest, though he couldn't quite make sense of it. She turned away then, letting the moment dissolve into the lantern-lit night around them. The river below rippled softly, as if keeping their secret safe.

Xun

The scent of lotus seed and rice paper still lingered on me when I Smokedrifted back to my quarters after dropping Jin off. I unconsciously twirled around once, setting my lantern down on the tea table. My joy had rubbed off on Mo, who glided round and round me in glee.

I didn't bother drawing any Lighting glyphs. My thoughts were still swirling somewhere between the bridge, Jin's laugh, and the taste of mooncakes. So, I didn't pick up on the malevolent energy until it was too late.

A shadow lunged, pressing a forearm against my throat with just enough pressure to steal my breath. My back hit the wall hard, head still dazed from the impact, when I felt an agonizing burn on my dominant hand, instantly melting the skin on my fingers.

Smokeacid.

The empty bottle was tossed heedlessly onto the floor with a clang as I winced, unable to scream.

"You looked so radiant earlier when you got your new robes," Kai murmured against my cheek. "But when I dropped by for a visit, you were gone. Thought I'd wait in here. See what the naughty Princess might be up to."

From this position, I had no leverage to push him off. My lungs seized, not from the pressure, but from memory. Of all the times he'd strangled me to the brink of oblivion. Of Shan. Pinned, struggling, dead.

No, not again.

In the close proximity, I could smell Kai— a stench that would haunt me to the end of all realms. I wheezed for air, panic spiraling, when a flicker of warmth curled beneath my sternum. *Mo.* Reminding me that I wasn't alone. Holding me together to stay conscious for as long as I could.

But when Kai started tugging at the cord around my waist with his free hand, I became exactly what I'd always been: *useless* and unable to do a thing. All my training with Xiao. All my years at the Weavers' Academy. All the way I'd crawled out of hell on all fours, along a path of molten fire. All of it went up in smoke in the face of the raw fear consuming me.

Just as I thought I couldn't hold on any longer, the door burst open. A fist collided hard with Kai's face, sending him staggering back.

"Get away from her," Jin snarled.

I immediately scrambled forward, fumbling around with my good hand to yank Jin back by the collar as my vision was still recovering from the lack of air.

"Jin—NO!" I wheezed, blocking in front of him.

Even with my daily weights training, it still felt like holding back a raging beast. Only when I was hissing in pain from the burn on my hand did Jin stop struggling against me. But with his fists still clenched, fury radiating, I didn't dare release him.

"Touchy," Kai sniggered, wiping the blood trickling from his lip with a thumb. "Just testing for palace security loopholes is all. I take my job as an *Imperial Guard*"—he stated his title emphatically, straightening his collar with a self-obsessed smirk—"very seriously, you know."

I thought Kai had made his point. That I would just need to hold Jin back until the threat passed. But Kai had now decided that Jin would make a fun, new target, and continued provoking him instead.

"Didn't realize *you* were the one watching over this section of the palace, little Warrior. Always the first to rush to her rescue. Oh …" Kai tutted, holding up a finger mockingly, "don't tell me … is it just *her* that you're watching so closely?"

"Oh? So, this wasn't your first time trespassing on Her Highness's quarters?" Jin spat, still heaving ragged breaths. I had to force him back once more.

Something flickered in Kai's eyes when he realized he was walking into a trap. Turning sharply, he stalked out without another word, jaw tight.

The moment he was gone, Jin spun toward me and grabbed my wrist, holding my burned hand up for closer inspection.

"Are you—"

"I'm fine," I said, carefully but firmly prying his hand off mine. My voice was even, but I wasn't.

I should've seen this coming—the public humiliation that Kai was hoping to see at the Trial didn't happen. Instead, my triumph had gained me some incipient support at court. Of course that would've triggered his spite. I'd let my guard down and forgotten where I was. Who I was. Just like Father had reproved me for.

"I'm fine," I repeated, more so to myself.

I knew Kai. Unfortunately, I knew him well. If he'd become set on painting a target on Jin's back, he wouldn't stop until he'd *completely* destroyed Jin.

"You need to head back to your quarters now," I said, turning away from Jin. When I heard a protest coming, I held up a hand, curtly halting it.

"*Not* getting on my roof. *Not* go looking for Kai. *Your own quarters*. I can take care of myself," I added coldly. "If you fail to show restraint, I can't risk having you help out with my investigations any further."

The silence between us was deafening.

I couldn't bear to look at his face. Falling apart was not an option right now, even if my heart was searing more painfully than my hand. Eventually, he left.

Once I'd steadied myself, I went looking for Yue. In an ironic twist of fate—considering our old inside joke about Smokeacid and everything else that'd happened between us—Yue was the one who treated my burns. Right up till the end when she finished wrapping it in a clean bandage, she didn't ask any questions. And just like that, we were even.

Afterward, I grabbed a blanket and used my pendant to return to the haunted cottage. Given my injury, I had to draw the Activation glyph with my other hand. Unsurprisingly, it took many attempts.

I didn't think Kai would be back so soon—not after all that. But I knew sleep would be elusive while his odor pervaded my room. So, I made a makeshift bed in the cottage courtyard and lay beneath the blanket of stars. And there it was again—that strange sense of peacefulness that always settled over me here. In the midst of ruins tucked in a lavish palace.

When I woke the next morning, I realized it was the best sleep I'd had in years.

A week later, once all the students had returned from family celebrations, the student Weavers accepted an invitation to observe the Martial Academy's drills and spars. Yue was good at her craft. Though my hand remained bandaged, it was almost completely healed in next to no time. I just had to artfully stay out of my parents' eyes until the scarring had faded.

Reigning Fire

During sparring rounds, a ripple of whispers chased through the courtyard like smoke. Kai lounged near the edge with his arms crossed, eyes scanning. Then he spoke just loud enough to carry.

"Careful how close you get to royalty these days. You never know who else might have left their scent."

A few things happened simultaneously then. The training blade in Jin's hand twitched. Holding my breath and carefully looking straight ahead, I silently implored him not to react. Sensing the shift, Ruo moved closer to Jin, on high alert.

Then Grandmaster Shao approached, and the threat blew over. For now.

That evening, back at our haunted cottage after keeping our heads down all week, Jin exploded, "I could *kill him*."

"You won't," I said firmly, looking him squarely in the eye. "That's exactly what he wants. A reaction. A scandal. The smallest spark, and he wins. And if that happens, I'll end up with much worse than a burned hand. You'll learn that defending me at court isn't often Father's top priority."

Perhaps I *had* taken after Lady Linhua, after all. It was as if I knew exactly what to say to get Jin to do what I wanted him to. Stay where I wanted him.

"You shouldn't have to endure that. You're a Princess." Jin paced around agitatedly.

"You're a Princess, *for fuck's sake!*" he growled.

The irony was never lost on me.

I smiled, cold and hollow. "Now, you've had a glimpse of the inner palace life. When power's at stake, nothing's too precious for sacrifice. Not even Princesses."

A sensory-intrusive memory invaded my mind. One where I could smell Kai's body odor. Feel his rancid breath grazing my neck. See his bared teeth as he purred, *All that cleverness, all that power … and yet, you are still my plaything.*

But then Jin's concerned face drifted back into view, and the memory of Kai slithered back to the sunless deep where it'd come from.

I softened my tone. "I know it's really hard for you to process any of this. But I've survived many things. Including ones I was certain I wouldn't."

I didn't know if there was anything I could realistically say to Jin that could take the pain from him. But I had to try.

"So, I just need you to trust me that I'll be fine in the end, OK?"

His breathing was still ragged, but he'd stopped raging. Not out loud, at least.

The laughter from the river still echoed in my bones. But it felt like it belonged to someone else now.

锦

jǐn

阳

yáng

Jasmine K. Y. Loo

Chapter Fifteen

重明鸟

CHONGMING BIRD

When Jin and I were finally ready to return to the Forbidden Archives a few nights later, we didn't have high hopes of finding anything substantial. The deeper we searched, the more fragmented the records had become.

The risks involved also grew exponentially. Mo couldn't sense clearly in the deeper sections, where too many glyphs were layered on top of each other. So, she might not be able to alert me of any incoming danger in time. But that was often how the most valuable secrets stayed hidden: behind the crumbling edges of scrolls no one dared reach deep enough to touch.

We took every precaution—sticking to the times between the rostered patrols, Silencing glyphs layered over the doors, cloak drawn tight over us whenever possible. Even then, each step forward felt like wading through quicksand, the air taut with the threat of apprehension.

So far, we'd been fairly lucky in all our trips to the Forbidden Archives. My pendant allowed us to bypass the guards stationed at the external entrances and the Smokecraft securing the internal doorways without needing counterglyphs. There was always a chance that the Unlocking glyphs could trigger the security alerts, even after appearing to work.

But that night, we had no idea how close we were to being caught. We were in a large chamber deep in the Archives, past the safer points of retreat, when we heard the muted shift of footsteps. Way too many of them to be a pure coincidence. Muffled voices followed closely after.

Ad-hoc patrols.

Jin signed something from the other end of the chamber, but I couldn't make out what he was saying. Then a new sound came. More boots. We would be cutting it too close if we stayed where we were.

When I saw that Jin had kept to his word and vanished under his cloak, I tucked myself into a tight space between a column and a wall, replacing the Lighting glyph on my collar with an Obscurant glyph.

Elongated shadows passed over the stone wall beside me as the guards moved by, slow and searching. But their rhythm sounded off beat, validating my suspicions that they weren't the usual patrols in here.

Could be Kai's work. *Does he already have something on me?* I thought, panic rising in my chest. *No, he's diabolical, but also an asshead. He wouldn't be the one to catch me.*

Swallowing hard, I started channeling my anxiety to Mo to keep my breathing even and soundless. Moments passed, then more. I knew I should have Smokedrifted back to the cottage. That was what Jin and I had agreed on, if we ever got split up. But my mind was racing.

What if Jin didn't manage to leave? He would have to follow the guards at their heels to leave when they disabled the Locking glyphs at the exits. What if he couldn't do that without risking discovery? Being able to stay invisible didn't mean he could walk through walls and leave.

If I left and found he wasn't back at the cottage, it would be even riskier for me to return for him without his cloak. For all I knew, I could rematerialize right in front of a troop of guards. Or worse, Kai. I clearly hadn't thought this through as well as I'd believed. But self-reproach wouldn't get Jin and me out of here.

I waited longer, until finally, the hallways outside seemed to clear. I'd barely turned to step out before I stopped in my tracks. Right near where I was hiding was a glyph, almost imperceptible, especially in the dark. It looked like an old Locking glyph—the kind you would only find on ancient doors—etched on what was supposed to be a solid stone wall. As I reached out toward it, I felt pulses of Smokeveil powers beyond it. They might feel old, but I was certain they were still extant.

That was when I felt movement behind me. My body shifted instinctively before my mind caught up. If Kai thought he could get me the same way a second time, he would learn how gravely mistaken he was. I turned swiftly, thrusting an elbow toward his face. He parried the blow, but my other hand was already locking onto the back of his neck, shoving him down and ready to ram a knee into his chest.

"Wait—it's me!" Jin exclaimed in a stunned whisper that froze me mid-motion.

He blinked up at me, his eyes wide, hands still raised in a defensive position.

"What the fuck was that?"

"Reflexes," I muttered, panting slightly. "It's … complicated." Then I pointed to the glyph I'd just discovered to distract him from asking any more questions. "Look what I found."

Leaning close, Jin squinted his eyes at where I was pointing.

"There's a hidden space behind this wall," I said in hushed undertones. "I don't think it's on any official maps of the Forbidden Archives."

We used my pendant to cross over to the other side of the wall without triggering the Locking glyph, and rematerialized at a dark, narrow passage. I nodded at Jin, and we went down it vigilantly. To our surprise, the end of the tunnel opened to an expansive chamber, lit by the reflection of soft blue light swirling from a glass dome above.

We stayed just before the threshold to survey our surroundings. This space was unlike anything we'd seen in here. Contrary to the other crumbling, dust-choked rooms littered with latent forbidden relics and dossiers on the erased and forgotten, this one looked as though it belonged to a royal from another era.

Ornate screens carved with qilin and phoenix designs framed the back wall, lacquered bookshelves lining the sides. Though the shelves were in disarray, scrolls and papers haphazardly stuffed or scattered across the floor, the space wasn't dirty. The air, while heavy, wasn't stale. The floor tiles had been swept. The low-set writing desk in the center gleamed softly in the glyphlight. Someone had been regularly maintaining this place.

Yet, much to my dismay, in the far corner of the room was a man, sitting cross-legged and gently rocking his body back and forth. Loose parchments filled with glyphs and symbols I didn't recognize had been strewn around him, covering almost every inch of the floor.

Jin looked a different direction, tapping my shoulder to get my attention. But he froze when the man in the corner began humming. Just a single line from an old battlefield song in a broken, looping rhythm:

"八百里分麾下炙，五十弦翻塞外声 ..."

Reason implored me to retreat immediately. Yet I found myself stepping forward, the pulse in my throat swallowing the sound of his tune. When the man noticed our presence, he stopped humming mid-line and stared at me. There was something piercing in his eyes—recognition, yes, but something else flickered there, too. Unease that morphed into awe. A reverence so intense it made my skin crawl.

Then his voice cracked. A single word, hoarse and splintered, repeated over and over again: "Bashe ... bashe ... bashe ..."

Jin shifted uneasily beside me. "Bashe? As in the giant snake from the old myth scrolls?"

But I was too astounded to answer. My gaze hadn't left the man's face. His features weren't entirely unfamiliar—he looked like someone I'd seen before, or perhaps *many someones*. There was a particular curve to his face, a slope to his brow ...

Something pulled tight in my chest. I thought of my grandmother, the late Empress. Though I was still young when she'd passed on, her portraits still hung in the palace halls. And suddenly, I could see it in this man before us—those same eyes, the same sharp line of cheekbone.

And then I saw it in someone else. My father. This man looked like an older mirror of Father. My throat dried, my pulse faltered as realization dawned on me. This man wasn't looking at *me*, not really. His eyes held no confusion, no attempt to place me. Because he thought he already had.

He thought he was looking at Prince Yan Yun.

The taste of bile rose in my throat as I recognized that he was family. No, not just family. He was their *son*. An uncle I'd never been introduced to. A royal Prince the world didn't know existed.

A rustle across the room caught our attention. Perched inside a tall glass enclosure on one of the shelves was an Emberkin with four glowing eyes, smoky feathers etched in silver-blue.

A chongming bird—caged in Lifeng glass.

So, that was what Jin wanted to show me before.

Distantly, I felt my hands tremble, but I desperately wanted to say something to the man. Ask some questions, at least.

Who had put him in here? How long had he been here? Had anyone ever tried to help him? What did all those symbols he'd drawn mean? Was there ever any hope for him to have a life out of … here?

Was this what I should be expecting for myself?

I had so many questions, but my voice had deserted me. With my head starting to spin, I decided I'd seen enough. It wasn't safe for us to stay any longer. Not without knowing when the maintenance crew for this room might turn up. Something we hadn't previously accounted for.

Jin was about to speak, but I stopped him, signing, "Not here."

And we backed out of the room slowly, the man's resumed chant echoing after us.

Once we Smokedrifted back to the abandoned cottage, Jin stammered, "Xun—what the hell was that? That Emberkin ... What we read before. Did we just see—"

I shook my head dazedly. "I need to think. Let me," I said, holding a shaky finger to my lips.

Jin fell silent.

Ignoring the icy chill in my hands, I didn't for the life of me know where to begin. So, I started with what I knew. Silently recited key facts of what we'd learned at the Academy and what we'd discovered so far.

Emberkin were smoke-born entities drawn from the Smokeveil, anchored by the Weaver's will and temperament. Hence why those compatible would only choose to bond us when our essence had settled into something nameable—within a year after our Binding Rites. They were supposed to take on the shape of real-world creatures—beasts of flesh and fang. Anything else was a sign of spiritual interference. An omen. A warning. So, based on what we were taught, Mo and I were meant to be anomalies.

Two years had passed before I'd found an opening to start searching for answers. About why I'd bonded a phoenix Emberkin—well over a year *before* my Binding. Why I was different. Why my difference was deemed such abomination.

Just as we'd finally began finding some clues, I saw Lady Linhua's nine-tailed fox Emberkin.

Not a real-world creature.

And tonight, Jin and I just saw a chongming bird Emberkin with our own eyes. The legendary four-eyed bird blessed with sight that uncovered patterns others couldn't. To see the world in a different light.

Also not a real-world creature.

His bonded human looked just like my late grandmother, who was only supposed to have three sons, including my father. The man was living in a secret chamber with his chongming bird Emberkin, shut off from the world. I highly doubt he'd put himself in there.

Assuming my theory was right. That he'd mistaken me for Father … He had repeatedly called me bashe—a mythic giant snake with a green head, black body, and an insatiable appetite. A depiction of the complexities of morality and justice. A representation of the coexistence of both light and darkness.

The man was referring to Zhu Feng. He'd meant he wasn't just any snake Emberkin.

Zhu Feng was a bashe.

In just a matter of weeks, I'd discovered that both of those who'd brought me into this world had bonded mythical Emberkin, just like me. Father had been *the* most powerful person in the Empire all these years, since he'd become Prince Regent. He'd known all this time that we weren't an anomaly.

And yet, we were still outlawed.

I gave a humorless chuckle. We hadn't even been officially outlawed. Our Emberkin had simply been scrubbed clean from all formal records. Described as an embodiment of evilness and danger, even in the sealed records within the Forbidden Archives.

Why would Father do it, then? Why would he have bestowed these relics upon us? And along with them, the power to search. To uncover.

Once again, I found myself trying to make sense of a man whom I could perhaps never make sense of.

Because he could TAKE BACK what he's given away anytime he wants to, a small voice within me answered, *if he doesn't like what we do with the power he's bestowed.*

It begged the question: How many of us were there, truly—within this palace and beyond?

The weight of it all—the lies, the lineage, the way history had buried us—pressed down on my chest like a boulder. My feet moved, but I couldn't feel them. The memory of the man's eyes, wide and wild, was playing on a loop in my mind. He looked like he wouldn't hurt a fly. Erratic—yes, perhaps—but harmless, just like his chongming bird Emberkin. Aside from being unusual, what had he done to deserve being trapped in a miniature Lifeng prison?

The man hadn't seen me. He'd seen a ghost. And I was the only one who knew who that ghost really was.

At least now I'd witnessed what they did to children who didn't fit. Children like me. I scoffed.

My pulse was steady, even while my mind was fraying at the edges. It was so steady it felt wrong. Like the stillness before a storm, when even the wind held its breath. The coldness seeped into my bones; the numbness spread to my extremities.

And when the trembling started in my knees, I thought I could will it away. But the truth dragged me under like a tide, and I crumpled.

Jin

Jin watched her sink to the floor. It happened so suddenly, so silently, that he barely had time to reach for her. Her fingers gripped the edge of the dilapidating bed frame like it was the only thing anchoring her to the world. He'd seen her keeping steady through pain, poison, fire. But this? This unraveled her.

He didn't speak. Just lowered himself beside her, knees creaking on the floorboards. The silence felt sacred. Shattering it with words would be like snapping the spine of a holy tome. Then he saw her hand twitch, just slightly, like she was reaching for something that wasn't there.

And then *it* appeared.

From the shadowed space beside her, something coalesced into form. Jin held his breath as the smoke took shape. First eyes. Then beak. Then fire.

A large red-and-orange creature that moved like smoke and shadow but glowed with an inner heat emerged before them. It reminded him of the fire she'd conjured that day in the arena—the illusion that had burned itself into his memory but never touched his skin. Jin's hand instinctively went for the hilt of a blade he wasn't carrying.

Then he stopped. Because he saw that Xun didn't flinch. Instead, she leaned into the phoenix like it was an instinct, like it'd always been there for her. The Emberkin curled protectively around her—serpentine and sinuous, wings tucked, tail coiled. Its body never quite solid, never quite fully visible. But it was both majestically beautiful and hauntingly terrifying.

"Mo," she whispered tenderly, not to him.

Jin's throat tightened.

So, this was the real reason they were investigating unregistered Emberkin. What she'd been hiding. Not because she didn't trust him, but because she knew that walking in on certain secrets could invite peril to their doorstep. For the both of them. Perhaps even for those connected to him. *His family*.

His heart was gripped by fear. It wasn't that he thought she would take on all the risks of probing into forbidden knowledge without a solid reason. But *this*?

Jin felt a rush of something he struggled to name. Wonder, dismay … and grief. Not for himself, but for *her*. He wanted to reach for her. To tell her she wasn't alone, that he would follow her into whatever hell this secret might lead to. But some fractured, frightened part of him was holding him back.

This wasn't just a creature but a revelation. The manifestation of anything resembling celestial entities in the Mortal Realm was inconceivable. And the mortals obliterated what they didn't understand.

And yet, it was also her. Mo, the Emberkin who'd clearly been guarding Xun in silence all this time.

He hated the part of him that recoiled. Hated even more the part that understood why he did. He could already feel the war starting inside him. He wanted to protect her. He wanted to run. He wanted her to be safe. He wanted her to be his.

But above all, he wanted Xun to live. Not in the shadows, not under a curse, not as a myth they hunted down. He wanted her to live stably, brightly, magnificently. Even if that meant carving himself out of her future ... he was going to do it. With shaking hands and a bleeding heart.

As much as it killed him, he'd come to the painful conclusion that he wanted her to have a glorious marriage with someone worthy of her title, of her bloodline. Someone the Empire would celebrate, not condemn.

He wanted her to be able to walk through the palace gardens, hand in hand with her children, without fear. To have peace, power, and protection—so there would *never* be an opening for someone like Kai to come near her ever again.

Jin wanted to watch her build a legacy of peace in this very Empire—*hers*. That was the Empire he would fight for, because *she* was the reigning Empress he wanted to guard with his life.

So, even though he wanted her more than he'd ever wanted anything in this world, he'd decided that this was the kind of love he had for her. Till his last dying breath.

But suddenly, he saw how this would end.

Xun would be hunted, feared, and exiled. There would only be the shadow of a phoenix circling above her and the constant trepidation of discovery. Or worse … he couldn't bring himself to imagine Xun being shut away in a secret chamber by herself for the rest of her life.

Like that man.

And if that happened, Jin would never be able to reach her again. There would be nothing he could do, just like *that night*. He grimaced in pain at the memory. He knew why she'd been callous toward him. He knew and yet, *there was nothing he could do*.

He'd told himself he would never touch her again. Not since he recognized what a dangerous addiction that would be. To have touched something that could never be. To have held it in his hands, knowing it might well be the very last time he ever could.

And yet, in spite of it all—against his better judgment—he reached out from behind Xun and pulled her into a tight embrace, rocking her gently from side to side. She let him. And she let her tears fall silently onto his arm.

She'd let him in to her real world, in more ways than one that night. And perhaps *that* was the most dangerous addiction of all. The more he was allowed to see who she really was beneath all that façade, the more he wanted to see all of this girl in front of him. To be the one she leaned on. To be the one who could share the load of her burdens and secrets.

Holding Xun, he wasn't sure if he was trying to keep her from falling apart or himself from unraveling. But they just stayed that way without a word between them. He wished they could stay that way forever.

But a life in hiding was *not* going to be her destiny. Jin could never accept that. He looked down at the pendant hanging across her chest. At his cloak still folded on the chair. At their soot-scrawled plans on the desk.

He gritted his teeth as he strengthened his resolve.

There *had* to be a way. And Jin would find it, even if it meant rewriting every rule in the realm that made her a threat.

mò

Silently

Chapter Sixteen

海枯石烂

WHERE SMOKE TURNS TO STONE

Xun

The summons came with no explanation. Just a formal scroll delivered to my Academy quarters, with Father's seal pressed cleanly onto it. I was to present myself in his private study by the Hour of the Dragon.

Master Dan was already standing before Father's desk when I arrived, his expression unreadable. Father didn't look up right away. Just continued writing something with his brush, attentively.

I curtsied and stood at attention, waiting. Whenever there was a third person present, Zhu Feng had never stayed anywhere but coiled around Father's leg, so that the top half of his body was never visible. Finally, Father looked up.

"So, you have yet to bond an Emberkin," he stated plainly, his tone deceptively light, yet sharp.

I kept my face neutral. Even with Mo steadying me, Father had a kind of energy that could make even the most skilled Weavers feel compelled to dry swallow when he took on that tone.

"Your Binding Rites were nearly a year ago," he continued. "Is Master Dan not fulfilling his duty?"

My eyes flicked to Master Dan, who gave the smallest shake of his head. Not in denial, more in warning. I understood. The wrong answer could shift the weight of suspicion toward him.

"He has done all that he can," I replied.

Father's expression didn't change. "And you? Are *you* doing all that you can?"

I said nothing, just looked at him. I wondered if there could ever be an alternate reality, where he overturned all the misinformation about Emberkin and the social classes, instead of condoning it and continuing the cycle of lies. Where I could excitedly tell my father all about Mo and proudly present her to the world.

But that was not the reality. Because that was not what my father had chosen.

He regarded me for a long time, just as I did him.

All my life, I'd waited, hoped, prayed—that one day, in a moment like this, our signals might finally cross. That somehow, through the silence, we would manage to understand each other at last.

"You were never meant to disappoint," he finished with a stern reminder before dismissing me. Of course, he never had anything else to say to me.

I left the study in silence, my footsteps echoing down the corridor. The polished stone floor gleamed with imperial perfection, as if nothing imperfect had ever walked its halls.

At the turn near the western courtyard, I nearly collided with Yan Lu, my younger cousin. The all-round prodigy, as I was being relentlessly reminded all our lives. Everything about Lu was a validation of how brilliant he was—from the sesquipedalian prose in his writing all the way down to his Emberkin.

Though we were both students of the Weavers' Academy, we rarely crossed paths with each other. Being in different years helped with that. Everyone knew we were related by our royal blood, that much was true. But it didn't mean he would want to be *associated* with me. That was an important difference there, one that boy genius knew all too well.

From a distance, the contrast between us worked in his favor. But if he were seen mingling with me? Others might start questioning *his* judiciousness, instead. Most days, I would feign ignorance and keep things diplomatic between us. But not today. Today, I had nothing left to give him. To anyone.

Lu blinked at me, caught mid-step with a heavy scroll three times the usual rolled-up circumference tucked under one arm, and an intricately carved layered pastry carrier with sundry tea cakes carried in his other hand.

"Ah, Cousin Xun," he called with a polite bow that was just a fraction too deep, too precise. "Didn't expect to see you here, since I've been summoned. Uncle usually clears the halls after one of his … motivational chats. But these should cheer him up," he said with a grin, holding up the dessert carrier.

I didn't answer. Only squeezed my trembling hands tightly together behind me to steady them, hoping Lu would get lost. Regrettably, he wouldn't.

"I was just on my way to present some findings on the glyph distortion patterns in the lifewarden towers," Lu added breezily. "You know how it is like—one moment you're solving cross-domain fluctuations, the next you're being asked to rewrite archival protocols."

He gave a modest shrug that was anything but. Then, that calculating gaze flicked to me. Not hostile, not necessarily unkind, either. Just … evaluating.

"You look tired," he said commiseratively. "But then again, it *has* nearly been a year, hasn't it?"

A beat passed before he smiled again—that maddeningly perfect smile that made me want to slam those dessert trays he was carrying into his face. Yet, I still wasn't able to utter a single word, let alone an intelligible response to his cleverly veiled mockery.

Is making others underestimate you really a ploy, or just something you tell yourself to make the truth hurt less? I asked myself. I swallowed the sting that my own voice had deserted me, even when there was no one here to rob me of it this time.

"I suppose we all rise in our own time. Though some of us are … called upon earlier." Lu bowed again, this time with one foot already turned toward his next destination. "Take care of yourself, cousin."

I watched him walk away, his steps unhurried, his confidence effortless. In that moment, I understood what the court saw in him. The future of the Empire. A prodigy sculpted by palace tutors and court strategists. Every gesture studied. Every flaw polished out before it ever had a chance to form.

I turned in the opposite direction, toward my own path. One that grew darker by the day.

Jin

The air in the abandoned cottage was colder than usual as they were entering the heart of winter. To avoid creating any smoke that could give them away, Xun had drawn some Heating glyphs in the space between them. She sat across from Jin at the low table, her face half-lit by the shimmering glyphs.

In light of the recent developments, they'd agreed that instead of rushing back into the Forbidden Archives to search blindly like a pair of headless chooks, they should first try to work out a practicable plan.

"What happens," Jin asked, "if we don't figure it out in time?" With Xun's seventeenth birthday less than two moons away, the anxiety had been robbing all the air in his lungs.

She didn't pretend not to grasp his meaning. "Then I'll most likely fade into the background," she said matter-of-factly. "Become the forgotten Princess, like an aunt of mine. The disappointment that the rumors have always whispered about. Lie low for a few years, then probably get married off in a political arrangement to some noble household. Whoever's most useful to the Empire at the time, really. And the Empire would sigh in relief that the inconvenient daughter is finally out of the way."

The bitterness in her voice was palpable, even when she tried to keep her tone light. She gave a soft, humorless laugh. "Maybe it's for the best. Yan Lu is far more suited to the throne, anyway. Ridiculously smart, charming, and obedient. Everything I'm not. In this Empire, bloodlines only get you so far. It all still comes down to competence. A lineal heir is strongly preferrable, but it isn't a must."

"No," Jin said, shaking his head. "You don't get to give up. You're born to rule, *not* be a pawn."

She looked at him, weary. "You don't understand what it's like. Every move scrutinized, every word weighed. And now this … with Mo."

Jin heard her. But at the same time, he got the sense that she was secretly grateful he would never understand what it was like. Maybe because then, he would always get to be the blessed sunshine that he was, like the meaning behind his name—Jin Yang.

There was a night when they'd lain side by side on the old cottage's courtyard, stargazing together. It was then that she'd told him how much she loved his name. "Like the sun that's just *there*," she said, "without needing anyone's permission to *be*. To shine. To warm skin and thaw hearts."

He'd never given his name much thought before then. But what he loved was how she called him Jin. No one else had called him that until she started to. It made him feel like *her* Jin.

"Then help me understand," Jin said to her now, trying to keep the edge of desperation out of his voice. "Tell me how Mo works. Tell me everything."

Xun hesitated. Then slowly, she began to explain about the Dream Realm. About how she could cross over because of Mo. There, she'd learned things she never could have in the Mortal Realm. That was how she'd met Xiao, who was instructing her in combat and Swordcraft. Jin recalled the time when she'd almost smashed his face in the Forbidden Archives, having mistaken him for a palace guard.

He listened on, trying not to show how much it was all rattling him. It was the first time he'd resented being a non-Weaver. Simply because he didn't understand enough about that world to know how to fix any of this.

Finally, he said, "Maybe you should stop."

"Stop what?"

"Crossing into the Dream Realm. Just for now. We don't know how that bond was formed, or how much is already set in stone. If there's any chance we can find a way to undo this …" he trailed off.

The look on her face said she understood. She nodded slowly. "So, that's what you think the solution might be." Her voice was quiet. Not out of grievance, just a bone-deep weariness.

"I don't *want* it to be," he said. "I want you to stay just the way you are, but if it keeps you safe—"

But Xun was already turning away before Jin could finish his sentence. He could feel her walls coming back up. Mo, still curled in the shadows near her elbow, let out a low hum, as if wondering what to do with Jin's cluelessness.

The silence stretched between them. Xun never knew this, but Jin had seen her before they'd first met. Once, when he was helping Grandmaster Shao deliver a message to Master Dan at the Weavers' Academy. Long before the Trial and the Archives and all the secrets they now carried, Jin remembered watching a girl. Standing alone on the periphery while others were forming coteries of friends and allies in the courtyard.

She hadn't said a word, just stared up at the clouds like they were maps only she could read. Jin remembered thinking she didn't seem lost. Just ... alone. Like she needed to single-handedly carry all the burdens heavens had unloaded upon her.

Then he thought of the image of her kneeling on the floor, shaking. Yet still never once asking for help. Never made him promise to always stand by her.

Once he'd realized the full gravity of the situation, he often considered the potential repercussions to his family. At the same time, he knew if she'd asked—all she needed was to ask—he would be pledging his undying loyalty to her. Consequences be damned.

He hated how familiar her forlorn expression was to him. Hated more that he'd done nothing about it. He wouldn't make that mistake again. Not this time. Not when it mattered most.

Xun finally broke the silence. "You think I can live without Mo."

He didn't know the answer to that. What he knew was that he couldn't live in a world without Xun.

Where he could no longer see her, or even catch the occasional glimpse from afar. He didn't tell her that. He couldn't. But if letting go of Mo meant keeping her safe—if it meant preserving a destiny that was rightfully hers—he would ask her to try anyway. Even if it meant she would never forgive him for it.

Xun

Crossing into the Dream Realm had never felt like this before. The moment the smoke curled around my ankles, pulling me in, I knew something was out of place. From the outset, Xiao and the qilin drummers weren't waiting before me, and for a beat, the tendrils of unease spiraled around me. Was I truly alone?

Then the mist dispersed, and Xiao was there. They didn't say a word, but the set of their shoulders, the way they shifted their gaze to the mountain behind them, then back to me again—it was a summons. *Don't question, don't argue, just follow along*, I imagined them saying.

Though I wasn't exactly in the mood to embark on a deadly slog through completely unfamiliar terrain in the middle of the night, it wasn't as if I was in the mood for much else anyway.

But it wasn't a sheer ascent. The path was worn; a memory trail carved into dreamstone and myth. My shoes were barely making a sound against the cool stone and snow. And the wind embraced me from behind, so that my coat was being pulled forward like a security blanket holding me.

The further we climbed, the more the Dream Realm blurred with the corporeal in the Mortal Realm. I thought I saw flickers of glyphlights from the palace. Heard the distant echo of Kai's laughter, sinister and cruel. Glimpsed the flick of Mo's tail vanishing around the corner, like she was watching us from somewhere further ahead.

I didn't know how long we'd been climbing—maybe moments, maybe a lifetime. But the ache spreading up my legs felt real, even in the Dream Realm. A part of me was disgruntled at Xiao. They could fashion weapons out of thin air in this realm, but apparently shoes fit for the journey were out of reach. Maybe that was the lesson. That ready or not, you had to *climb* to understand, to see clearly.

Finally, we crested the ridge.

The peak wasn't exactly what I'd expected. There were no statues, no altars, no token of significance in any shape or form to mark the climb. The clouds curled around us, brushing my cheeks like a mother's caress—not mine, but what I imagined a regular mother's caress to feel like.

And below us ... the world. From my vantage point, the palace was but a speck, the river a ribbon, the Archives concealed by shadows and stone. The mountain bore witness to it all, unmoved and constant.

Xiao kneeled beside me and placed something on the ground. A single river stone, polished smooth, etched with layered glyphs whose glow pulsed like old memories. Not unlike a Smokemirror, or perhaps the origin of one. When I reached for it, the surface shimmered, forming not illusions but remembrance.

I saw myself. As a child, as I was now, as I could have been. I saw Mo, Jin, Shan, my father, mother, Kai. Saw the endless nights I'd stayed up to work just a little bit harder, hoping I could be worthy. Saw all the terror, fury, sorrow, and grief I'd been channeling to Mo—just to get through one more moment.

I saw my well-intentioned but misguided endeavors to protect those dear to me. And in turn, the meaninglessness of it all reflected back to me.

I saw my relentless, soundless howling into the void, felt the utter absence of the slightest reverberation in return. The images didn't speak, yet each echoed with something deeper than words.

Xiao rose, as if acknowledging that this was a moment for me, and me alone. As they turned to leave, I caught a glimpse of their silhouette through the fog. For an infinitesimal moment, it felt like the outline of someone I knew better than anyone but couldn't quite place. Like I'd been struck with a pang of intimate familiarity from someone else's memories.

I relinquished the compulsion to chase down paths without solid ground. Just breathed, deep and slow, looking out at the world beneath me in quiet reflection. I should've felt perturbed that Xiao was leaving me here alone, but I wasn't. For once, my mind wasn't trying to choreograph ten steps ahead and was content to just stay in the here and now.

In time, I'd come to the insight: not all bonds were meant to be severed. Some were meant to endure. To rise. To reign. While I didn't have all the answers, I knew now what I *wouldn't* do.

I wasn't broken; *I was forged*. If my choices meant re-entering the fire, then let it be.

Jin

Jin's cloak fluttered around him as he slipped into the private quarters at the Weavers' Academy. Just like him, Ruo had been assigned her own room since their Concordance Trial victory, courtesy of Xun.

He felt like he was losing his godsdamn mind. When Xun had turned up at their cottage the night before, she'd simply announced the cessation of all their investigations. That at the end of the day, she was either going to be an insignificant pawn or a more significant pawn, which made no difference to her. And that was that. Without even waiting for him to respond, she'd activated her pendant again, leaving an utterly bewildered Jin behind to rage at ghosts.

He'd considered storming into Xun's quarters under his cloak and dragging her back. But he knew that he couldn't *make* her activate her pendant to bring them back to the Forbidden Archives. And without Xun, there was no way he could bypass all the security to get in there by himself. Which was exactly why he'd ended up in Ruo's quarters tonight.

He'd waited in the corner, invisible, until she'd entered and closed the door behind her. When he'd revealed himself, Ruo had nearly flung a teapot within arm's reach at him. Nearly.

"Are you insane?" Ruo hissed, eyes darting to the door before swiftly drawing a Silencing glyph next to them. "You're lucky my first instinct wasn't to attack with Smokecraft. What were you thinking, sneaking into a Weaver's room?"

"Sorry," Jin said, trying to steady his voice. "But I'm obviously here for a reason."

She crossed her arms. "This better be good."

"I need a favor. A big one."

Ruo raised an eyebrow. "Bigger than saving your ass at the convergence battle?"

He smiled wispily. "Much bigger, unfortunately."

Frowning, Ruo asked, "What do you want?"

Jin took a deep breath. "I need to access the deepest layers of the Forbidden Archives. Not just the surface—the innermost layer. And I can't do it alone, not even with my cloak."

"Very funny."

Ruo started turning away, but Jin stopped her. "Please, Ruo. You're the only one I can trust with this. And if you say no ... I'm out of options."

Ruo gawked at him like he'd grown three heads. "You've lost your fucking mind. Do you have a death wish? No—do I look like I *share* it? Why not just ask Xun? Princesses might have better immunity against execution," she blurted, all in one breath.

"Please," he pleaded earnestly. "If you have any way at all, this is the time. I'm desperate, Ruo. More than I've ever been. I can't tell you why. Not because I don't trust you, but because it'd put *you* in danger."

She glared at him. "Like you weren't already putting me in danger."

A long silence ensued as Ruo was studying Jin skeptically, as if still contemplating if this was just an elaborate prank. He hoped she could see that he wouldn't be turning to her if it wasn't urgent.

Heaving a sigh, Ruo produced a small object, wrapped in cloth, from the drawer of her nightstand. She unwrapped it to reveal a smoky-gray orb with veins of glimmering silver, no bigger than a plum.

"This is what I picked from the Vault," she said.

He reached out, puzzled. "What does it do?"

"The Seeker's Eye," she said. "One use only. It'll show you the path to what you're seeking, so long as your intent's clear. Creates a one-time portal that leads you to it and back, bypassing any Smokecraft barriers along the way. Once it's used, it's gone."

"You're sure about giving this to me?" Jin asked, torn between his guilty-conscience and desperation.

"You fucking owe me big time."

He accepted it reverently. "Thank you. I swear I'll never forget this. When there's something I could do to repay you, just say the word." A brief hesitation. "But ... I can't use it myself, can I?"

"No. It needs someone trained in Smokecraft to activate it." Then, casting a glance at Jin who continued looking at her expectantly, she asked, incredulous, "You want to do this *now*? As in, right this moment?"

"I have no choice. Time's running out."

Tilting her head up to the ceiling, Ruo looked as if she was musing on what she'd done wrong to give others the impression that she was a saint. But without another word, she set the orb on the floor and drew a precise set of glyphs in the air, saying a single word Jin didn't recognize.

The glyphs ignited as they folded themselves into the orb. It pulsed once. Then again, brighter. This time, a soft thread of light unfurled from its core, slithering across the ground like silk spun from lightning.

Standing up, Ruo planted her hands on her hips. "The thread will lead you to what you seek. But be careful, it won't protect you. And in case you haven't noticed, it glows like a constipated dragon's tail. I'll watch from here, but if it smells like trouble—poof, I'm gone. I'm helping you, Jin, not dying for you."

Jin knew she wasn't joking, but that was only fair. He nodded solemnly and turned to follow the light.

"Oh, and Jin," she added casually, "if you die, I'm getting that cloak."

He almost laughed. Under normal circumstances, he would have. Instead, he only vanished beneath his cloak and stepped into the dark. The thread of light shimmered beneath his feet as he slipped through the ancient, dust-veiled corridors of the Forbidden Archives. This far beneath the surface, the air grew biting, its mustiness permeating his nostrils.

Jin's breath was shallow as he fought his body screaming for him to turn back to safety. Every few steps, he paused to listen, but there was nothing. No guards, no whispers, no creaking doors. Just the thud of his heartbeat in his ears and the steady glow of the Seeker's thread winding ever forward.

Eventually, the path led him to a low, narrow arch. Unlike the outer layers' crumbling grandeur, this one was made of plain stone, rough-hewn and dark. Jin ducked beneath it to emerge in a vaulted chamber. A circle of faded torches lined the walls, enchanted to burn cold blue without smoke. The relic thread stopped at a pedestal at the center of the room.

With no time to waste, Jin reached out to the scroll resting on the pedestal, praying it wouldn't trigger any security measures. When nothing seemed to happen, he immediately perused the ancient text as quickly as his eyes could go, his heart sinking with every line.

While he didn't understand the glyphs, it wasn't hard to see this wasn't just a method of unbonding, but a torturous means of erasure. A tearing apart of the soul—agonizing and permanent. *Forbidden.* Which probably said a lot, considering the Empire wasn't exactly celebrated for its benevolence.

It described techniques that severed the soul's bond with their Emberkin through ritualized trauma. A process not designed to heal, but to contain, expunge, and censor. Jin gripped the edge of the pedestal until his knuckles turned white.

This couldn't be what she deserved. And yet … this was what her enemies might force upon her if they found out about her secret. A chill ran down his spine. Could anyone already know?

Backing away slowly, Jin rolled up the scroll, his hands trembling, before dropping it disconcertedly back on the pedestal. He was hell-bent on finding a solution to all of this, but this was where the relic orb had led him. It was like someone had put a nail to the coffin of any hopes he might have held.

He dazedly stumbled all the way back to Ruo's quarters, unaware he wasn't sheltered under his cloak. He thought of Xun's hands, unshrinking even when trembling. Of the way her voice dropped when she was guarding something fragile. Of the fire in her eyes when she didn't realize someone was watching.

This was what they would do to her.

He barely noticed the portal closing behind him.

Grabbing his arm, Ruo asked, concern lining her face, "Did you find what you need?"

"How strong are the Silencing glyphs here now?"

Ruo frowned. "Well, I've reinforced them when you were gone, in case all hell breaks loose. We could have a battle in here, and no one would hear a thing."

At the confirmation, Jin dropped to his knees and gave a guttural scream.

There was no cure, only a weapon. One that could be used against her, not for her. And he … he couldn't fix this.

DREAM REALM

梦

mèng

境

jìn

Chapter Seventeen

轮回声

THE SOUND OF UNDOING

Xun

Instead of inner palace attendants, Father had sent guards to escort me to the Imperial Arena. While a routine summons wasn't generally accompanied by a squad, it wasn't impossible. Sometimes, special circumstances might call for extra protective detail. Yet something in the Imperial Guards' demeanor told me their mission wasn't to protect me. But they didn't bind my hands, or shove, or threaten. I was still a princess of Yan, after all.

The guards didn't leave my side when we arrived at the same expansive, sunlit space where the convergence battle of the Trial was held. Tiered seating platforms surrounded its perimeter, with towering walls behind them demarcating the boundaries of the space. This time, however, there was no crowd, no students. Just a scattering of nobles and high-ranking ministers, each flanked by their Emberkin.

My stomach turned; this couldn't be good.

Father stood by Master Dan at the center of the arena, their expressions unreadable. Councilor Wu posted himself off to the side, his vulture-like gaze flicking between me and the dais.

It didn't take long for me to detect Kai's presence. Leaning insouciantly against one of the pillars behind the dais, his eyes met mine and crinkled with a slow, venomous smile. His commanding officer shot him a disgruntled look but stifled a rebuke. Something cold coiled in my gut.

"This is a procedural matter," Father said, his voice carrying effortlessly across the space with the Amplifying glyph on his throat. "The Healers and Weavers have recommended an experimental method to help strengthen the connection between your soul and the Smokeveil. Given your delayed bonding, this should help clarify your potential." He gestured toward the ceremonial dais before him.

"Understood," I said.

My voice didn't waver, but my heart was thumping so loudly, it was as if someone had drawn an Amplifying glyph over it. This didn't sound like anything I'd heard of before, so I hadn't anticipated this. And I hated surprises.

"The ceremony required the bonded humans of the strongest Emberkin across the Empire to be present. Hence," Father explained, indicating toward the dozen high-born officials around us. "Though you will feel some discomfort, as far as we know, the procedure is not harmful."

As far as they know.

The dais, inscribed with glyphs and ceremonial calligraphy, had been blessed with holy water drawn from the Temple of Smoke and Rain, deep within the southern mountains. A large copper brazier burned at each of its corners, releasing curls of sandalwood smoke into the air and creating an illusion of four smoke pillars erected around the dais.

Ascending with the last of my composure, I kneeled on the cushion prepared for me like the obedient puppet they'd raised me to be. Two senior Smokeveil Weavers—clad in robes embroidered with cloud-and-smoke motifs—stepped forward deferentially, their eyes downcast. One held a vessel of consecrated spring water infused with moon lotus, a rare herb said to bridge the divide between realms.

The other Weaver began to chant, low and rhythmic, his voice barely louder than my thunderous heartbeat. I nearly missed his instruction to hold out both my hands before me, palms facing up. In response, the Imperial Guards stationed nearby started closing in around the dais, making it crystal clear that this wasn't a request, but an edict.

When I obliged, the Weaver placed a polished jade rod onto my hands—a relic used to fortify newborn Emberkin bonds. But I was already bonded, even if they weren't cognizant of it. What would this mean for Mo and me?

As holy water was being sprinkled onto the glyphs encircling me, I felt the world narrowing, pressing in on me. The air thickened, heavy with unsaid truth. Even in the absence of ropes and shackles, I could feel the weight of every eye on me. Sensing my unease, Mo shrank further behind me. Though I always kept her carefully concealed from others with my Smokecraft, she still often hid behind me or up my flowing sleeves whenever we had company.

I told myself I would do this. Endure whatever they had in store for me. Father was only doing this out of swelling desperation. If I couldn't bear with it to the end, it would only pile disgrace onto the growing mount of dissatisfaction Father was already harboring toward me. Especially with an audience present. There was no telling what would be next.

But then it started—the searing pain like a simultaneous assault of fire and ice through my veins. As though the Smokeveil wasn't just brushing against my soul, but perforating, scorching, slashing. Biting down on my lip to keep from screaming, I tried my hardest to let go of the relic, but to no avail. My fingers wrapped tightly around it against my will. It didn't take long before something within me buckled.

Within the same breath, a burst of gold and flame erupted from within me, followed by a shriek that echoed through the arena, not human. Then came a pair of wings that spread far enough from behind me to reach the periphery of my vision. *Mo.*

I heard the gasps. Saw the nobles rising to their feet. My Emberkin—radiant, burning, unmistakably *mythic*—had been revealed to the rest of the world. That was when I knew—

This was the end for me.

Jin

Jin hadn't meant to run. Not at first. He and Ruo were walking across the Academy courtyard when a student Weavers passed them. She muttered something about a ceremony in the Imperial Arena, the Princess being prepared, on the "Regent's orders."

Jin didn't wait to ask questions. He was already sprinting by the time Ruo was calling after him.

"Jin! Jin—*wait*!"

But he didn't wait.

He didn't *think*.

He didn't even go fetch his cloak.

When he reached the outer rim of the Imperial Arena, there were already guards stationed before the entryway. Jin ducked through a side stairwell, narrowly avoiding one of the posted sentries. Then he found a spot in the spectator platforms where he could take cover while still see the center dais.

And there she was. Yan Xun, put on her knees, shaking uncontrollably. Next thing he knew, a blinding flash lit up the entire space. A phoenix burst into view behind her, wings fanning in a magnificent arc of fire and smoke. It was all unfolding so rapidly before him that he fleetingly thought he'd imagined it. But the gasps around the arena confirmed otherwise. Everyone present had *seen* it.

"Mo ..." Jin breathed, his stomach turning cold.

A piercing scream from Xun flooded his mind, seizing his heart in a suffocating squeeze. He stepped forward, ready to heave himself over the ledge of the low wall separating the audience from the arena. Even knowing full well he would be intercepted by guards, he didn't give a damn.

But just as his foot lifted from the platform, a sharp glyph flared silently against his temple. He caught one last glimpse of Xun—crumpled, flames licking the edge of her robes, the phoenix rising like a scream behind her—before the world went dark.

Jin awoke to the sound of his own pounding fists against a glyph-sealed door. Xun's screams still echoed in his head, but he was somehow back in his own quarters in the Martial Academy. It'd all happened so quickly that if he hadn't heard her voice from the other side of the door, he wouldn't have realized it was Ruo who'd knocked him out cold.

"You'll just bruise yourself, asshead," came her voice from outside.

"RUO!!!" Jin roared. "Open the damned door!"

He could hear the scrape of a chair leg shifting as she sat down.

Slamming his shoulder against the door this time, he bellowed, "*Ruoooh!*" Then he cursed so loudly he could hear her leaning away from the door. "You *knocked me out?!* She was—I have to—she *needed* me!"

"No," Ruo said calmly. "She *needed* you to stay alive."

Jin froze.

"She gave me that *order* after the Mid-Autumn Festival," Ruo continued, her voice tight. "For me to keep a close eye on you. Said if I ever saw you contemplating something stupid—*public*—that invited execution, I was to knock you out. No questions."

"You don't understand what you just did," Jin growled, pressing his forehead to the door.

"I do," Ruo said, gentler now. "But so did she."

He turned and slumped against the door, heart racing. The image of the phoenix, of Xun's crumpled body, of that twisted smile on Kai's face … Did this mean Xun had seen this coming? No. She was just worried he would hunt Kai down and kill him. That was what her order to Ruo was about.

Xun wasn't wrong; he *did* want to. He'd been deliberating whether the consequences of murdering a half-royal could possibly fall on him alone, without implicating his family.

His mind was pulled back, unbidden, to the week before the Mid-Autumn Festival. Some of the other Martial Academy students were excitedly chatting in the courtyard, comparing travel plans and holiday dishes. Jin had lingered nearby, pretending not to listen, knowing he wouldn't be going home again this year. Not that anyone had ever asked.

Yet, the next afternoon, he'd found a mooncake by his bedroll. Just one. Left without a note, wrapped in oiled parchment, still warm. He hadn't seen Xun leave it, but he knew it was her.

When he saw her later that day, she'd simply carried on as usual, as if she wasn't the only person in the world who could see through his longing. He never asked how she got it. Just savored it slowly, bite by careful bite, like it was something sacred.

And now, she was gone.

Fucking Weavers with their fucking Smokecraft. Even his fucking windows were sealed shut.

"How long are you going to keep me in here?" Jin asked Ruo, his voice deadpan.

A brief pause, then: "For as long as necessary, until I'm confident you won't do anything rash."

Jin flopped onto the floor in resignation. This was *not* how it was supposed to go. He was supposed to find answers—find a *solution* that was supposed to *work*. Yet the answer he'd found wasn't a way out, and they were still heading straight for his worst nightmares all the same. There was no way out.

He needed to know what had happened to her. But he couldn't ask. Because if he was going to like the answer, he wouldn't still be stuck in here. He *couldn't* bear to hear she was dead.

All he could do was curl into a fetal position and sob his heart out.

Xun

They'd given me my old annex in the inner palace for my house arrest. Not out of kindness, but logistical practicality. I was surrounded by those same white-tiled floors, silk-screen doors, high lattice windows. Except this time, there were no attendants, no gardeners, no private tutors. Not a single footstep could be heard in the hallways, unless it was a guard on patrol.

This wasn't the soft, dusk-lit stillness I'd grown to appreciate over the years, but rather a quietness that cut, not soothed. I could hear nothing and everything at the same time. My own breath. The wind scratching against the paper windows. An indistinct drip from a rain spout outside.

But I couldn't see a thing. Not the room, not even the shape of my own hands. The Imperial Healers said the blindness might be temporary. *Might.* There were no promises. No one wanted to be the first to say the word "permanent." Just that the trauma from the ceremony might have overloaded something delicate, like the nerves in my eyes. But that they were hopeful it hadn't severed anything deeper beyond my eyes. Then proceeded to assure me that I was otherwise in good health. How comforting.

What I did know for certain was this:

Mo was gone.

Captured and imprisoned in Lifeng Pagoda.

I hadn't seen it happen, but I imagined she didn't even attempt to flee and hide. Though Emberkin couldn't stray too far from their bonded Weavers, Mo could have flown and stayed as high above me as her bond allowed, well out of reach of anyone below. But Mo had never left me in danger, not once.

That was probably how they'd coaxed her into a containment vessel of Lifeng glass, forged for one purpose only: to confine Emberkin who didn't play by the Empire's rulebook.

For the first time in over two years, I couldn't feel Mo's presence. But I could still feel the weight of her body curled across my chest on cold nights, wings folded tight, warm against me. I chuckled when I thought about the little huffs of smoke when she sighed in her sleep. Wept when I thought of the way she always shifted closer whenever I stirred, as if she could sense my unease before I did.

And in my mind, I could still hear the flutter of her wings, once a constant filling the space above me. I'd always thought it sounded like paper catching on fire—soft, then sudden. Memories of her pervaded every corner of my consciousness, like ash that refused to scatter. Lying on my bed, I reached out to the empty space above me and pictured her disappearing into the rafters, the trail of flame sweeping behind her like a silent promise. That no matter what, we would find our way back to each other.

It was hard to imagine I was once fearful of her presence. But now I knew Mo was just a mirror. What I'd been unable to bear was the reflection of myself. Broken and aberrant.

Without Mo, the Dream Realm was out of bounds. Even so, I'd made a futile attempt to seek some wisdom from Xiao. The mentor who'd guided me through the roughest parts of life without uttering a single sound. But no, it was like walking blindly in an unending tunnel that led me nowhere. If Xiao couldn't help me, no one could.

Now, there was only silence stacked on silence.

I didn't know if Jin had been in the arena that day. All I could think of when it was happening was the pain. The kind that blurred everything else into white noise. That filtered out faces, voices, everything but the burn. And yet, in the quiet, when my mind wasn't drifting to Mo and Xiao, it was going to Jin. As tears started trickling down my face, I prayed with all my might he hadn't witnessed any of it.

Had Ruo kept her word? Was she making sure he would stay out of it, like she'd promised?

I hoped so.

Jin was foolhardy sometimes, and obstinate in ways that made me want to scream. But he was also kind and clever. Once, when he was giving me secret self-defense lessons, I'd accidentally torn a seam in my sleeve. I could've mended it with Smokecraft but stopped short when Jin started pulling out some thread and a needle from his pack. Then, without asking if I wanted help, he just kneeled before me and started stitching, neat and methodical. Like it was the most natural thing in the world.

When I asked why he just happened to have needle and thread, he said, "Sometimes, all you can afford is to fix what's right in front of you."

Perhaps he'd said that because he didn't think it was something a Princess could relate to. But it'd struck a chord with me more than he would ever know.

He *was* so much more than the world allowed him to believe. If only he would keep his poise and stay out of trouble, he could carve something out for himself. Something honest in this muddied world. I hoped he would, even if he hated me for what I'd done. Even if he could never forgive me.

Dying for love wasn't the hardest thing to do—it would only take a moment of valor. Living with grief, on the other hand, was an invisible kind of hard— the kind that earned no reward, no recognition.

As for me, I supposed it would only be a matter of time before I would be accustomed to the silence, given I would have the rest of my life to. Based on what I'd seen and what I now knew, being held in a lifelong house arrest was a very likely possibility.

All my life, I'd barely had any time to myself. I never knew any children's games because I'd never played them. I was always busy learning something, always working *harder* on what others considered important. What I wouldn't have given for a solid night of sleep back then.

But no one had ever taught me what to do with free time, which was now in abundance.

If one could even call this free time.

In time, all my ghosts began materializing to keep me company. They were the only things I didn't need sight to see. Some lurked in the corners, quietly accusing. Some lingered by the shadows, whispering haunting truths I'd been trying to bury. Others paced, restless and demanding. A few pressed in too close. I never had to ask their names; I knew them by feel. By the pressure in my chest just before it caved. The tremor of my lips just before the pain broke free.

I saw the part of me that had died when Kai first assaulted me. The part that had died with Shan. The part that had died a bit more with every silence from Father. The part that had died when my mother's spell broke. The part that was destined to die when I dared want someone I could never have. The part that had lost Mo and Xiao.

Now that they were all out here with me, I realized I could hardly tell myself apart from the ghosts I'd spent my entire life tucking quietly under the edges of my being.

Perhaps that was the trick of it.

You didn't become a ghost all at once. You shed yourself in layers … until one day, there was more memory than person.

Perhaps I'd been dead for a long time and just didn't know it. Not until the sound of my own undoing started echoing louder than everything else.

SMOKECRAFT

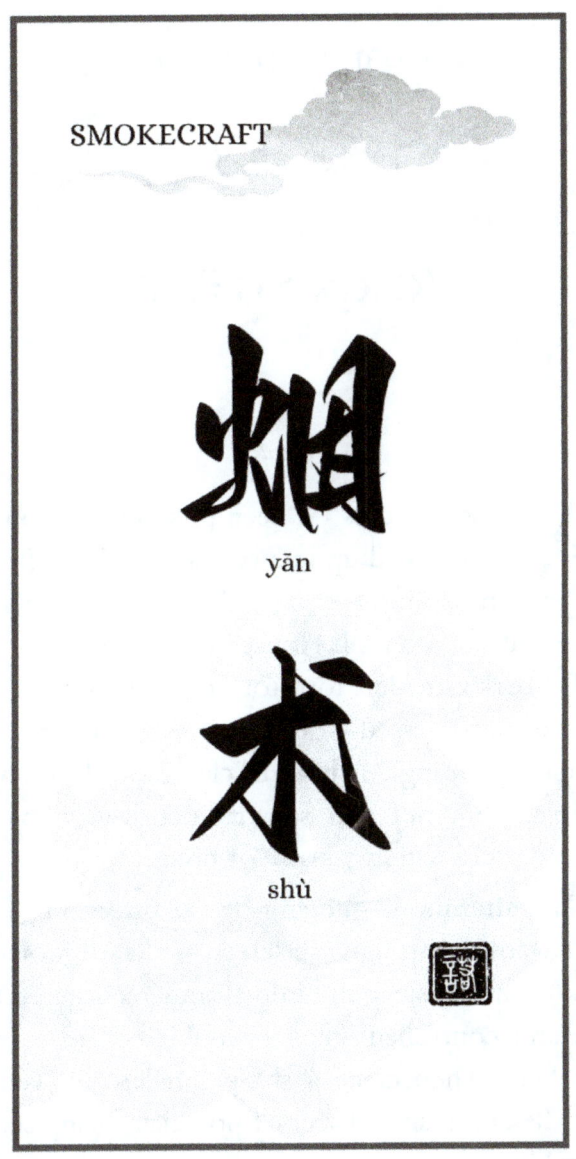

yān

shù

Chapter Eighteen

燃如观火

REIGNING FIRE

Xun

As mortified as I'd been to stumble upon the man locked up in a secret chamber with his Emberkin, I now realized there could be worse things, after all. House arrest, blindness, and no Emberkin made a torturous combination.

The days passed—or I assumed they did. I'd stopped counting. My internal clock had always been reliable, but grief and sensory deprivation played strange tricks with my sense of time.

One afternoon—judging by the direction of the sun's warmth through the screen—I heard footsteps I hadn't heard since my imprisonment began. Delicate and controlled steps I would recognize from anywhere. Then came a sharp inhale, followed by a sniffle and a soft clatter of porcelain being set on the table.

"Mom?" I said. The word surprised even me. I hadn't called her that in years.

Lady Linhua let out a shuddered breath.

"I've pleaded for days," she whispered. "I thought they would never let me in."

I didn't respond.

"Here," she said, moving toward me. The bed creaked slightly as she sat. "It's just a calming tonic. It'll help with your nerves. Help you rest." She lifted the bowl and gently brought it up to my lips.

I drank, only because I didn't have the strength in me to argue. It was bitter and earthy—some kind of root infusion, probably with dried chrysanthemum. When she dabbed at the corner of my mouth with a handkerchief, I could feel the tremble in her hands.

"You're so thin," she murmured, her voice breaking. "My poor girl. I don't understand how this happened. How it all … fell apart." She was crying, and saying all the things you were supposed to say when you didn't know what to say at all.

"Listen, Mom," I said softly, cutting through her tearful moping. She stilled. "I need to ask you something, considering this might be the last time we ever see each other."

I was met with silence. Except this time, I couldn't rely on my sight to decipher it. Turning my head in her direction, I tried to face her squarely for this.

"Have I ever been the number one in your heart? Ever? Even just once?"

She sucked in a sharp breath through her teeth. "What—Yan Xun, don't be foolish. What kind of question is that?"

"An important one. I just need you to answer me honestly. Please."

Her voice crumbled, and the tears returned.

"Of course you have. Of course. My heart has always—*always*—belonged to you, my treasure."

She pulled me into a hug, arms shaking. I let her. I didn't return it, but I let her. I decided it was the last hug I would accept from her. Because from here on, I wouldn't have a mother, no matter how this ended. I inhaled her scent one last time—a smell that used to anchor me through the roughest of storms.

Before I finally understood she was the storm.

After a while, Linhua pulled back, reaching for the empty bowl.

"One last thing," I said. She paused expectantly. "Your hairpin. The pearl one with the orchid stem."

"My favorite?" she asked.

"Yes. You know how I love my hairpins. Treat it as a last bit of dignity for a fallen Princess?"

A long pause ensued, before I heard a rustle of silk. Then a quiet clink as she pulled it free from her hair. Leaning in close, she gently coiled my hair into a simple knot, holding it together with her pin.

"It suits you more, anyway," she said, smoothing the strands framing my face.

I gave no response. There was nothing left to be said between us. Straightening, she smoothed her robes and lingered for a moment, oblivious to the fact that I could no longer see nor feel her performance. Then I heard the door open before closing again.

And the silence returned, inflaming the grief that was roiling in me—the final surrender of the mom I'd believed I had. Gently tracing the outlines of her pin, I waited for sleep to claim me in mercy.

Ruo

By the time the rumors reached the Academies, they were already ablaze.

"The Phoenix Princess had been claimed by a celestial beast—an omen of imbalance, of divine punishment."

The nobles whispered of Smokeveil corruption, of unnatural bonds. Of sullied bloodlines mixing with powers that they were never meant to hold. And fanning those flames, always just behind the screens, was Fu Kai.

Ruo heard it all. Every gossip, every shift in public sentiment. But she made sure Jin heard none of it. Each day she stood outside his quarters, a quiet sentinel for a hurting friend. Every nosey visitor turned away. Meals delivered personally, even if they were barely touched. Because if he ever found out what happened to the girl he would've died for … he wouldn't live long enough to do anything about it.

As days passed, even Jin's own squad began questioning his peculiar confinement. She didn't suppose anyone expected he still had anything to do with the Princess after the Trial. Even Ruo herself was mildly surprised when Yan Xun had come to her with the request. But Ruo was beyond relieved when Grandmaster Shao granted her permission to handle the situation with Jin as she saw fit.

Jin hadn't spoken a single word since that day. In fact, she'd barely heard a sound from inside. No more crying. No more screaming. Just silence—so dense it made her ears ring.

Ruo started doubting herself, wondering if she'd agreed to Yan Xun's request too quickly. If there was more she could've done before everything had fallen apart. If there was ever a chance to save Yan Xun, had she helped Jin instead of knocking him out. But then she remembered Yan Xun's words—clear, earnest, and final: *"Whatever you do, no matter the cost, don't ever let him run into fire. Please."*

So, Ruo held her silence. Kept her post. Honored her promise. Even when her fingers itched to knock. Even when her chest ached from the stillness in Jin's room. She even spent most of the nights outside his door, knees drawn to her chest, glyphs glowing around her to keep the cold at bay. Sometimes, she tried envisaging what she would do if it were someone she loved in there. Wondered if she'd ever loved anyone the way Jin loved Yan Xun.

There had been rumors Ruo couldn't unhear. *Experimental rite*, they said—spoken by attendants and students who didn't know she was listening. Everyone was openly speculating on Prince Yan Yun's final verdict for the Princess. Some whispered of Fu Kai being seen frequenting the Regent's private study since her arrest.

Weighed down by guilt, Ruo once started to write Jin a letter. Just a few lines, nothing grand.

You deserved to know. You deserved to fight for her. I'm sorry.

But her hand had trembled halfway through, and she'd crumpled it. Because this wasn't about love or even justice anymore. It was about survival. And the reality was, she couldn't protect both Yan Xun and Jin. So, if silence was the only shield she could offer Jin, she would hold it up like a sword.

Xun

Many more days had passed since I'd last had a visitor. Still no word from Father. No verdict. I began to wish for a conviction—anything to end the uncertainty. No sense in delaying the inevitable.

I was perched on the edge of my bed, hair still wet from the washbasin, when I felt it. A shift in the air. An instinctive tension in my gut. A shadow crossing the screen. Then the door creaked open. Measured footsteps too stealthy for a guard.

Then came his voice.

"Even when blinded, you still manage to look like a little queen," Kai purred, his voice curling through the air like poison smoke.

I didn't humor him with a reaction. Of course, he wouldn't miss the chance to witness my undoing in person.

"Still not going to scream?" he asked, a tinge of disappointment in his voice. "Most girls would."

"You're not most men," I said flatly.

He chuckled at what he took as a compliment. "No. No, indeed, I'm not."

The silence between us thickened.

"You know, I was only expecting to see you publicly humiliated beyond redemption at the ceremony, when you still couldn't bond an Emberkin after all that fuss. But you did me one better, my darling."

Just as I thought, asshead.

"Then when your father told me," Kai continued, slowly strolling closer, "he's finally made up his mind … I offered. Told him a Princess deserved a dignified end. A family farewell."

I didn't take the bait. My father was many things, but he would never have agreed to my execution.

"He agreed."

Then, from beneath his robes, Kai drew something slender and gleaming. Metal sang in the still air.

The Emperor's short sword. A Yan family heirloom.

"I thought it was poetic," Kai said, "to let your own kin end what should never have existed. And just look at how pretty this is."

He turned the sword around in his hands to admire it.

"I wonder if I'd be allowed to keep it afterwards," he mused, running a finger along the blade as if testing its weight.

Fear was a luxury of the living.

"So pretty, indeed," I agreed.

It only took a breath before realization dawned. Kai's gaze snapped up, stunned, right as I jammed the pearl hairpin into his eye. Turned out the Imperial Healers were right about my blindness being temporary, after all. It was hasty of me to pre-judge their competence.

Kai stumbled back, roaring in pain and clutching the side of his face.

The pin stayed put.

Prisoners under house arrest weren't allowed personal effects. No letters. No ink. But I'd surreptitiously asked for Lady Linhua's favorite hairpin weeks ago, when I'd thought it might serve an entirely different purpose. For a dignified end, perhaps. A cleaner one. One of my own choosing.

So, I'd told her having the pin would bring me comfort. That it reminded me of my mother. I'd said it all without so much as a blink or a shift in my gaze. Shan would've been proud of me.

But in the end, the pin had found its target just fine.

As soon as Kai staggered back far enough, I kicked the sword out of his hand, catching it mid-air by the hilt.

"Most men would've screamed, Fu Kai," I said, almost kindly. "You're not so special, after all."

Baring his teeth, he reached for the hilt of his own sword, a standard issue for palace guards. But before he could draw it, I swung my sword in a broad sweep before me, locking into an offensive stance.

Even through his agony, the puzzlement still shone through on his face. But if he could still make facial expressions, he wasn't in enough pain. *Not yet.*

Reigning Fire

"You have three breaths to decide if you want to do this with or without the pin still in your face," I said, offering him a choice. Something he'd never offered me.

Kai took a breath's time to contemplate. Decided to pull it out on the second. Unfortunately, a single breath's time wasn't enough for him to recover from a fresh wave of anguish.

Staying true to my word, I launched forward on the third breath's time, slashing across his dominant arm. It was metal against bone and sinew. This time, I got to watch Kai's survival instincts kicking in. To see it in his eyes, his body, his breath.

He parried my next strike and drew his sword with his non-dominant hand, holding it up clumsily in a defensive stance. Before he got to do much with it, however, that arm was sliced wide open, too. Then, circling behind him, I dragged my blade across the back of his knees.

When he dropped to the floor, I faced him again to deliver a kick squarely in his chest, throwing him backward until he hit a wall. The very same wall he'd once pinned me up against, over and over. Some would say karma was a beautiful thing.

But in that instant, *I was karma*.

"You *bitch*!" Kai spat. "You think you'll ever get out of this alive? You're a fucking nobody, and you always will be!" He tried his best to glare at me with his remaining eye, his breathing ragged.

Just then, a deafening explosion shook the palace, and the earth tremored. Anyone with intact survival instincts would've paid attention. But sadly for Kai, he'd long broken mine. I paid it no heed. Dropping to one knee, I looked him straight in the eye.

"Fu Kai, do me a favor," I said, enunciating each word clearly. "When we finally meet again in hell, do tell me what it's like to be *slain* by a fucking nobody."

At the last word, I drove the sword deep into his chest, an inch away from his heart. Leaning in close, I whispered in his ear, "This is for Shan."

Then, holding his gaze, I twisted the blade, slow and cruel.

"And this is for me," I told him, loud enough to be heard over his screams.

I'd intended to watch the light go out of his eyes, but a bright flash at the edge of my vision distracted me. I blinked up at the source to find … Mo.

And I gave a true, unguarded smile for the first time since she'd been taken.

But instead of gliding toward me, Mo drifted upward to the roof—through the roof—growing in size with every flap of her smoky wings.

I watched her rise, her beauty astonishing me just as much as in memory. When the last of her tail disappeared from view, the entire roof above us went ablaze. Not an illusory fire, but one that brought heat.

Reason screamed for me to leave immediately, but there was something incredibly cathartic about watching the flames dancing down the walls of my childhood chambers. The gilded prison for my youth, my innocence, my hopes and dreams.

For all my ghosts.

I should've felt scared. But I was dazzled by the roof's falling embers, like fiery raindrops from the heavens, drifting in slow motion.

Yet, even as I tilted my face up, the flames had never touched me, not once. They danced, yes—ravenous and wild—but never toward me. As if they had a spirit of their own. That was when I realized: this wasn't fire unleashed in rage, but one with purpose.

Fire that knew exactly what needed to burn.

So, I allowed myself a few more moments before drawing my sword back out. Turned out I didn't need to wait for Kai to be in hell before he would burn. Finally, I left, never once looking back. Something in my gut told me Mo would come find me when she was ready.

Walking out, I'd expected Warriors. A coordinated ambush. Distress signals, at the very least. Though the bells did sound, I found myself moving through empty halls, in a palace that was never vacant. It was only starting to make sense when I saw the Lifeng Pagoda, its roof torn open, flames licking the top floor. Thick smoke billowed in a towering column, reaching all the way to the heavens.

Given how Mo's fire had spared me, I would expect most other Emberkin in Lifeng to be safe.

Phoenix fire didn't devour the innocent; it unearthed the rot, set ghosts free.

Father and the rest of the Empire would be busy dealing with all the Emberkin reuniting with their bonded humans.

My uncles would be paying a visit soon.

Jin

The warning bells were already screaming when Ruo unsealed the door. She didn't say a word, just gave him a look, urgent and grim, before stepping aside.

Jin didn't wait for an explanation. He barely registered the chaos outside as he broke into a run, with only a single intent in mind. Then something finally caught his attention, enough to pause.

The Lifeng Pagoda, devoured by flames.

From the eastern courtyard, the top floor was scarcely visible through the rising smoke—its roof split open like a wound, hungry flames licking the air in ribbons. Warriors and palace guards were rushing past him from all directions, orders barked, gates locked down. But Jin kept moving. He didn't know where he was going, only knew he had to find her.

He made it into the inner palace, past the courtyard wall, past the annex gardens. He should've been stopped, tackled, surrounded. Only he wasn't. Then, at long last, he saw her. Emerging from smoke and fire like a vision from an impossible dream.

Xun.

She walked unhurriedly out of a corridor, as if just strolling around the gardens, her old annex swallowed by smoke and flames behind her. There were splatters of blood across her soot-smudged face and robes. Her eyes stared blankly ahead as if she was no longer behind them, her hair disheveled. And held loosely on her side was a sword, blood still dripping slowly from its tip in a calming tempo, a stark contrast to the violent sight.

On her other side, a long trail of ash chased her moving fingertips—dancing and curling through the air, like it was alive. Slowly, it gathered into form. Mo sharpened into shape, wings folded and head bowed gently at rest, perching on Xun's wrist like she'd never left. Though she looked much smaller than she had before, Jin knew it was Mo from the way she was leaning into Xun.

She was real. She was alive. She wasn't a fiction of his imagination. Jin's breath caught in his throat, and he moved toward her before he could think.

"XUN!"

She stopped in her tracks, looking as if she'd heard a voice she never expected to hear again. Like the voice of a ghost. Only when he reached her did he see life steadily returning to her eyes.

Gripping her shoulders like he was trying to grab hold of smoke that would surely dissipate in time, he frantically scanned for injuries. But he paused when she slowly lifted a hand to his face—fingers warm from fire and fury but still gentle. Too gentle.

"Where I'm going," she said slowly and carefully, "you can't follow, Jin."

Even with tears pricking her eyes, her lower lip quivering, she was still smiling up at him. But that only made his heart twist more savagely.

"The life you wanted for me, that future … it was never mine to live. I've never chosen any of this. But if I had a choice now …" she paused as her thumb brushed his cheek, "I'd still choose it. Just to meet you."

Jin's throat closed around something sharp. He reached up and covered her hand with his own, anchoring it there, just for a moment longer.

"Then stay," he whispered, choking back tears. "Stay, and we'll find another way. You and me—we always do. Let me help you, let me—"

Xun's hand trembled under his, but she didn't pull it away. "You know there is no other way."

And she gave Jin a look—soft, broken, and infinite.

A tremor passed through him, sharp and sudden, like his body had finally caught up to what his heart already knew. He wanted to scream, beg, break something—anything just to stop this moment from slipping through his fingers. But when he looked into her eyes, he knew.

There was no stopping her. Not this time.

"Thank you," she whispered, dropping her hand.

And something broke in Jin.

"NO!" he shouted, his voice cracking. "No, no— if you walk out of here, Yan Xun will be no more!"

At those words, her lips curled into a smile, so beautiful and tragic it nearly dropped him to his knees. Then a bubble of laughter escaped her. A soft, aching sound—haunting and sweet and crumbling all at once. And once she'd started, it was as if she couldn't stop. Even through the tears now pouring down her face, she continued to laugh.

And without turning back, she walked away. Through the burning garden. Past the fallen walls. Into the firelight that would become legend.

Jin watched her until the smoke swallowed everything whole. And still, he stood there, hand pressed to the fading warmth on his cheek, as if it was the only thing left tethering him to the world.

EMBERKIN

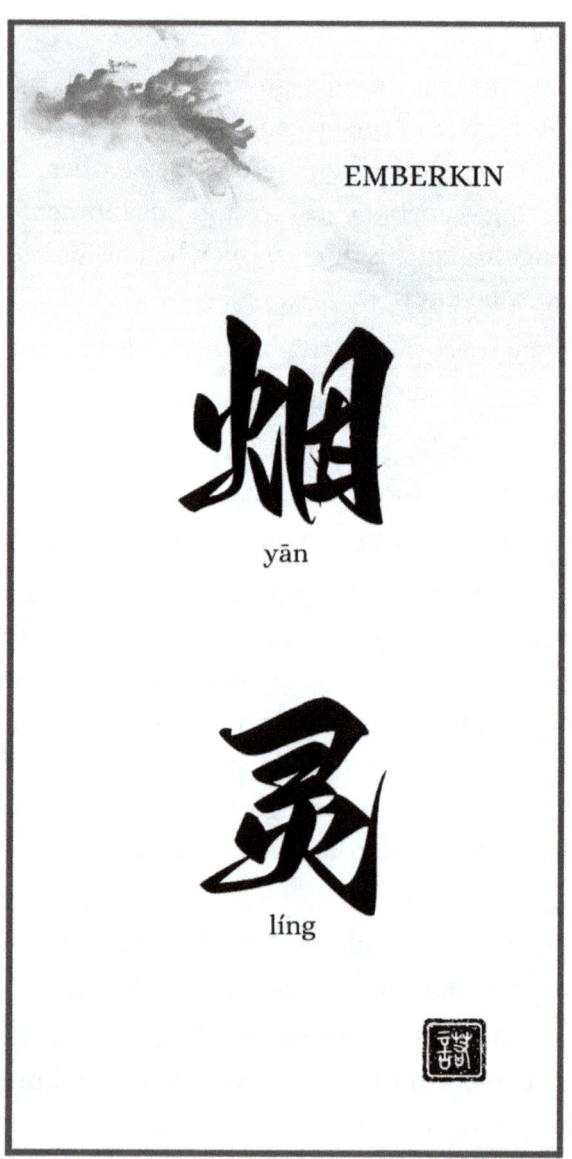

yān

líng

Reigning Fire

结语

EPILOGUE

Xun

I thought I would have felt thoroughly lost. Curled up in some heavens-forsaken place, wondering where I could go next. But once I'd left the palace grounds, my heart held a clarity I'd never thought possible. Like I'd always known where I was going, even when I didn't think I did.

With most troops dispatched to round up the Lifeng escapees, the palace was put under lockdown. On my way out, I'd encountered a squad of Imperial Guards stationed at the gates. But as far as I could tell, none of them were Weavers.

Instead of accosting me or sending out a distress signal, they'd simply stared at me and my bloodied sword, then at each other. While I no longer had the commanding power of a Princess, my Emberkin did just set a good part of the palace on fire, unleashing a complete pandemonium like none had ever seen. Lifeng wasn't invincible, after all.

I didn't rush to clarify that neither Mo nor I understood how our powers worked, just stared straight ahead while they contemplated their next move. After a long stand-off, their Commander gestured for the gates to be cracked open, just wide enough for me to slip through.

Perhaps they'd sensed my preparedness to kill my way out of there, if it came down to it. Yan Xun would never consider taking innocent lives, but that was no longer who I was.

So I'd left, reeking of slaughter and smoke. I had nothing but the clothes on my back and the short sword that was once a family heirloom of Yan Xun's—now mine. Alas, my relic pendant had been confiscated when I was put under house arrest. But I focused on more pressing needs, like obtaining proper boots for my long, unforeseen journey, and a scabbard for my sword. Considering its original was left in Kai's robes.

Taking flight into the nearest woods, I found a stream to wash up in, then went hunting. Life as a Princess had never been what others imagined, laced with hidden adversities most would never even glimpse. Still, I'd never had to worry about how I would find food. So, this had all been … a steep learning curve, to say the least. But I'd been adapting as quickly as I could.

One step at a time, I told myself.

I wondered if this precious relic sword had ever been used before it'd come into my possession, or if it'd simply been displayed. But I doubted anyone expected it would one day be used for hunting and skinning beasts. Its hilt was so exquisitely designed that I had to use Smokecraft to dull its colors to black whenever I was in town.

Even in remote towns, I still came across whispers of the Empire's "Demon Princess" perishing in a fire—by heavens' will, they said. It was strange how reassuring it felt to hear the news of my own death. Regardless, it wouldn't be prudent of me to be roaming around with a sword that looked like it didn't belong in the Mortal Realm.

Learning to improvise, I fashioned a sword scabbard using some pelts and resilient tree roots I'd found, before heading to a small town nearby to trade the rest of the skins for a different attire. A pair of boots fit for the journey ahead and some regular linen robes that the people wear.

It was surprising how at ease I felt in my new robes, as if letting go of a weight I hadn't realized I was carrying. All my life, I'd only been allowed to wear silk. Linen was "for peasants," they would say. Even under house arrest, they'd dressed me in plain white silk robes. But I'd never truly felt like I could breathe freely in silk. Something about its texture made it feel as though it could slip off me at any time, much like my sanity.

Mo was all too happy to bear witness as I ceremoniously burned my silk robes, once I had new ones to take their place. Since she'd broken out of Lifeng prison, I realized there was probably more to what I could do with her and my powers. Who would've thought that phoenix fire was the nemesis of the impenetrable Lifeng glass?

This was all uncharted territory for both Mo and me, since there were next to no records available on mythic Emberkin. But I hoped we would learn more about our powers together in time. Sometimes, I wished Xiao would simply give me the answers. But so far, everything I'd been taught was on their terms.

Since my escape, one of the many things that continued haunting me was that I'd left without freeing the man—most likely my uncle—and his chongming bird Emberkin from the concealed chamber. But in time, I'd come to the painful conclusion that I couldn't save the world. And if all I could do was save myself ... perhaps that was alright.

Perhaps that was enough.

It wasn't exactly an easy task to find a legendary mountain without so much as a proper name. It'd taken a few moons of trial and error before I could locate the fabled Great Smoke Falls and get to the foot of the mountain it was plunging from. But having a mission to focus on helped dull the pain in my heart. If I could occupy my mind enough, I could almost forget how it hurt to breathe whenever I was reminded of walking away from the person who mattered most to me.

The ascent took another moon or so, and it was nothing like the climb I'd made with Xiao in the Dream Realm. The thick and dense undergrowth concealed the depths beneath, often making the terrain wildly unpredictable. My body was now covered in more scars and calluses than I could count. The stings and burns were real, but I didn't mind them. Finally, what was on the outside mirrored what had long been true within.

At last, here I was—at the peak of the enigmatic mountain that, according to legends, touched the edge of Smokeveil. Mo soared high above me, relishing that great sense of freedom we'd never had. More than once along the way, I'd wished I still had my relic pendant on me. Just so I could skip the arduous mount. But now that I'd made it to the top—once again, with nothing to mark the occasion—I realized I wouldn't have it any other way.

But I did wonder ... or perhaps "fantasize" would be more apt. About what could've been, if I'd made a different choice in the Relics Vault that day. If I'd instead picked something that would let me look into someone's future, for instance. Would I be able to see

Jin's face again right now? To rest in the knowledge that he could heal. Find happiness again. *Live*.

I surmised that he must have resented me for forcing his hand. For leaving without him, simply because I selfishly refused to live with the torment of witnessing yet another soul that would perish for me. Neither of us had ever talked about it, but we'd both known the ending of whatever was between us since the very beginning. In one way or another.

Long before we'd met, we were already fated never to be. Beginning from the day he was accepted into the Imperial Martial Academy. From the moment a ten-year-old Jin had signed a Spellbinding agreement to pledge his services to the divine ruler of the Empire. Until death.

Even if the Empire never called upon his services—whether due to unsatisfactory progress or any other reason—he would be bound to never serve another soul again for the rest of his life. To abscond would mean his soul would slowly corrode away.

His soul had never belonged to himself. None of ours had, which was perhaps why so many of us within those palace walls no longer had one.

Jin and I could never offer each other what we didn't own.

Standing here now, I could feel the raw buzzing of Smokeveil powers. Mighty yet merciful, unlike what I'd experienced at the ceremony that marked the start of my official downfall. So, I thought I would try … even if it was sheer folly. To ask if the heavens could give me a sign, just to reassure me that Jin would be alright. A plea for any answer that might ease my guilt and trepidation.

But neither the mountain nor the heavens answered my pleas.

When the biting cold at the peak started threatening to turn my veins into frozen rivers, I turned to leave, a deep dejection pulling at my feet. I'd made my choice, so it was only fair I should live with the cost. If it meant Jin would survive, I could live with the burden of never knowing.

And that was when it came to me. Something else that had been at the back of my mind.

My name.

Not the name I was bestowed, but one that stood for who I was, who I would be from here on.

Finally, for the first time in my life, I would have a name that felt like mine.

Yan Ling—the flaming bearer of all my ghosts, past and present.

yàn

líng

SELECTED CHINESE IDIOMS
& CULTURAL NOTES

Presented in order of appearance

*Note: The following explanations contain brief cultural and thematic insights into the chapter titles. While care has been taken to avoid major spoilers, some interpretations may hint at the emotional tone or events of each chapter. Consider reading this section after completing the story for fullest impact.

深藏不露

shēn cáng bù lù | Ch. 3 title | "Hidden depth that's never revealed"
Describes someone who keeps their true talents, emotions, or intentions hidden. Reflects deliberate concealment of power or knowledge so deep that others may never know it's there.

烟雨濛濛

yān yǔ méng méng | Ch. 9 title | "A misty drizzle, veiling the world"
A poetic phrase evoking soft rain and emotional ambiguity. Chosen for where secrets and feelings blur like mist.

梦幻泡影

mèng huàn pào yǐng | Ch. 12 title | "Like a dream, an illusion, a bubble, a shadow"
A phrase describing something beautiful yet fleeting—insubstantial, like a passing dream. Chosen for where reality and illusion blur.

万丈深渊

wàn zhàng shēn yuān | Ch. 13 title | "A bottomless abyss"
Often used to describe a state of extreme peril or despair—a chasm so deep it swallows light. Chosen for where buried truths resurface, dark and consuming.

海枯石烂

hǎi kū shí làn | Ch. 16 title | "Till the seas run dry and rocks crumble"
Signifies eternal devotion or resolve. Used to highlight unshakable bonds, even in the face of time and ruin.

轮回声

lún húi shēng | Ch. 17 title | "Sounds of reincarnation"
A poetic term evoking the cyclical nature of existence, describing the echoes from past lifetimes or actions repeating through time.

燎如观火

liáo rú guān huǒ | Ch. 18 title | "As obvious as watching fire"
Describes when something becomes unmistakably clear or impossible to ignore.

ACKNOWLEDGMENTS

I want to thank my husband for being my tether to the real world every time I disappear into writing. Thank you for reminding me to do the basic things that keep me alive—like eating and drinking—when I forget them entirely. For following me to the ends of the world, no matter how wild the journey I decide to take. I'm a luckier girl than Xun because I have you.

Reigning Fire